Acclaim for
SHADOW

"Wildly entertaining. Heart poundingly swoon-worthy. Stunningly vivid. *Shadow* satisfies every YA fantasy we've ever had regarding Peter Pan. This gorgeous conclusion to the Heirs of Neverland series will have you clapping you hands and declaring, 'I believe!'"

— CAREY CORP, *New York Times* bestselling author of
The Halo Chronicles and The Doon Series

"Kara Swanson has poured her whole heart into *Shadow,* and it shows. Darker and more emotional than its predecessor, *Shadow* will be a satisfying, bittersweet finale for fans of *Dust.*"

— LINDSAY A. FRANKLIN, award-winning author of *The Story Peddler*

"In this intriguing sequel to the Peter Pan reimagining, *Dust,* Kara Swanson crafts a dark Neverland riddled with secrets. *Shadow* delivers lush storytelling, vivid characters, and heart-pounding action that will transport readers to a magical world and capture their hearts along the way!"

— LORIE LANGDON, author of *Olivia Twist* and
the upcoming Disney Villains series

T0284166

Books by Kara Swanson

The Girl Who Could See

Dust
Shadow

KARA SWANSON

Published by Enclave Publishing, an imprint of Oasis Family Media, LLC

Carol Stream, Illinois, USA.
www.enclavepublishing.com

ISBN: 978-1-62184-173-9 (printed hardback)
ISBN: 978-1-62184-175-3 (printed softcover)
ISBN: 978-1-62184-174-6 (ebook)

Cover design by Kirk DouPonce, www.DogEaredDesign.com
Typesetting by Jamie Foley, www.JamieFoley.com

Printed in the United States of America.

To Orrie and RJ—
For crawling into the darkest places with me,
lighting a spark, and showing me I could
ignite.

Fairy tales do not tell children the dragons exist.

Children already know that dragons exist.

Fairy tales tell children the dragons can be killed.

— G.K. Chesterton

1

PETER

Neverland

Falling out of the sky is far less fun than it sounds.

One minute I'm soaring past the stars, barreling through a veil of color and magic and snatches of children's voices and whispered dreams—and then there it is. It spreads out below me in familiar rugged curves that I know better than my own shadow.

Neverland.

I angle toward the island, trails of Jeremy's packet of pixie dust lifting my body, when I start to stutter. My body wobbles midair, and I check the store of dust, only to find that it's almost gone. I try to coast, treading late-afternoon air, but the last shred of dust flickers out.

I drop.

Spiraling toward the roiling, dark stretch of Neversea below like some rock shot from Slightly's slingshot, I flail in the air but can't seem to slow. All hints of airy pixie dust gone.

Blast it all!

When I had Tink, there'd always be plenty of dust to make it to Neverland. To drift lightly down to perch on the trees and spy on

Lily's tribe—or kick one of Hook's cannonballs out of the air. But this time, without her, it took much longer to even to get a bead on the island. Neverland usually calls to me, like a siren's lure drawing me closer—but instead my Never Never Land pushed me away. Hid.

As I plummet past the stars, through the clouds and biting wind toward the thrashing Neversea below, I suddenly realize why.

This whole island is angry.

It's in the chilled air. The way the water kicks below me. The skeletal silhouette of the island.

I slam into the icy waves like a cannonball. They knock the breath from my lungs and batter my skin as I sink. Cold numbs my body before I can beat for the surface. The Neversea wrestles control, swallowing me up.

The island isn't just angry—Neverland is afraid.

Its fear leaks through the water around me, weighted and churning with such panic it makes me nauseous. This is nothing like the crystal clear, warm depth I'm used to.

I force myself to strike for the surface and break through. I shake wet hair out of my eyes as the water continues to swell and writhe around me, almost thick and slimy as it attempts to drag me away from the island. Neverland's craggy shores rise in the distance, not as far as I'd thought, but even from this vantage point, something is off. The color is leached from the shore, the sand dark and the trees lifeless and charred.

Not very promising.

I wrestle with the Neversea, fighting to make it to that shore.

I almost crow out of habit, but of course my Lost Boys won't answer. Or if they did, it wouldn't be to help me. No one here would want to pull me out of this water. More likely they'd shove me back under.

As I get closer to the craggy shoreline, my body aching and creaking like a blithering ship, I see something fluid and glistening slide through the water a few paces ahead. And then the flash of a rippled, sharp fin. I halt, bobbing in the frigid water, not daring to breathe.

Good gad. I hope the sirens aren't hungry.

I'm only a few feet from shore, so I push down my uneasiness and continue swimming, trying to keep the dangerous undersea creatures well within view. Suddenly, an oily tail slides past my leg.

My skin crawls, and I wrench away. *Oh no . . .*

I angle around whatever clipped my leg and swim faster, desperate for that shoreline. Suddenly a sharp lance of pain tears across my side. Another cuts through my right shin. I grit my teeth.

Not good, not good, not good.

Thin streams of crimson fill the murky waters. The scaly creatures circle me, sharp talons protruding from thin fingers and tangled, oily hair obscuring pale faces. My chest caves in, too tight to breathe.

Don't just wait for them to add seasoning and take a bite!

My heavy and stinging limbs stir back into motion, legs pinwheeling as I swim as fast as I can through the thick water. But the sirens easily keep pace, taking their time as they try to tear me apart. A claw slices through my arm. Teeth puncture my leg. A webbed hand pulls at my hair.

They're toying with me.

"'Ey, chums! We used to be mates, remember? I used to feed you pirates?" My voice is breathless and raspy, salty water snaking down my throat. "Remember those grand ol' times?"

But the sirens are fast nearing a frenzy. I'm only five feet from the dark stone beach rimming Neverland, but two webbed fists circle my legs and pull me under. I can't kick away. They're far too strong.

Dark, thick water fills my vision. Other webbed hands pin my legs and circle my arms, wrenching me deeper as I writhe and fight.

Only a shred of air is left in my lungs. Every fiber of my being is blooming exhausted. Somehow, I've always been able to hold my breath longer in the Neversea than I could on Earth—but now my chest is already screaming.

I kick at the slithery grips holding my ankles, losing my shoes in the process, and when my head snaps up, one of the sirens hovers in front of me. Charcoal tendrils of hair curl through the water around her pale features. The large, hollow eyes staring at me from her gray skin are more dilated than I remember, but it still clicks. The scar on the right cheek, the sharp jawline, the thin lips . . . I know her.

"Nyssa?" All the sirens freeze.

She drifts closer and makes a clattering, hissing noise. The other sirens let go and drift back a pace.

My lungs burn, and my eyes are blurred, but I see her scales have become dull and warped, almost slimy. No longer the familiar glossy ebony. Come to think of it . . . I glance around and realize that all of these sirens seem different. Thinner, bonier, duller. Their tails a little shriveled, their scales lackluster.

I turn back to the siren in front of me. The others hover in the water around us, their tails swishing deftly, deferring to her. She is their queen, after all. And one of the few sirens I've ever really respected. But this is not the Nyssa I remember.

"Peter . . ." I mumble, gesturing to myself, and she tilts her head again. A spark of hope ignites—maybe she'll remember. Maybe she'll let me go.

But her panicked eyes remain unchanged, and she shakes her head.

Great.

Her thin, rubbery lips pull wide to reveal rows of sharp teeth. I kick toward the surface with my last shreds of strength—but it's too late. She lets out a long, haunting wail.

A dozen sirens bare their teeth and launch at me, ready for the kill. Frenzied and furied and ready to tear me to shreds. I'd seen them do it to pirates before but never thought this was how I'd go.

Squeezing my eyes shut, I roll into a ball.

Sorry, Claire. I didn't even get to you.

Some rescuer I am.

A webbed claw burrows into my shoulder, but before their teeth can tear through the skin, one of them screeches.

A small tunnel of bubbles flashes past my cheek.

My eyes fly open, and I see dozens of small threads of bubbles through the water around me. I drift upward, not even sure how I haven't lost consciousness yet. As I near the surface, I can make out the sound as small projectiles continue to cut through the water, scattering the sirens. The sirens hiss and bare their teeth but quickly slide backward through the water and away from me.

Bullets.

Someone is firing into the water.

It's a miracle they didn't hit me.

I can just make out the water lightening above me, and then a hand reaches down.

I manage to get my numb fingers into the proffered grasp. I'm dragged up onto a rugged wooden slat.

I roll over, hacking and gasping for air. My ears ring, and I can't even lift my head to see who is turning me on my side. Gradually my vision clears.

I'm on a makeshift raft of driftwood, and someone is hunched at the front, pulling on a length of crusty rope. Pulling us to shore. I start when I see the rusted pistol lying beside him.

My hazy brain riffles through the list of anyone on this island who could possibly have access to a gun. Was I just scooped out of the siren's hold to be caught by one of the pirates?

Clenching my jaw, I get to my knees and reach for the gun.

"You should rest. You just almost drowned. That fall didn't look fun either."

Fist around the handle, I stare at the figure who continues to steadily pull on the rope, hand over hand, drawing us to shore. He's lean, with shaggy dark hair and a stained brown shirt that seems a bit too big for his shoulders.

"Who are you?"

He doesn't even flinch when I nudge him with the muzzle. "Not going to answer if you're waving that at me. Not that there's any bullets left. Used them all saving you from those sirens." His voice is low, even-toned. He just continues hefting on the rope. There's something familiar about the easy, languid movements and the way his voice doesn't waver.

I set the gun back down just as he pulls the raft up and jumps ashore, ragged pants rolled up his shins. He gestures for me to get out. I lurch off the makeshift raft and wade clumsily to a shore almost as black as siren scales, the cuts littering my skin stinging with every painstaking movement.

My mysterious rescuer drags the raft up onto the sands. One shoulder slumps, head ducked and thick hair hanging into his eyes. When he rubs at his nose with the back of his hand, a familiar tick, I stare. It can't be.

"Tootles?"

Warm almond eyes rise to meet mine, and he reveals a familiar half smile that for a moment gives me a flash of who this boy used to be. Not quite the smallest, but always the quietest, Tootles had a soft, disarming way about him.

That was one of the reasons I was shocked when he aimed an arrow at a Wendy-Bird and sent the young Story Girl tumbling from the skies. If Slightly had shot the arrow, I wouldn't have been the least bit surprised. But Tootles? The lad really had the worst luck, and he'd been ready for me to plunge the arrow into his own chest as punishment for the accidental shooting.

And I might have, if Wendy hadn't stopped me.

"It's been a long time, Peter."

His words abruptly bring me back. I try to step toward him, but my legs finally give out. I sink into the dark sand and stare at him. "I thought you were dead. I was sure Connor had . . ."

He trudges toward me. "He certainly tried. But I'm quicker than I look."

That I know.

As Tootles reaches a hand down to help me to my feet, hope starts to rise. If Tootles survived, who knows what else could still be intact?

He looks older, quite a bit older, like all of the Lost Boys do. Another reminder of just how broken this island has become. Not to mention that time runs differently here anyway.

Tootles eyes the nasty cuts and bite marks that really sting now.

"We'd better get those cleaned up." Something about the iron in his tone makes me pause. This Tootles's grip is strong and calloused, skin littered with thin scars that hadn't been there before. His eyes are haunted, his languid movements weighted.

"What happened to you? How long have you been here? And thanks for not letting me become siren chow, by the way," I add as he leads me across the beach. We pause near a thick, charred tree for me to lean on and catch my breath. The obsidian sand lining the beach fades into the coarse ground around the trees, and there are strange darkish veins cutting across the dusty terrain. Something is seriously wrong with this place.

"Speak quieter," Tootles tells me as he tears strips from his oversized shirt to bind up the cuts running streams of red down my skin. "The pirates patrol this beach about this time every day. We should find somewhere to hide."

I skirt a glance around. "I don't see—"

Tootles's hand clamps over my mouth. "Trust me."

Point taken.

He gestures for me to follow him, and I try to match his silent footsteps through the charred, twisted remnants of the jungle and toward a large rock covered in slimy moss. He brushes a dangling curtain of the moss away to reveal a small nook in the rock and motions for me to duck in. He follows close by, letting the veil of moss fall over the front of the secret alcove again.

"We'll wait a few minutes for them to pass, and then I'll take you home."

Crammed in against the slimy back of the rock, it's jarring just how thin Tootles has become and the way his bony shoulders and ribs jut through his threadbare shirt. He obviously hasn't been eating well.

My own ribs sting every time I breathe, the patchwork of small gashes making it hard to focus and sucking away my energy.

Still, I'm desperate to ask: "What's going on, mate? What's Connor done? Do you know where Claire is?"

He shushes me again, still peering out through the veil of moss, keeping impossibly still.

I pull my knees to my chest, trying to breathe through the biting pain that keeps flaring up. At least his makeshift bandages have stopped the bleeding for now, and it's only the slices on my shoulder that seem especially deep.

Silence hangs over us, and when Tootles finally speaks, each word is weighted enough to ground a pixie. "Connor has near-total control of the island. Neverland is dying, Peter."

He traces a strange dark vein that skitters across the ground beneath our feet. His voice is so hushed I have to strain my ears just to catch it. "The creatures here are all terrified. You saw it with the sirens—they're changing. He's mutilating it all."

Searing anger boils through my bones. I launch to my feet, bursting through the veil of moss. "That's it! I'm going to go find him and Claire and—"

But Tootles grabs my arm and yanks me back inside, smacking a hand over my mouth.

"Are you *trying* to get killed?" He spits the words at me. "If you rush after Connor like this"—he lets go of my arm to gesture wildly—"he will destroy you without a second glance. You won't save Claire that way. Plus, there are things you don't know."

I've never seen Tootles lose his cool, let alone the wild, frantic intensity that fills his words. "What else am I supposed to do?"

"Let me get you safely to the hideout. And then I can teach you how to survive here." Tootles's eyes grow very weary. "This isn't the Neverland you know, Peter. This isn't your dream world any longer."

My head sinks to rest on my knees as I stare at the ground, back pressed against the curve of the rock. I study the thin, dark veins spiderwebbing through the dirt. I hate to admit it, but he's right.

Every child visits a dreamland when they sleep. On rare occasions, when reality truly is too horrible for a little mind to bear, sometimes that dreamworld becomes more than a dream.

I'd been just a tiny boy, crying under my bed, when an impetuous pixie knocked on my window. I couldn't jump off that sill fast enough. Never looking back.

But this Neverland isn't my escape anymore. This place has become the world of Connor's nightmares, connected to him in the same way it used to be tethered to me.

And just as my dreams created this place . . .

Connor's nightmares are tearing it apart.

2

CLAIRE

Neverland
Before

I never thought I'd see Neverland like this.

Chained to the *Jolly Roger* like a caged bird. An iron cuff circles my ankle, with a thick, crusted chain trailing from it. I stare out the muggy window of Hook's stifling cabin at the arching landscape beyond the anchored ship.

I never thought I'd see Neverland like *this*.

Hollow. Shattered. Dark and foreboding.

The door to Hook's cabin swings open, and the tall pirate in the crimson coat steps into the room. Holding that infernal cane with the sword blade hidden inside.

I kick against the iron clamped to my right ankle. "You have to let me out!"

I expect him to say what he has every time we've had this argument for the past three days. Tell me this is for my best and that at least I'm being fed and safe . . .

That word makes me want to spit in his face. I don't want his forced sense of safety—I'm not safe, I'm his prisoner. I've been locked in his cabin ever since we docked here in Neverland. He hasn't even let me see my brother.

It's not time yet, Hook keeps saying. It's not the right time for me to meet Connor, but it will be soon.

Right.

"Patience, love," Hook says as he unlocks the massive bolt tying the chain to the bed, giving me more slack. Without glancing at me, he gestures for me to follow as he strides out of the cabin and clips across the rough deck.

Cautiously I peer around the doorframe. Hook has taken the chain, tossed it around the mast, and locked it with a rusted old deadbolt.

Wrapping my arms around my worn, pale blue cardigan, I cross the splintered deck of the *Jolly Roger* in bare feet. Movement on the ship lessens, and most of the pirates sneer. Slightly sends me a sympathetic look, sweat glistening over his freckled shoulders as he helps move large crates and tosses them into a small dinghy bobbing on the tide. Nibs is the only other Lost Boy not ashore, and he stands with his back to me, unwavering at the stern of the ship. He hasn't been able to look me in the eye since Hook tied me up.

The hopelessness is suffocating. I watch Hook move closer, picking up the rope slack in his gloved hand like it's nothing. Like I'm just some animal he can take for walks.

Catching sight of the pistol in his waistcoat, I make a desperate grab for it. I've attempted to snatch a weapon several times before and know he's probably too quick for me—but I have to try *something*.

Hook easily sidesteps me, waggling a finger. "Now, now, that's not—"

He's interrupted as a massive wave slams into the side of the boat. I'm thrown roughly to the side, and my knees and palms hit the deck hard. The pirates fight for their footing. The water has kicked up without warning, and on the island, the trees tremble so violently several of them snap in half.

An earthquake?

After the waves still, Hook stretches a hand to me, but I avoid it, pushing myself to my feet, dusting off my ragged jeans. He only shakes his head. "As much as you may hate me for it, I'm doing this for your good. Things are unstable. You would not be well received."

"So, you're keeping me prisoner?" This time I do spit on his nicely pressed coat.

The captain trails his hook down the side of my face. I jerk away, but not before he smirks. "You'll thank me for this one day, love."

Stop trying to placate me.

Another earthquake volleys through the island, and the ship tosses dangerously again, but I use the moment to spin away from Hook, eyes burning as I blink back angry tears. Thin flecks of gold drip from my skin, trailing down my wrists and leaking from my fingertips.

I don't notice my heels rising from the deck until I drift a few inches off the ground. I glide over the deck. For a moment, hope lifts my heart like the whisper of dust lifting my body—but then there's the sharp tug of iron chafing raw skin. And I'm reminded I'm tied down by metal that I haven't been able to burn through, no matter how many times I've tried. As much as I want to see Connor, perhaps there's also a part of me nervous of what could be out there that would stay a pirate's hand and keep them moored so far from shore.

My heart drops, and my feet hit the ground.

I sense Hook's eyes on me, but I ignore him and limp to the edge. My ankle aches from all the times over the past few days I've tried to fly. To pull away and get off this blasted ship. But I've never been able to, and now, like an animal beaten down so many times it's lost its fight, all I can do is lean against the rail of the *Roger.*

Out of my periphery, I instinctively keep tabs on anyone who might come close. In case any of the pirates want to try poking at the caged birdie again. Thankfully they're keeping their distance, probably on Hook's orders.

The captain has crossed to the stern, where he can still watch me, but is now deep in conversation with Nibs.

A flash of anger tightens my fists clutching the rail. I glare out over the roiling water. The shore of Neverland is a rocky, spiked landscape so close the spines of haggard trees and the mist coating distant mountains are visible. A faint gray tint of smoke curls over the western end of the island. If I squint, I can make out a flicker of tiny lights darting through the trees. The sky is overcast, the sunlight dim and faded. An echo of a long-forgotten beauty that has since died.

Even the wind that raises goosebumps on my arms feels haunting and sapped of life.

But somewhere out there, across that foreboding shore, is Connor. *So close.*

If only I could get rid of this chain.

Another swell of fury ripples through me, and at the smell of burning wood I glance down to find thin, charcoal flakes of dust scattering, leaving charred burn marks across the rail.

I shake off the dust and try to settle my mind. There has to be a way to burn through this chain.

But before I can seek out a private place to give it a try, a voice cuts through my thoughts.

"It didn't always look like that."

I glance up to find Slightly beside me, peering wistfully at Neverland. His freckles stand out against his pale skin, and a shock of hair falls into his eyes. For a moment, I have a flash of what this Lost Boy may have looked like as a child. Carefree and loud and adventurous.

Slightly is the only Lost Boy who drifted nearer and nearer to me on the trip over, genuinely seeming interested in friendship. He'd sneak me extra food and even bandaged up my hands when I ripped my palms and fingertips raw trying to burn through the chain to no avail.

He's the only Lost Boy who doesn't seem quite as afraid of Hook . . . or as coated in guilt as Nibs is.

Slightly's mouth tilts into a reminiscent smile. "It used to be so bright and vibrant. Even on the days that Peter was gone and the cold came, it was nothing like this."

"What changed?"

He blinks rapidly, shooting a glance toward the captain. "Hook is right—believe it or not. He is trying to protect you. There are things here that are far more dangerous than you know. And it's gotten even worse than the last time we were here."

I study him for a long moment.

"You don't want to be here either, do you?" I ask. "You're trapped too, like I am."

He presses his lips together, sliding a hand into his pocket, and then darts his eyes around the ship.

He sidles a little closer. "It's all become so complicated. But you . . ." He takes something small and slender out of the pocket. It glints in the sunlight. "You can get away if you want. You can just fly away."

I keep my voice low. "Not with this chain, I can't." I palm the thick, metal links.

"But if I unlocked it, you could run. Fly. That's something none of us can do." Slightly leans into me. "You can get away, Claire. Fly home. Go somewhere they will never find you. Leave all of this behind."

My brow ripples. "Leave? I still need to find—"

But Slightly quickly shakes his head. "*No.* No, you can't stay. You have to get away before Connor finds you. Promise me, Claire. Promise you'll fly to Earth and never look back."

Slightly glances over his shoulder again, and this time Hook stirs, gray eyes narrowed and cold.

Uh oh . . .

I quickly bend my leg and balance my foot against the side of the ship, high enough that Slightly can get to the cuff circling my ankle—and the small lock pinning it in place. His hands shake as he slides the slender knife into the lock slot and starts picking it.

"Promise me that you will fly as far away from here as you can," he implores.

He's too slow with that blade. Hook is only steps away. I nudge the knife aside.

"Let me try!" I close my eyes, fill my palms with the chain, and unleash the pain. *Please, please work.* I can feel Slightly trembling beside me, and something about his fear enflames my anger. Nothing about this world is what I expected. This ship is a cage— and I can't free them if I can't save myself.

Fierce determination cannonballs through the ashen specks

that pour from my skin. The dark dust burns through the heavy chain in seconds. It falls to the deck.

But Hook is here.

Slightly jumps in front of me, blocking the pirate captain.

Hook raises a dagger, glare locked on me. "Don't you dare—"

Too late, you old codfish.

I catch Slightly's desperate eyes one last time, and he mouths, "*Fly!*"

I leap onto the rail and don't even bother to glance back at the captain. My future is ahead. I drop off the edge of the ship. Shining, golden dust erupts from me. I'm finally unleashed from my cage, and I've never felt lighter.

Hook shouts orders, and a bullet zings past my ear, but they're far too late. Every fiber of my being crackles to life. My back skims the whitecaps, and then I spin onto my stomach as dust ignites the air around me. I fly faster and faster, fingertips skimming the water as I zoom toward Neverland.

I can faintly hear Hook bellowing after me, voice filled with anger and edged with alarm.

But I pour on more dust and soon leave the pirate's echoing voice behind as I cross into Neverland. I fly through the thick jungle and am soon swallowed by the spines of dark, charred trees. I don't stop, don't slow down, just keep flying faster and faster. Deeper and deeper.

The island closes in. Shriveled, twisted branches claw out, scratching my face. The sun fades as eerie, thick mist swells around me, and soon I can hardly see. Even my dust feels masked and stifled here. I pour out more to stay afloat.

I'm not quite sure what I'm flying toward, looking for—but my gut says that whatever lies in the heart of this Neverland will find me.

I let my feet drop and keep pressing forward, quickly making my way across cracked, craggy ground. I didn't realize the jungle on this island would be so thick. Strange dark veins spiderweb across the jungle floor. Shrieking howls of animals break the eerie silence every few minutes, but the unnerving sounds are muffled. A shiver crawls over my arms, and as dread sets into my bones, it almost looks like the trees bend in toward me. Like the mist grows thicker. The island gets colder.

Pulling my tattered cardigan more tightly around myself, I force my mind to clear. To steady. *There is no danger here, not yet.*

And with that single thought, as my calloused feet step over snapped twigs and cold ground, the mist thins. Warmth starts to soak in all around me. The trees lean away, this time shifting forward, as if gesturing me onward.

Almost as if the jungle is reacting to *me.*

But that's not possible . . .

Right?

Or maybe Neverland really is a place where the never is possible.

I slow down, feeling I've put enough space between me and the pirates. As I near one of the sharp, angular trees, I reach out to touch it, but before my hand can brush the bark, the tree visibly flows toward me. A thin branch presses into my palm. It's a slow, languid movement—almost sad. Like a sick puppy nuzzling your hand.

I stare up at the tree. "How on earth . . . ?"

But I'm not on Earth. This *is* a fantasy world. Maybe even the trees are aware.

I trail my fingertips along one of the thin, spindly offshoots of the branch. It shivers under my touch, and that odd cold soaks into my skin again. "Shhh . . ." I whisper instinctively, moving closer to the tree. Thin drips of gold spill from my fingers.

As my pixie dust flickers and lands on it, the slender gold flakes soak in, and the tree warms. It stretches, like a haggard old man waking from a years-long nap, and a rich brown color returns to its darkened bark.

A little smile tugs at my mouth.

I move my hand along the reaching branch and then place both hands on the trunk. Another flash of chill skims over my body, but warmth again returns as more of my dust soaks into the tree. A faint hint of green starts to flicker at the edges of the branches. Tiny leaves unfurling. Small pink buds, barely the size of my fingernail, press their heads up.

Relief. I'm not sure if the whisper of sensation is coming from the tree or me.

Suddenly, a blast of angry wind rips through the jungle, bringing with it a rolling cloud of dark mist. My skin crawls, muscles going tight. The ground shakes again, and I cling to the tree. The color has already been leached from it, the hint of leaves now shriveled and dying.

The island convulses around me.

I almost crash to my knees. The ground shakes and rolls beneath my feet. My chest is so tight I gasp for air, eyes watering.

This feels like a panic attack. But it's not just me—it's this place.

Something is so very wrong here. Something about this island is . . . built into my bones. As if these are more than just trees and ground and mountains. Something deeper. Something unexpected.

And right now, it's screaming for me to run.

I stumble back the way I came, but the ground is rolling so

heavily I almost trip. Gasping, I use a bit of dust to keep my footing and run away from the dread that lifts through the icy ground.

The shadowed mist swallows me, so cold that ice forms on the ground.

Thud, thud, thud.

New footsteps. Not running but marching forward determinedly.

I don't know if it's Hook or some other unseen threat, but from the way terror fills my veins, and the way this whole island trembles, it's not good.

Not safe . . . not safe.

I force my legs to move faster despite the stray rocks and scattered sticks cutting at my bare feet.

A vine shoots out of the mist and wraps around my shin. Another appears from the opposite direction, and I wince as it wraps around my sprained ankle. Fear spikes through me. *No!* More dark vines slither like snakes across the ground and spiral up my legs.

I try to rip them away, but more rough vines wrap my wrists. Shooting up my body and winding around my chest. Holding me in place. My head twists around, frantic to understand what is happening.

"Let me go!" I cry out. "What are you?"

Shadows seep all around me. The mist darkens markedly, and a tremor ripples through the ashen trees.

A figure steps forward, silhouetted by the mist. He lopes closer, the mist clinging to him. The vines wrapping me perceptively shift toward him.

I struggle against the stiff hold of the thick vines. "Get me out of these!"

He doesn't say anything, just glides closer, head bent forward so that his long, pale hair hides his features. Bile rises in my throat, and the island ripples again. His skin is sickly pale, and he seems too thin.

"W-who . . . ?" I can't seem to get the word out.

He steps right up to me. Slowly, painstakingly, he lifts his head, paralyzing me by the haunting expression in those eerily familiar blue eyes.

I gasp.

"I'm here, Claire."

3

PETER

Neverland
Present

This Neverland is twisted and fragmented, everything turned around and wrong. North is south, south is west, and the stars are hidden day and night. Yet as Tootles guides me through the thick, ashen foliage and past the spiral of smoke from Lily's village, I know where we are going.

At least, I think so, until the blithering earthquake starts. It spirals through the quivering jungle, and the ground dips and bends like some giant beast waking beneath our feet. The sky darkens, storm clouds moody and thickening. I fight for my balance as thin cracks splinter across the craggy ground underfoot.

"Peter, just wait—" Tootles begins, but I ignore him.

This is *my* island. My chest twists with every ripple underfoot. I don't know what in the blasted heck is happening to this place, but I refuse to let it hold me back.

Stubbornly keeping my head up, I force my way forward. The ground bucks back at me, and I lose my footing. I fall forward but manage a stiff roll to cushion my fall. When I leap back to my feet, I don't see the tree branch swinging my way before it's too late.

Blast!

I grit my teeth and keep moving forward.

Tootles catches up to me as I shoot a glare at the dark trees surrounding me, spindly branches clawing skyward. *Lay off, would the lot of you?*

"This whole place has got its blasted knickers in a twist."

Tootles shakes his head. "You said it, not me." He jogs on ahead.

The island begins to settle down, apparently finishing up its latest tantrum. Tootles cuts through a craggy field and nimbly leaps over a small stream I think I recognize—though now it's filled with murky, dark goo.

Certainly didn't dream up *that*.

We skirt around a grove of dead flowers—and I remember this patch of trees, twisted as they are. And the cluster of rocks we used to climb on.

We're close!

My pace speeds up, and I round the corner excitedly because I *know* it's here.

But the shriveled, warped tree standing in the middle of the charred ground is nothing like I remembered.

Our tree is so haggard that you almost can't make out the slender holes chiseled into the side. I'm a tangled mess of threads of relief and homesickness knotted up in disbelief at how shriveled it's all become. Footsteps dragging, I go over to the hollow tree and trace a uniquely shaped hole winnowed out in the side. "This was Cubby's . . ."

Tootles knocks a calloused knuckle against the rough bark. "Yes. His chute was the biggest and the only one still usable. I only recently moved back here—it's been so long, the pirates don't even bother to keep tabs here anymore."

Skin growing cold, I circle the tree. I can make out a few more of the tunnel entrances, but the shapes that had once been carved out to perfectly fit each of the Lost Boys have now been nearly swallowed up as the tree has twisted and bowed.

But I'm curious. "How did you survive for so long?" Tootles rubs at the back of his head. "Moved and hid a lot, mainly. Watching, learning how the pirates and Connor made do. Learned to work around them. For months, I'd have to find a new hideout practically every day. At least I know the island better than nearly anyone else and could set up traps and warning systems near some of the hideouts."

"Including the booby traps and trip wires we had around this old place?"

"Especially those."

Noted. Careful where I step and what leaves I tug on, I continue circling the tree. I stop when I reach one hauntingly familiar cutout shape. Even shriveled as it is, I recognize the entrance that I'd carved out for myself. Bending down, I press my hand against the side of the small tunnel. Even if the tree hadn't contorted like this, I would never be able to fit in this hole.

I'm much too big now.

Something about that realization makes my temples throb. So much has changed. Far more than I want to admit. When I try to unravel even one thread of that blooming mess, I find that it's wrapped like a noose around my neck. The past doesn't play nice.

"Ready to go in?" Tootles is not watching me but scanning the jungle around us.

Ah—right. We're probably exposed here.

Pushing aside the disappointment, I muster a lopsided grin. "You bet! Lead on, chap."

He levels me another one of those long, perceptive glances. Then he turns and goes back toward the larger hole that had once been Cubby's.

With practiced fluidity, Tootles leaps feetfirst into the hollowed entrance. I can hear the faint rumble of his body sliding through the tunneled-out chute and down to the underground hideout beneath.

I step up, take a deep breath, and then duck inside the cutout. "Here goes nothing." Feetfirst, I jump in.

The chute is still very small and my shoulders are almost too broad. I squeeze my arms over my chest and somehow manage to scoot through. I thud out on the other end, landing on the hard-packed dirt floor.

As I leap to my feet, I'm riveted by the look of shock on Tootles's face. He's even paler, lifting a finger to his lips.

"Hey, let's not do that . . ." He's speaking in an oddly hushed, even-tempered tone, but fear cuts beneath his words.

My brows clash together. "What?"

I start toward him, but Tootles quickly shakes his head, gesturing for me to stay still.

"Take it easy. Let's not do anything brash."

His wide gaze is fixated on something behind me. Over my shoulder.

Every nerve on high alert, I swivel on my heel. My mouth drops open at the form hovering against the edge of the dirt-walled hideout. It's a little more ragged, a little dimmer, and a heck of a lot smaller than I remembered.

But that is definitely my shadow.

And it's holding a knife.

My stomach drops, and the bottoms of my feet burn where the

scars used to be. Guessing my shadow isn't very happy about me cutting it off.

I put my hands out. "Whoa—mate—let's talk this out."

Tootles gestures to the dark, almost transparent silhouette. "Yes, c'mon, Shadow. You've already been told it wasn't entirely his fault."

My mouth drops open for the second time. "You have talked about this?"

My gaze darts between the Lost Boy and the small, impish shadow stalking toward us. It slides across the floor, knife forward.

I shoot Tootles a dour look. "It's not *entirely* my fault? What kind of codswallop have you been—"

But Shadow darts forward, grabbing for my ankles and swinging the blade.

I leap backward and slam into Tootles. We both go flying, knocking over a few wayward dishes and a ramshackle chair. I land on my back, knocking the wind from my lungs. My eyes shoot open, and I come face-to-face with my shadow.

It's dangling above me, splashed across the curved roof of the hideout.

This is it.

He's going to drop down and gut me like a fish.

Because, let's be honest, I probably would do nothing less if someone had decided to chop me off.

I brace for the swipe of the blade, squeezing my eyes shut—

Nothing happens.

And that's when I realize Shadow has dropped the knife.

He's not looming over me—he's writhing against the ceiling. No, not writhing—laughing! Shadow is literally rolling on the roof. Laughing his blooming head off.

I bellow curses up at Shadow, and he continues miming laugher, pointing a small hand at me. And because this shadow is my own blasted echo, I know exactly what he's saying:

You should have seen the look on your face when I jumped at you, y'duffer.

I'm not sure if I'm shaking with fury or shock or stress or all of it, but when I pry myself off the ground, I toss a few choice words at that impish fellow.

Of course my boyish shadow-self would have a morbid sense of humor.

I'm finally able to catch my breath, the chill skimming my skin waning as I realize that maybe this shadowed nuisance isn't going to kill me after all.

Hopefully.

"Okay, so . . ." I turn toward Tootles and point to Shadow still clinging to the ceiling. "Explain how *this* happened."

Tootles shuffles his feet. "After you cut off your shadow and escaped—I think he fell. I found him all tangled up in the twisted branches of a tree, barely moving. I brought him back here, and pretty soon he was skittering around everywhere and getting into all kinds of trouble." He gives his head a shake. "He's a bit of a nuisance, but over time, Shadow sort of . . . kept me company."

As he casts a knowing glance at the shadow, Tootles's expression lifts with a small smile. I have a sudden idea of how lonely Tootles must have been while I was gone. The only Lost Boy left here, the only one who hadn't joined Hook.

When I spy Shadow again, he's slid down from the ceiling and lounges like a slip of paper on a cracked chair at the far end of the room. The large chair that I'd once called my throne. I'd perch in it like a proper royal and order the boys about. But now the makeshift throne has become dull and spider-webbed and a little shrunken, like the rest of this place.

I slowly turn in a circle and take in the hideout. Hard-packed dirt walls that used to be covered in moss or freckled by small flowers are now instead only marred by dark, jagged veins. Even the tree roots that used to curl out of the walls and create a perfect place to hang one's slingshot are gone. Dust cakes the ground, and the thick woven matts we'd rigged to sleep on have been piled in a corner to make a thicker bed for Tootles, and others have been propped at an angle as a makeshift chair.

Even the table and chairs we'd hand carved and strapped together with coils of rope are chipped and sagging.

Clearly Tootles has tried his best to patch up what he can, but this underground sanctum that used to be so full of life and rustic color and vibrancy and laughter and boys' games is now . . . dusty and forlorn.

Everything, that is, but the weapons that are within arm's reach near the exit of the hideout, where I see Tootles stow the pistol he's been carrying. Boxes of stored vegetables and dried meat are also stacked against the wall. I spy a pile of torn rags and needle and thread. I doubt it's for sewing clothes—more like sewing up wounds.

This place has been transformed into a bunker for survival.

A sharp pang shunts through my chest. My head starts to ache.

I scoop up some of the ointment and shredded rags from Tootles's stash and gingerly shove off my hoodie. "Mind if I . . . ?" I gesture to the slices that sting along my torso. He ducks his head in a nod, quickly crouching beside me and together we make quick work of binding up the cuts. The ointment not only helps the wounds heal but takes the edge off the pain.

Once I'm all fixed up, I tug my hoodie back on and slowly rise to my feet.

Tootles stares at me for a long minute, like he's going to say something, then lets out a long breath. "I'll find us something to eat." He wanders toward the mess quarters of the hideout.

I scan the hideout again, starting to feel a tad more optimistic at the thought of grub. But then I see the tiny nook nestled in the corner of the hideout. My chest locks up.

I try to toss a lousy attempt at humor toward Tootles. "You didn't give her home to another pixie, did you?"

But Tootles's reply is somber. "Peter, there aren't many pixies left."

I sputter. "What? What does that mean?"

He's scrounging around inside a large tub filled with some kind of dried fish. "Most of them haven't survived. They're too frail for how tumultuous Neverland has been with all the anger and doubt that Connor brought here."

In a haze, I head toward the small alcove carved out of the hideout's wall. A slender drape of woven, shimmering white strands handmade by the pixies themselves still falls over the entrance to the tiny home.

And I know, even before I gently lift the thin curtain and peer inside, that Tootles has taken good care of her.

Her memory.

I try to hold back the grief that is welling like a blasted storm inside of me.

Not a speck of dust mars Tink's small home. Her bed made of seabird feathers is stacked nicely. Her tiny thimble seat and the seashell mirror rest delicately in one corner. The tiny crown of dried berries I'd once made her lies beside her bed. I lean closer to take in the intricate drawings she'd spread across her walls. Painted by a tiny pixie hand and in a shimmering gold ink she'd stolen from the human world, silhouettes of Lost Boys circling the little place. Grinning and playing and meaning everything to the tiny pixie.

A pang pierces through me when I see that even Connor is pictured here.

Then I spot myself. Painted in the center of the curving wall, hands on my hips, large grin and dancing eyes.

And she's painted herself there too—a tiny fluttering thing perched on my shoulder.

Peter and Tink. The way it had always been. The way it was supposed to be.

In a world where the pixies had filled the island with light and life.

Not in this world that snuffed their very lights out.

As I stare at this empty place where Tink used to be, the wall I'd built to hold back grief splinters.

I break.

I can't pretend this is all fine. That I can still fix this, make it what it used to be.

I can't bring her back.

Can't bring any of it back.

It feels like a white-hot poker has suddenly been rammed through my temples, and my entire body shakes. My knees crumple, and I collapse to the floor. But it's the thick, wet tears dripping down my cheeks that are the most shocking. Salty and gushing from my blooming eyes.

It's all so wrong.

Tears flood down my face. My nose runs, and droplets dribble off my chin. I can't make it stop.

The world seems to spin. But it isn't until things begin to clatter around, chairs sliding and Tootles tripping across the floor, that I realize it's not just my head spinning.

The whole room spins. Rocking and shaking with my sobs.

The island is grieving with me.

Maybe my connection isn't as distant as I thought.

I'm not sure how long I continue to weep, glad that no one else is around besides Tootles and Shadow to see me grieve just how lost of a boy I truly am. How much has been torn away. Crying for Tink and her people. Everything I somehow ripped apart without ever realizing it.

When the tears finally ebb, a bit of strength comes back into my muscles, and the massive ache in my head has dulled as well.

Scrubbing at my face with a mucked-up sleeve, I gulp down deep breaths. My feet are unsteady as I stand, but at least the floor has stopped rocking. Shoving thick tendrils of reddish hair out of my eyes, I find Tootles staring at me.

"I don't think I've ever seen you cry before." His own eyes glisten. "Not even when Wendy left."

I wipe at my face. "Yeah, well, I don't think I've ever blubbered quite so much before." I point a stern finger at him. "And if you tell anyone—"

But Tootles throws spindly arms around me and clumsily pats my back. "It's all right, Peter. We all need a good cry sometimes."

Good ol' Tootles.

I reel back and wipe my leaking nose. "You sound like Claire."

"I think I'll like this Claire." He smiles.

I narrow my eyes at him. "Whoa, there. She's mine, mate."

Tootles colors. "That's not what I meant—"

"Don't fret, chap." I clap him on the shoulder. "I won't tell Tiger Lily you said that."

That makes him blush more, and I'm glad to see that his soft spot for the tribal princess is still there. At least some things don't change.

The familiar banter helps soothe the ache in my chest. Tootles offers me water, and after I guzzle it, a new kind of determination settles over me. I may not be able to bring the pixies back, but I can try to save whatever is left of this place and Claire. "All right, mate. I want to hear it—all of it. What is really going on here? And how did you survive for so long? I can't imagine Connor has been happy with you. Or Hook. Or anyone, really."

Tootles sits on one of the less rickety chairs. "It hasn't been easy." He slowly rolls up one of his baggy sleeves, and as he does so, I see the thick, jagged lines of roughly healed scars tracing up his thin arms. Nasty-looking scars—some of them deep enough and jagged enough that he must have stitched them up on his own.

I wince just thinking about it.

"Connor's connection to Neverland is unlike anything I've seen. He's learned how to wield the island like a weapon." He rolls up his other sleeve, revealing thin spirals of jagged scars. "One time, he tried to catch me by wrapping me up in thorny vines. And he told the sirens to drown me. Another time, it was a tree branch to my head."

He pulls back hair from his temple, revealing another scar disappearing into his hairline. "Connor already has control over nearly every tree and vine and inch of broken ground. The rivers flow with ink, and the sun rarely shines through."

Tootles braces his hands in front of him and looks straight at me. "If he gets what he really wants—total control of the island no longer split between you, him, and Claire?" His eyes grow dark. "He'll have access to more magic and devastation than anyone could ever come back from."

I slump to the floor, back against the packed-dirt wall. "And no one has tried to do anything? Even if only to slow him down?"

Tootles shakes his head. "They're all terrified. Even Hook. And a few months ago Connor kidnapped a tribal healer from Lily's people. Not even their warriors could stop him."

I'm surprised. "A healer? Why would Connor need a tribal healer?"

Tootles pinches his eyes shut. "I'm not sure. The healer refused to help with whatever Connor wanted. No one has ever seen him since, and his apprentices went into hiding. I've heard rumors from the few pixies who've been able to sneak on board the ship that Connor is researching into Dark Stars and Blood Bonds. I have no idea what that means, but I do know one thing."

He opens his eyes, and we both speak in unison. "It's not good."

I chew over everything he's just said. "Well, there's only one thing to do." Getting to my feet. I trail my gaze from Tink's little alcove, to Shadow plastered against the wall behind Tootles, and back down to the Lost Boy.

"We have to get Claire back before Connor can do anything dodgy. Once we have her back, we'll figure out what to do next. How to fix the island and rescue that healer."

Tootles looks at me a moment, then kicks back his chair as he abruptly rises to his feet. "That was actually a decent and not totally foolhardy idea." There's a ghost of a grin as he knocks me on the shoulder. "What did you do with the old Peter Pan?"

I blink. "I think he's finally growing up. Just the tiniest bit."

I expect another headache to swell at those words. For the

island to splinter and kittens to cry or some other dramatic nonsense. But instead, nothing shifts. Except the look on Tootles's face. For the first time, I think I see hope in his gaze.

"This new Peter may just be the only one who could actually pull this off."

4

CLAIRE

Neverland

The vines slither away, freeing my body—but I'm more entrapped, more frozen than ever. I can't feel my legs, throat closing up as I stare at the boy in front of me. No, not boy. The man.

It's been over six years since I last saw him. Since he disappeared.

This Connor I barely recognize. But the shattered look in his eyes is far too familiar. I take in the pale blue of his irises and the way he stares at me.

Like I'm not the only one trapped.

His skin is so pale it's almost bluish, and for a moment I think maybe he's cold and that's why he's shuddering, shivering. But then he looks away, and the hair hanging over the right side of his face shifts, and I see the dark veins. Thin, inky spiderwebs climbing up his neck, pulsing beneath his skin and spreading out, crossing his jaw and up his cheek.

Instinctively, I reach out to touch his face. I feel his cold skin beneath my fingertips. Connor whips away. *"Don't."*

I take a trepidatious step nearer to him. "Are . . . you okay?"

He's turned a little away, and after a pause, he faces me fully on. As he takes me in, a slow, fragile smile warms his face. He reaches out a hand. "Sorry for scaring you."

I stare down at his hand, pale, and the faint bluish hint of his dark veins beneath the white skin—but familiar too. The soft scar on his palm he got tumbling down the stairs in one of our foster homes.

I put my hand into his. "It's really you?"

Warmth seems to surge through his skin as he clasps my hand tight, voice a little raw. "Yeah. It's me."

And with that, I vault into him, letting go of his hand and wrapping both arms around his neck. Pulling my brother into a hug so tight neither of us can breathe, but I don't care.

I've found him.

I can't even speak, relieved, disbelieving tears welling in my eyes and swelling my throat shut.

"Please don't let this be a dream," I murmur, so quietly.

But Connor has buried his face against my neck and whispers back, "It's not a dream. I've missed you, Claire-y."

I bite my lip, hearing the old nickname. A few tears trace a path down my cheeks and wet his pale skin.

We stay like that for a long time, but it's still not long enough. Not long enough just *holding* my brother after spending what feels like an eternity wondering if I could ever get him back.

But everyone who told me it was hopeless was wrong. I've found him. And I'm never losing my Connor again.

Releasing a long breath, I lightly pull back, staring up at him, taking him in again. All the questions suddenly flood my mind. "How did you do that? With the vines? And how . . ." I wave a hand at the twisted, craggy world around us. "What happened here? What happened to you?"

His pale lips quirk slightly. "So many questions, as always." He dips a shoulder. "The vines were . . . to keep you safe. This island isn't so friendly. I didn't want you to keep running or to get hurt. Or to run from . . . me." The last word makes my whole heart ache.

I squeeze his hand again, voice trembling. "Never, Connor. I'd never run from you."

It's the first time I've used his name aloud.

His eyes lighten as he watches me, and then he gestures to the island around us. The mist has ebbed away, but the sky is still dark, trees gnarled and bent toward us. Neverland frail and skeletal. "Peter and I didn't get along so well, and the island got kind of sick." He's avoiding my eyes.

"It's okay—you can tell me all of it. What really happened with Peter." I look up at him, waiting for him to meet my eyes. Finally, his icicle-blue eyes drift down to meet mine. I try to coax the answer from him. "What kind of sick? What do you mean you didn't get along?"

He glances over his shoulder, and I follow his line of sight and see two figures approaching us distantly through the mist and shriveled palm trees. One of them walks with a slight limp and a familiar curve of a hook on one arm—the other I don't recognize. But it seems feminine.

Hook and . . . who? My skin crawls. I take the faintest step back from Connor, hoping he'll follow me. Shelter me. Something. The minutes stretch on, and I begin to think Connor won't answer me, just stand there, a little bent like the bedraggled trees around us.

His voice is low. "You know how sometimes there are things you lock deep down? Things that hurt too much to look at?"

A shiver snakes up my spine. "Very much."

He gives a little nod. "Figured you would. Well, here, in

Neverland . . ." He lifts his eyes to the shriveled palm fronds rocking against curved trunks. "Those things you bury deep down—they don't stay buried long. They sort of bubble out and seep into everything. Whether or not you want them to."

A cool breeze raises goosebumps along my shoulders, through my ragged cardigan. "What kinds of things, Connor?"

He shrugs and takes slow steps, tugging me along with him, finally putting distance between the approaching pirate and stranger. "Things I've been working through—but I don't have enough control over Neverland to really manage them right. The whole island is sick because of that. If I could control it"—he brushes a hand over the veins that spiderweb up the side of his face—"I could probably fix a lot of this. Instead of it just leaking out."

He's still dancing around the real truth. Feeding me bits and pieces, but they're not quite fitting.

"How can the island help you with the . . . things you've suppressed? Control what?"

He leads me deeper into the jungle, but I notice that the sun has actually begun to filter through the clouds here. "Where are you taking me?"

He grins down at me, pulling me with him a little faster. "You'll see! I can't wait for you to meet them. I'll explain everything after. They've been so excited to see you!"

"They?"

He seems almost giddy now. "Just wait and see."

We've left Hook far behind, but I can't help but notice how the jungle seems to ebb and flow around Connor. Trees angling toward him, dark puddles shifting out of the way of his steps. "What did you mean about control of the island? Is that how you moved those vines?"

He ducks around the arching arm of a tree and gestures for it to lean back for me, and it does. "We're both connected to the island, Claire. The same bond we've had since we were just children and the same bond Peter has. Only ours is much stronger than his ever really was."

We walk quickly, skirting past some towering palm trees and jumping over a small rippling brook. "Bond?"

He pulls up to a stop, behind an arching mossy cluster of rocks. "Why else do you think Neverland speaks to us? It's the magic in our veins. It's why whenever Peter left, Neverland would freeze over, and why when he'd return, it would thaw out." Connor is talking not as a boy who read a bedtime story, but as someone who observed it. He kneels down and places a palm against the ground. "It's why the whole island breathes with us. Why it sings to us and does what we ask." Two vines shoot out of the underbrush, slithering toward us. I jump back.

Connor waves a hand, and immediately the vines fall still. "Don't worry. They're not dangerous. They're just doing what I told them. You could probably control the island, too, if you tried."

I remember the tree that had reached toward me earlier today. I eye the vine. "Could Peter do that?"

"With the vines? Or water?"

Water?

Connor shakes his head. "No, that's just us. Because we're from here—part pixie and part siren." He braces a hand against the mossy curve of the largest boulder. "Though, I think you got most of the pixie side while I got the siren. I can't do the thing with the dust. It's pretty cool, though."

My jaw goes slack, eyes locked on him— "Wait...*siren?* What do you mean?"

"What, did you think you were full pixie? At that size?" He gives an odd little laugh. "We're descended from the most magical creatures of Neverland—it's why your dust has darker properties. And why we're connected to Neverland at all and share the same bond with the island Peter does."

And while it's *shocking*, to say the least, my brother's revelations seem to click into place. If we are part siren and part pixie . . . it would explain a lot.

"How did that even happen?"

He rubs at his forehead. "Something about a siren trading in his tail to walk on land . . . and a pixie giving up her wings to be his size. They died when we were very young, though no one will quite tell me how. But it doesn't really matter. What matters is what we can *do*." His eyes brighten. "I'll show you everything and teach you what you're capable of too. But first . . . you have to see this."

He starts to climb up the mossy boulders, beckoning for me to follow. A little uncertain, I brace one foot against one of the lower rocks and clamber up after him. He gives me a hand up, and soon we're sliding over the other side, a short drop to the ground. I land soundly on my bare feet, dust myself off, and lift my eyes to take in where he's brought me.

My jaw drops.

We're nestled in a small glade of some kind. A circle of trees rim the area, but instead of shriveled and bent, they're actually woven and curled together like an intricate latticework. Moss glides down from the boulders and sweeps across the ground, speckled with little flowers that have opened delicate white petals.

But it's not the scenery that makes me gasp—it's the flickering, golden little balls of light that flutter across the mossy knoll and set the latticework of trees alight. Like fairy lights strung in a circle around us, but they're alive. Real. Tiny pixies that drift through the air leave drizzles of pixie dust everywhere the eye can see.

"What is this?"

"Pixie Grove." A curious little smile appears. "Do you like it? I made it for you. The Pixie Tree isn't too far from here."

I can't seem to take it all in. "It's incredible." The pixies begin to drift in toward me. Small, bobbing bodies that leave behind trails of glorious, gleaming dust. My own dust lifts from my skin and joins the cool late-afternoon breeze, igniting the air with glimmers of gold. A few pixies reach me, and they pepper my arms and neck with butterfly kisses, whispering greetings and sweet nothings.

Connor drifts closer, but the pixies seem more taken with me. "Welcome home, Claire," he whispers.

My eyes well up. Seeing all these pixies filling this grove, seeing this part of my family in their homeland. Their gleaming light and the way they flit and soar. It reminds me of the first time I met them in Kensington Gardens.

"If this was all here"—I blink back my tears—"why did you let Hook keep me trapped on the *Roger*? Why didn't you try to let me out?"

Connor's scraggly hair falls over the side of his face again. "I told you, the island isn't very safe. I was hoping I could make it more beautiful before you saw it."

I nuzzle one of the pixies back and gently catch one that tumbles out of my hair. I watch them chatter and chide each other and chuckle.

Finally, I turn. "I'm not fragile, Connor. I can handle the reality of this place. I'm just glad the pixies are okay."

There's a slight tick in his jaw, and the veins across his features pulse a bit, growing darker for a moment.

I point to the dark veins spiraling up his face and abruptly ask, "What is that, Connor? Does that hurt?"

He won't look at me.

"Will it go away?"

He remains silent as I persist. "Can I help you somehow?"

That captures his attention. "Actually, I could use your help, Claire."

"Of course. What can I do?" A few more pixies fly in little swirls around my body, creating streams of pixie dust that loop around me. Out of my periphery, I can see others of the small winged creatures break off into pairs and go dancing and skittering across the glade. A few grab my fingers and start to pull me toward the middle of the grove.

The ground underfoot is silky with moss and clusters of those bunched white flowers. Pixie dust is scattered throughout the air and sinks to the moss, igniting the whole grove like dangling sparks of sunlight. A gentle breeze whistles through the hem of trees, softly rustling tropical leaves.

I humor the pixies as they tug at me and dance through the air around my head, laughing at their antics. I glance over my shoulder at Connor, who is following on my heels. His icicle-blue eyes watch me unwaveringly. "Yes, there's one thing I could really use your help with," he responds.

"What's that?" The pixies begin to spin me, and I smile, batting a few away that tug too hard on my hair. I don't mean to ignore Connor who is standing stiffly by, watching, but I can't help getting caught up in the moment. "You aren't going to dance?"

"Not my thing."

"Suit yourself." I give a little spin.

He rubs again at the veins climbing the side of his neck. "Maybe after you give me your connection to the island and I can finally manage some of this, I'll feel like dancing."

I almost trip over my own feet, swinging around to look at him. "After I what?"

"Give me your connection to Neverland," he restates. "I need a bit more control—once I have that, I'll be able to make all of Neverland like this." He gestures to the glade, and I suddenly freeze.

I just found out about my connection. About how whole I am here. And he wants me to cut that away?

My pulse kicks up, and I scan the latticework of trees, thoughts tripping and scrambling, trying to find a way this fits together— but suddenly the weave of trees doesn't look so ornamental.

It looks like the walls of a cage.

My chest tightens.

I made this for you. Connor's words ricochet in my thoughts. One pixie is tugging on the hem of my shirt, while a few more spiral around my head, but as I really examine the pixies and my surroundings, I notice something I didn't see before.

Their eyes.

Above the almost too wide smiles filling the pixies' small faces, their wide eyes are almost screaming at me. As they dart around, they seem hardly able to look at Connor. I realize though the pixies swirl around me, they fully avoid him.

Despite putting on a show for me, a tremor runs through their small bodies, and a haze of blinking red undercoats their golden shimmer. It's not the angry kind of red I've seen before.

This color means something else. Fear.

I made this for you.

One of the pixies that had been sitting at the edge of the grove suddenly beelines toward me. Her brown hair flurries around her green eyes, as she stops just in front of my nose. She vibrates a deep, eerie red—not just afraid, far angrier.

She stares me in the eyes and says one word that I understand perfectly:

"*Fly!*"

She spins and flies as quickly as she can toward the edge of the grove. But before she reaches the edge of the trees, they groan and snap and twist tighter, until they have bent in and woven so tightly together that they've formed a wall around us.

I turn to look for Connor and jolt to find that he's standing right behind me, those icy blue eyes darkened.

"What's going on?" Pale, almost-panicked dust begins to drip from my fingers.

He looks at the pixies that have all fled to the edge of the glade and are trying to squeeze out between the branches or starting to aim for the sky that is growing more overcast by the minute.

"I told them they shouldn't leave."

I still. "Why?"

Connor's mouth clamps shut.

My body hums, every nerve on edge. "Connor, *please* . . ."

His voice is toneless. "The rest are all dead."

I gape at him. "N-no . . . can't be . . ."

"It's true." His words are almost imperceptible. I see a flash of something dark boiling under his skin.

I grab his shoulders and give him a little shake.

"Just be honest—what has really happened here? To our world?" My voice is rising, raw, trembling.

He doesn't look at me. But slowly, the trees forming a woven wall around us begin to bend and sag and lean back. The remaining pixies that hadn't flown over the top flutter away. As the pixies and their gold dust disappear, the small glade suddenly feels very, very dark.

"I told you the island was sick," Connor mutters. "The pixies are fragile. Most of them couldn't take it. Peter never really knew how to manage this place either. He would just let the island wipe away anything he didn't like. Wipe away the memories. Until it couldn't, and his selfishness started to tear this place apart. I had to take control."

This part of the story is the first thing that truly makes sense.

His brows clash together. "He almost killed me for it. For having a stronger bond with the island—so I kicked him out. I sent him falling to Earth where he couldn't hurt the island anymore."

"It was more than he would have done for me," Connor adds. "But even with Peter gone, the island is still . . . splintering."

I watch as the dark haze fills his pale blue irises. "But you can help, Claire. You can give me what I need to fix everything. Will you let go of your connection and give me the full stream of magic I need to restore this island?"

A chill slithers down my spine.

This is my Connor, the one I've been searching for so long . . . So, why do I feel like his definition of *fix* and mine are two dangerously different things?

5

CLAIRE

Neverland

Connor watches me, waiting for an answer.

I take a step back, a sheen of dust coating my palms. The instant I'm out of his reach, his eyes narrow. Another flash of something roiling and inky beneath the surface. There's something else there. Something lurks below the Connor I once knew.

Something volatile.

"You can't just leave, Claire. You have to give me your connection to the island. It's easy—you just transfer that stream of magic to me. Like soaking me in your dust—but something far deeper, more primal than that. Giving up the cord that has always tethered you here." His voice turns pleading. "Don't you want to help me? It won't hurt, and you'll still have your dust and can stay in Neverland with me."

I take another step back and look at him. At the way the dark veins writhing up his face seem to darken a bit, at the desperation in his eyes.

I'm not quite sure that giving my brother more power will actually help heal an island that has been shredded by the connection he already has.

A low, dry chuckle fills the air from somewhere behind us.

"I told you she wouldn't do it."

In my attention locked so closely on my brother, I hadn't even heard the footsteps until they crunch through the underbrush behind me. I spin around and see someone stepping out from the rim of trees circling us. The waiflike silhouette that I'd caught sight of before. The woman who glides toward us is so ghostly pale that I wonder if she is mirage from the mist.

Connor shakes his head. "I guess you were right."

I'm confused as he moves away. The stranger comes closer. Everything about her, from her bony fame to her faded red hair, seems leached of color and sickly.

I instinctively wrench backward, crafting a bit of dust and primed to fly right out of this situation. "Who are you?"

Her pallid green eyes are hollow and look past me toward my brother. "As agreed, we do this my way now. We'll take her to Skull Rock."

Yeah, not a fan of that plan. A small wave of dust cascades over my arms, and I start to rise—but before I get very far off the ground, a wrinkled vine shoots up and curls around my ankle, locking me in place. I swivel toward Connor. "What the heck do you think you're doing? Who is this woman? What's going on?"

He almost seems mournful as he meets my gaze. "Don't hurt her too much."

But he's not talking to me. He's talking to *her*.

The woman's hollow eyes ignite with a sharp spark. She draws a long, slender knife out of her tattered skirts.

I gasp. "Get back!" I yell and kick at her with my free foot, but Connor twists his hand, and another vine wraps that leg. I'm pulled to the ground, onto my knees.

Pain jolts me, and I lift my head to my brother, eyes beginning to water. "Connor, please—"

But his expression has gone distant. He is no longer even looking at me, just watching the woman, who steps up and lifts her knife. Dark, angry, frenzied dust begins to swirl around me, whipping through my blue cardigan, but the woman doesn't even seem to notice as flecks sizzle against her shins. She lets the blade hover at my neck. I try to pull away, but she jabs the point close enough to prick my skin, and I freeze. More dust churns, but it's not burning through the vines fast enough.

She leans in close to whisper, "You may not be ready to comply just yet . . . but you will."

Then she slams the handle of the knife into my temple, and the world erupts with sparks. I drop to the ground like a ragdoll, head screaming and darkness pulling at me. My brother's eyes are the last thing I see as I fade into unconsciousness. He stares down at me with an expression as hollow as hers.

6

CLAIRE

Neverland

I wake up screaming.

Jerking upright from where I'm stretched out upon a cold, stony floor, I find that I'm locked inside some kind of cell. The room is carved out of rock, with a few small holes to let in light on one wall, and on the opposite side, a door made of roughly hammered iron is crammed into a rectangular-shaped opening. There's a bucket and threadbare blanket but nothing else.

Everything about this cell is harsh and cold.

A sob fills my chest.

I lift my hand and watch a few flakes of gold freckle my palm.

Closing my eyes and taking a deep breath, I force down my fear and reach for that hum of magic pulsing through my veins, burrowed in the marrow of my bones. Only this time, it's not just the warmth of my pixie dust that I sense—it's the whole island. Neverland's song. The melody is a faint whisper, a little breathless and afraid, but it swells and dances through my thoughts, whispering, *welcome home.*

It lets me know that even here, trapped in this cage, I am not helpless.

And I'm not ready to give up that melody just yet.

Pixie dust coats my skin, filling the air and rippling over my body. I rise off the floor and float over the ground. I peer through a small rectangular window at the top of the door. I can just make out the rough shapes of other cells built into the rocky surface. I remember what the woman said—

"We'll take her to Skull Rock."

Skull Rock. It's real. And apparently it doubles as a prison.

The Disney version never showed that.

Although I do think I remember something about Hook trying to chain up the Darling kids and drown them.

I shiver and sink down to sit on the dank floor, back against the curve of the chilled rock. I'm close enough to the door to hopefully be able to hear anyone coming or quickly fly up and peek out the small window again.

I'm not sure how long I've been sitting there when my ears perk up at the thud of approaching footsteps. I lightly float up to look out. Connor is leading a small group of people down the narrow hallway toward me. The tall, spindly woman who threatened me with the knife is on his heels, looking every bit as hollow and cold as ever. But behind them is someone more familiar—a certain one handed pirate. As they all stop in front of my cell, Hook glances between me and the woman who has already drawn a key from her pocket.

Hook offers to open the lock, and my eyebrows rise when, after he has done so, he places a hand on the woman's back to enter. It's subtle, but I still catch it.

Interesting . . .

As they lock the door behind them, I hover against the roof at the back of the cell, trying to stay out of their reach. But the ceiling is too low for much protection.

I let out a long sigh, deciding that it's probably better to reserve my strength. I slide down against the cool rock wall and sit with my knees tucked against my chest, eyes darting between the three of them. "What do you want with me?"

I stiffen as Connor settles against the wall beside me. As if it's a normal day and he's just my brother about to discuss the weather. Not like he locked me in the place to begin with.

He's calmed a bit, although those angry, inky veins still climb across half of his face. A tremor ripples through his body every few seconds, but when he speaks, his voice is cool and collected.

"We are both connected to this island, Claire. You and I—and Peter." His eyes seem to go darker and then clear. Connor shoots a look at the woman and then continues. "Peter gained his connection by creating this place. This island was his escape. But Neverland is our birthright—we were born here, Claire. Born with our very hearts woven into the fabric of Neverland, and so we share the same connection Peter used to have some control of."

It's not new information, but hearing him say it just like that, it sinks in in a different way. I watch my brother closely. "Then do you know who our parents were?"

He nods. "Yes, I discovered that much at least. Once we fix the island—I'll tell you what I can." My brother takes a step forward, eagerness humming in his voice. "Oh, there is still so much you don't know, Claire. Even about yourself. I can't wait to show you—"

A harsh, loud cough cuts him off, and he glances at the woman. She doesn't say anything, but her icy stare dominates the room.

I am getting a headache. I turn a fierce glare on the woman. "Who are you? You obviously know things I don't. What's so funny?"

Her expression goes blank. Connor puts a hand on my arm. "Claire, I wasn't entirely honest about why I needed your connection." But something about his touch feels hollow. Even the way he's sitting is too stiff, despite how casual he's trying to appear. Like he's playing a part. "If I can have the full strength of the connection to Neverland, I can change the rules and rewrite the way the island works and stop the decay. But it's more than changing the island."

He pauses, then leans in toward me and whispers, "I can erase the memories. Everything that is tearing me apart and bubbling up inside. I can start over, Claire."

I bite my lip and regard my brother. An eager, hopeful warmth that lights up his face in a way I haven't seen since I arrived. He almost looks like the little boy I remember.

I desperately want to believe him.

"What memories? How do I know this would really work?" Letting a bit more dust drift from my palms, I use it to leverage back to my feet and lean against the curving stone wall of the cell. "Does it have to be all or can it be just part of my connection? And how do I know that if I did give you some of my connection to the island that it would actually help you?" I press. "What would be the ramifications of losing some of that magic? Would it take away my dust?" As if on cue, a few flecks of pixie dust lift some of my curls from about my shoulders.

The woman speaks for the first time. "Giving up your bond with the island would not affect your natural-born magic, simply your impact on Neverland."

"How do I know what you're saying is true?" I narrow my eyes at her. "How can I trust you? I don't even know who you are. And you almost slit my throat."

"It doesn't matter."

I utter a mock laugh. "You want me to give up my magical connection to the island based off the word of some crazy stranger who knocked me over the head with a knife? No thanks."

Hook shoots me a cautioning look as he goes over to the woman and puts a hand on her shoulder. She visibly relaxes.

"I think you should tell her, Paige. Tell her why you know more about this island than even Peter does."

She goes very still, measuring me. When she finally does speak, it's very slowly, cautiously, as if she's not sure I even deserve to have a glimpse at the cards she's playing so close to her chest.

"I was the very first Lost Girl. Long before Wendy ever set foot on this island. Peter doesn't remember me, but I've been here from the very beginning."

My stomach drops to my toes. *No. Way.*

Something about her haggard appearance and desperate eyes hits differently now.

"And I know all about the connection to the island because I used to be tethered to Neverland . . ." Her eyes shift. "Before Peter tried to kill me."

I can't breathe. "Why would he do that?"

But there's a strange lurking suspicion as I turn her words over and over in my head. Her icy green eyes start to thaw.

She glances at Hook, and he gives a subtle nod. Her lithe body moves forward. I suddenly realize that while this woman is rather terrifying, I also recognize the fractured, aching expression that bleeds through the cracks in her cold demeanor. It's the same look Connor and I are both marred with.

This woman has suffered horrible things.

She leans down until she is at eye level with me. Her hair falls over her shoulders, ragged and tangled and a faded red. When she tilts her chin and gives me a weary almost-smile, it suddenly hits me why this woman seems so familiar. Why something about the slight tilt of her shoulders and red hair, the curve of her jawline and hollow expression is so haunting.

She reminds me of someone else.

"My name is Paige," she says, voice void of emotion. "And I'm Peter Pan's sister."

My jaw goes slack.

It's . . . insane.

Utterly insane.

But this island has been full of surprises.

She watches me closely, as if she expects me to recoil or bombard her with questions. I do nothing. I just sit here, studying her, seeing all the ways she suddenly seems so very much like Peter. And all the ways she is nothing like him. The gauntness that not only shakes her thin form but fills her expression. Until I know why she would lie, I'll play along.

I clear my throat. "What did Peter do?"

Her head ticks to the side, a hint of surprise in her dull green irises. "You are stronger than you look." She glances again at Hook, and I get the sense that he's told her about me. Her expression grows distant. "I came with Peter to this island many, many years ago when we first needed somewhere to escape."

How could Peter have not remembered he had a sister? That they arrived here together?

I glance at my brother, and he just nods.

Not exactly reassuring.

"James Hocken was one of the first Lost Boys Peter ever brought to the island. He was one of the oldest. If you choose to, you can grow in your own way here. Like the tribal warriors do. And so James and I did. We grew up together, and eventually, that childhood friendship grew into something more." As Paige continues, the pirate captain gently glides the blunt curve of his hook down her shoulder. My mind is whirling. "James and I fell in love and decided that we wanted more for ourselves than just this island. We wanted a future."

The wistful smile on her lips shifts into a scowl that makes my blood turn cold. "But of course Peter didn't want things to change. He hated the thought of losing both James and me. We quarreled and he . . ." Her knuckles turn white. "He attacked James, cutting off his hand and feeding it to that crocodile. Then Peter nearly killed me in his desperation to make us stay."

There's iron in her voice and steel in her gaze. "So, forgive me if I'm the first to just assume that you would give up your own power simply because your brother asked for it. I've seen family bonds cast aside like chum to be fed to the crocodile."

I can understand her dissonance, the hurt that fills each word, the way Peter's selfishness has torn her life apart. And if anything, it reminds me why I had to leave him behind in the first place.

The person Peter Pan always seems to care most about is himself.

But I am not here to talk about Peter.

I am here for my brother.

I'm near exhaustion but take Connor's hands in mine and look at him. "If I help you, promise me you'll make them let me go?"

His eyes gleam. "I'll rip open the door to this cell myself."

I let out a long breath and glance once again at Paige.

I dart a glance at Hook. "Once I tether Connor fully to the island and he's able to restore himself and Neverland, I'm done?

This is all over? He can come home with me?"

Hook wraps his hand over the handle of his cane and nods, expression dead serious. "Absolutely."

Paige doesn't say anything, just watches with those haunting, faded green eyes. So like Peter's—but hollow and sickly, like a withered flower that's been kept away from the light for years. And in that moment, I know there is only one choice.

Peter's selfishness, his determination to keep this world and these people all for himself, exactly how he wanted them, is what got us into this mess in the first place.

Maybe a single selfless act of mine can undo everything that has been shattered.

I look straight into Connor's eyes. "You will always mean far more to me than any amount of magic or power."

And it's true. Because I love my brother.

I take his hand and close my eyes and reach deep into the swell of light and air and hum of magic that beats deep in my chest like a second heart. The tether that I instinctively know how to find. The same pulse that tells me just how sick this island is. How exhausted and twisted and broken it is. Needing to be whole, to be remade.

So, I reach into that deep well of magic, that hum inside of me spreading out like a heartbeat through this whole island. Echoing through Connor, through the beat of his pulse beneath my palms.

And I give that to him.

Give him that tether of magic. That whisper of connection. I sever the heartbeat of Neverland that I've just learned how to hear and let the stream of magic flow away from me and into my brother.

I give the life pulse of the island to Connor Kenton. Let it soak into him like my dust.

And immediately my whole body grows cold. My own pulse

slows. My chest tightens, constricts. I watch the pixie dust shimmering and flecking my skin fade, dim, and disappear.

"Wh-what is happening?"

Sharp panic lances through me, and my frantic eyes latch onto Hook and Paige.

But neither of them are looking at me. They're staring at Connor, who has ripped his hands out of my grasp and risen to his feet. His whole body is pulsing. At first I think it's with light, but then I realize there's something eerie about the glow. The thin, dark veins that had spider-webbed up his face grow and spread, faster and faster. They race down his neck, over his shoulders, and across his arms. His skin becomes more and more pallid in between the ragged veins.

Then his blue-tinted skin begins to crack and ripple. Like a mask made of stone that slowly shatters.

It's like he's coming apart.

But he doesn't seem to mind. He throws his head back, taking in a deep breath, and I hear thunder strike overhead.

With a wild smile he raises his arms before Paige and Hook. The pirate captain falters back a step, hand tight on his cane. But Paige is gazing at Connor, beaming.

"It worked!" he exults, and she nods, pride shining from her.

"Yes. We're so close now."

I gape up at them, confusion stinging like the tears that are filling my eyes. "What is happening? I thought you said this would help?"

My brother turns toward me, triumphant. "This *is* helping me, Claire." He moves closer and leans in. "You're just not paying close enough attention."

For a second I think I see his eyes soften. For a shred of a moment his visage seems to waver, pale, cracked skin looking almost fleshlike. Then his eyes shift. Once again, he's this cracked, charred version of my brother.

He stands again and turns toward the door to the cell.

"Connor, wait!" I implore him. "You said you would let me out." I try to muster some dust to shove myself to my feet again, but none of the golden flakes come. Not even the pale ones that have plagued me since childhood.

What is going on?

Fear and anger fill me as I look at Paige. "Did you do this? Why can't I create the dust?"

She shrugs. "It's not a perfect science."

The alarm bells tolling in my head are deafening. "What have you done to me!"

Paige is nonchalant. "The healer we kidnapped and tortured gave quite a bit of information about this island and the darker sides of magic that could impact it. But even the tribes don't really know how the bonds work. Without your connection, you're nothing but a freakish hybrid. Your dust might replenish over time. Or not."

She turns away, heading for the door. I try to follow, but Hook's cane juts out and slams against my ribs, knocking me backward.

Panic pushes me back to my feet. "Stop! You promised! You promised you'd let me out!"

Hook doesn't even look my way as they step. The door shuts, and as Paige turns the lock, her haunting green eyes flash at me through the bars.

"We lied."

She and Hook walk off, neither flinching as I shriek at them. I throw myself against the door, fingers wrestling with the bars over the small window, screaming at them to let me out.

Connor is the last to leave. He watches me screaming and flailing and slowly shakes his head. "Someday, you'll understand why it had to be this way." He turns and starts to walk away, but then his steps slow. A shudder ripples over my brother's fractured body, and he glances over his shoulder at me. The skin along his face is marbled with the dark veins, chalky and cracked, but his eyes are clear.

"Pay attention," Connor whispers.

And then his eyes darken again, and with that, he walks away.

I am left forgotten in a cell deep inside Skull Rock screaming until my throat is hoarse.

Lost.

7

CLAIRE

Neverland
Two Months Later

I lose myself inside the cell.

I've been here for weeks. Time moves differently here. Trapped inside this harsh place of rock, it seems to wear on forever. I'm allowed a bucket of water for cleansing on random days. My hair had grown long and tangled, and I finally managed to work it out when one of the Lost Boys smuggled me a roughhewn brush. I pull my tangled mane back into braids that hang far past my shoulders. Most of the time I'm curled up in a ball in the corner of the cell.

Wanting to die.

Connor has never come to see me.

And that hollow absence only cuts and shreds open the deep wound created in my heart when he betrayed me. Stripped my magic and left me to rot.

I've cried. I've screamed. I've cursed his name.

But now I just . . . sit hollowly.

As hollow as this island. I can't even hear the ghostly after-echoes of Neverland I used to.

The only people I see are the Lost Boys who bring me food twice a day.

At first, they didn't talk to me.

Now, they are the only reason I even bother to eat and not waste away.

I've started measuring time by the space between their visits. I've found small ways over the weeks to maintain that human connection. Sometimes I tell them scraps of stories through the door. Sometimes they tell me any of the bedtime stories they can remember Peter bringing home all those years ago. Occasionally Slightly will fill me in on the happenings of the island, or the twins will sing me a shanty, or Cubby will sneak me a little pastry he made. They even managed to smuggle in some paints to me once, and I've been able to decorate the walls of this cell as best I can.

I rarely see Nibs. When I do, his eyes brim with guilt, and he hardly speaks to me. I'm not sure there's much to say anyway. I have forgiven him, and he knows that, but I don't think he can forgive himself.

"Psst . . . Claire."

At Slightly's voice, I step back from where I've been using a sharp piece of pottery to carve pictures into the circular wall of the cell—nothing particularly impressive, but it passes the time. I stow away the bit of chipping rock and give my little crudely made drawing of Big Ben a once-over before turning to face the door.

"What is it?" My voice is crackly.

He angles closer to the bars. "I have news. And something for you."

I draw nearer.

He scans the hallway, then shoves a fist through the metal bars. He looks around again, then slowly opens his hand.

I gasp. A tiny pixie sits on his palm.

She stares up at me with wide eyes, rustling her small dress made of a plush daisy.

She mustn't be seen.

"Quick, hide!" I tell her, reaching out. But she darts away from my hands and flies up to burrow into my braids, instantly disappearing in the thick weave of my dusty hair.

Well, guess that works.

Tears prick my eyes as I look at Slightly, knowing how much he's risking bringing me this little friend of light and color. "Thank you."

He flashes a quick smile and then leans in even closer. "And now for the news."

My throat tightens. I have no idea what this could mean. "Yes?"

"Some of the boys saw something today. *Someone* fall from the sky."

I freeze. The world freezes.

Slightly's voice is more hushed. "They think it's him, Claire. They think Pan is here."

I gape at him, and for the first time in what seems like an eternity my heart feels alive again. Its pulse beats wildly through me.

Slightly leaves as quickly as he appeared, as I remain standing there, staring out the bars that for so long have stood in my way. But I don't see the harsh panes of metal or the grungy rock walls that sap so much light.

My mind's eye is filled with a redheaded boy wearing a dimpled grin.

Although I'm not sure if I trust Peter Pan any more than I did when I boarded that ship with Hook, he may be my best chance of getting out of here.

I walk over to the corner of the room and the ragged blankets I've collected over time and thrown together into a makeshift bed. I lean down, shuffling under the corner of the pile, and withdraw a little scrap of material fashioned into a bound sack. It practically floats out of my palm, but I hold it in place. With my free hand, I reach up and nudge the little pixie from her hiding spot.

"Hello there, little one." I smile as she lands on my hand, perching at the edge of my knuckles. Her big green eyes peer up at me, her coloring a little duller than is healthy, but there's a spark of tenacity here too.

I like her already. That only makes the loneliness ache a little more, but I take a deep breath and gently extend the little bag toward her.

"I so wish I could keep you here to keep me company. But I've been waiting a long time for this moment." I shake the bag a bit, it almost sounds like the rustle of sand. "There's pixie dust in here—my pixie dust. It has taken me a very long time to gather even this much, so take good care of it . . . okay?" My voice breaks, and the pixie tilts her head at me. Not quite understanding.

But she flaps her little wings and reaches forward to grab the bag of dust, rising a bit into the air.

"I need you to fly far away from here with this. Can you take good care of it and go out and find someone trustworthy?" I take another deep breath, eyes smarting. "Can you give them this dust and then tell them to fly back to Earth?"

Her shocked little voice is like chinking wind chimes. I nod my head firmly, trying to set her at ease. "Yes, I'm sure. Please find someone trustworthy," I repeat, "that will go back to Earth, because they need to get a message to very specific people." I crook a finger, drawing her closer. She flits nearer. "You need to tell this person to go find Jeremy Darling and Tiger Lily, and tell them . . ."

Her round, twinkling green eyes are riveted on me. I bite my lip and whisper the words that Slightly relayed to me first.

"Connor wants to kill Peter Pan. And if Peter dies—so does Neverland and everyone on it."

8

PETER

Neverland

"Peter, there's something you need to know . . ."

There's a heavy note in Tootles's voice. I finish putting several small handmade bundled explosives that Tootles had stacked in a corner into a threadbare sack. Careful not to jostle them too much, I glance up at him. "Yeah?"

He talks as he works on quickly fashioning breathing tubes from several small, hollow reeds and curved metal pieces. "First of all, the plan is good and it should work. I've been preparing for this for a long time . . ."

I heft the bag. "I'll say. How long did it take you to put all of these together?"

"It gave me something to do over the past few weeks." He shoves back his floppy hair. "But, Peter, there's more. I told you that Hook has Claire hidden away deep inside Skull Rock. Now that the tide is up, our best bet will be to sneak in by swimming up through the lower entrance of the rock that is now underwater."

I bob my head in quick assent. "Yep, got that. And we use your explosives as a distraction to sneak inside."

We've been over this a dozen times. Clearly Tootles has already thought through this plan a hundred times more than that, between the gunpowder he's stolen from the pirates to fashion clever explosives and the breathing apparatuses he's making.

So why is he staring at me like he just lost a bloomin' puppy?

Tootles clears his throat, fiddling with the thin reeds in his hands. "It's not just that Claire's trapped in the rock. It's how long she's been trapped there."

I stare at him. "What do you mean?"

He fits several hollow reeds together with small curved metal junctions, then sets the breathing tubes aside. "Peter, how far behind Claire do you think you were when you got here?"

"Dunno. A couple of days, maybe?"

His eyes are heavy. "No, Peter. It was much longer than that. It was months."

Terror hits me in the gut like a sucker punch. "Wait— *what*? *Months*?"

Sweat beads his forehead. "Yes, Connor has had Claire trapped for over three months. If I could, I would have gotten her out a long time ago. No one really knows what they're doing with her."

I jolt to my feet. "Claire has been in the clutches of that codfish for *months*?"

I don't wait for him to reply. He's said enough. *Who knows what they've been doing to her.* All I'm suddenly seeing is red. My head is filled with the eerie echo of Claire's screams.

I race up the steps that lead out of the hideout, shove aside the creaking camouflaged door, and burst out into the spindly jungle.

My feet fly across the dry ground, kicking rocks away and snapping twigs.

Claire has been trapped here for months.

They could have been torturing her for the whole time.

I have to get to her.

There's a rustle in the jungle to my right, and I catch sight a glint of steel, but I don't care, just keep barreling ahead toward Skull Rock.

And then a streak of silver cuts through the branches, nicking me in the arm.

I spew a curse, pull up to a stop.

A slender, ornately engraved knife sticks out from the crusted bark of a tree.

I whip around to find a dark face peering at me through the trees. Thin silver constellation tattoos spiral up around the side of the warrior's features, rimming his ear and the hair cut close to his head. His charcoal eyes bore into me, two more blades spinning between his fingers.

Oh, great.

A hand grabs my arm and jerks me to the side. Tootles moves quickly to stand in front of me and faces the native warrior, hands palm up. "It was an accident to come this way. We swear by the stars we mean no harm. We'll leave this portion to you."

The warrior just stares at us, unflinching, but Tootles takes that as some kind of answer. He nearly wrenches my arm out of my socket dragging me back through the jungle, putting as much space between us and the stoic warrior as he can.

"Tootles, I—"

But he hushes me fiercely. He refuses to let me speak until we've reached the hideout again, and then he practically shoves me down the tunneled entrance of the craggy old tree.

I land awkwardly on my stomach, knocking the breath from my lungs. I barely crawl out of the way before Tootles comes barreling down.

He lands perfectly on his feet. His eyes are blazing, "Peter! What did you think you were *doing*? You could have gotten yourself killed! What good would you be to Claire then?"

I've never seen the Lost Boy so angry. He's shaking with fury. "You're lucky that it was one of the warriors that saw you and not a pirate. If Hook knew you were here, we'd be in real trouble. But not even Lily's people are in a safe place. Most of them would probably put an arrow in your chest if given the chance."

I wince. "How charming."

Tootles rakes his hand through his hair. "This is not a joke, Peter. You can't just do whatever you want anymore."

My mouth feels like cotton. "I know that."

"Do you? Do you really?" He points back toward the exit of our underground bunker. "Because what you did back there was utterly stupid. I told you this is not the Neverland you know. You have to be careful."

"Oh, trust me," I assure him. "I know the island has changed. But do you have to be such a wet blanket about it?"

"This is life and death, Peter! It's the only way I've survived for so long as the only Lost Boy not on Hook's leash." He swept his arm in a circle. "Even back before all this, I was the first of the boys to even have an idea of consequences. All those years ago when I first shot Wendy out of the sky."

I glance at him, surprised to even hear him talking about Wendy Darling.

Tootles's eyes grow more intense. "Although it was an accident,

SHADOW   69

I almost killed her back then. That's when I first began to realize that your way of doing whatever you wanted and forget the consequences didn't work. Instead, it was dangerous. And when everything went to heck with Connor and the rest of the Lost Boys taken captive by Hook, I was able to escape. I've stayed out of his grasp for all these years because I've been careful." He blows out a long breath, eyes fixed on me. "So, call me a damp squib if you want, but if we are going to rescue Claire, we're doing it *my* way. It's the only way we'll even get close. Understand?"

I hold his gaze for a long moment, as his words sink in, all clever quips gone, and then give a solemn nod. "Understood."

After all, he's managed to survive here for years on his own, with threats on every side.

Respect where it's due.

Tootles stands a bit taller. "All right. Grab that bag of explosives while I get the breathing devices. Then follow me."

I give another nod and heft up the bag of small charges. Tootles collects the rest of his gear. He's gaunt and on edge, always alert and poised to run like a nervous prey animal. So different from the boy I grew up with who was a little clumsy and always had the worst luck—frequently the last to a fight or missing out on our romps. A quiet boy with a shine in his eyes who just wanted to be one of the gang.

Just wanted to please me and make Tink happy.

This Tootles is different—aware and intentional, but still with a good heart.

And he has survived.

"**S**o, I just breathe like this?" I stick the curved apparatus of hollowed-out reeds inside my mouth.

Tootles nods, hefting the waterproof pack over one shoulder, and then puts in his own breathing tool. He steps off the bank of dark sand and wades into the choppy water. Just past him, Skull Rock rises above the churning waves. It looks just as creepy as it ever did.

Not sure if Shadow would have been much good on this mission, but the chap took off on his own before we even had the chance to ask. Figures.

Tootles was right, the tide is up and has submerged the lower portion of the skull-shaped rock, the yawning mouth, soundly underwater. Two massive eye holes glare at us from above water, with the strange curve of a nose hole resting just below. I just hope Tootles is also right that diving straight into the mouth of that gigantic, gaping cadaver is our best way in.

He has already waded into water so deep that it is up to his shoulders. He's using both his arms to swim forward and only pauses long enough to glance my way. He gestures for me to follow and then dives under.

The slender top of the breathing device is the only thing slightly visible as he swims forward, and to any unknowing eye, you'd just think it was a stray twig in the water.

I shift my attention from Tootles back to Skull Rock one last time, taking in the mist that swirls around it and the climb of ivy up the steep curve of the rock. Then I take a deep breath, plop the breathing reed into my mouth, and dive in after him.

Here goes nothing.

The water is so cold my whole body almost locks up once I'm submerged, but I shove onward with stubborn determination. The more I swim, taking in drags of air through the reed, the more I warm up. It seems like the water calms too.

After all, I still have some connection to this island, no matter how frail it may be.

I'm also pretty bloomin' thankful that the sirens stay well away from Skull Rock on account of the pirates. Not something we need to deal with right now.

It takes what feels like an eternity of Tootles and I battling the cold water and the choppy distance before we finally draw within a few feet of the towering rock. Tootles pops his head up, and I follow suit.

Salty spray of seafoam ricochets off the massive rock, and those gaping eye sockets glare down at us. I gasp for air as foamy spray slams into my face, but at least the spray provides cover. The distant shore is now just a ripple of mottled colors behind us.

I swim closer to Tootles, "Okay, so what now?"

He blinks back the water drenching his features and points toward the lower portion of the rock where the brunt of the foamy wash forms. "The entrance is below there. We've got to dive down and swim through that."

I eye the angry water we're going to have to swim through. If memory serves, the rock should split into a wide, bony smile a few feet down. If we can swim through that opening, there should be a cavernous space on the other side and steps to climb up inside the rock.

As long as we don't run out of air or get slammed against the Skull.

The familiar thrill of danger warms my clattering limbs.

"I'm a stronger swimmer. I'll take the pack," I tell Tootles. He tries to disagree, but I take it off his shoulder and sling it over mine. "All right, ready?"

His expression closes off, and he nods, voice flat. "Yep. I'll be right behind you."

I churn my legs to stay above another arching whitecap as I stick the breathing tube back inside the pack and clutch the bag's strap as strongly as I can. "Okay—here goes!"

I dive beneath the water. I kick fiercely, pushing through the slam of violent water and aim straight down. The sea tries to toss me toward the deadly curve of the rock.

Not a chance, mate!

I force myself deeper and deeper, then twist my body, squinting through the salty water that stings my eyes. The shadowed shape of the toothy rock smile appears ahead of me. I focus on the darker portion I think is the gap where I can swim through.

My lungs burn, but I keep striking forward. I aim for the opening, kick hard, and burst through the dark suction of water. The pull of the current fades away as soon as I'm inside the submerged lower portion of Skull Rock. My body screams for air as I push upward.

I break the surface and chug down a massive gulp of air. Wiping my eyes, I wait for my vision to adjust to the darkness.

I'm not alone in this echoing cavern.

And Tootles isn't here yet.

He has to come up any minute. Maybe he couldn't get through the wall of waves. But then there is a low, rumbled laugh from two massive pirates I now see opposite me. They're standing at the top of a carved stairway that recedes into a dark tunnel leading deeper into the rock.

One of the burly men holds a lantern, and he swings it out, trying to get a better view of me.

The other cocks a gun. "Well, well. Looks like the information was right after all. Go tell the cap'n that the boy is here, just like they said."

The first pirate hangs his lantern on a rusted hook sticking out of the rock and lumbers up the walkway to disappear through the tunnel. The other one aims the barrel of his large gun straight at me.

"Cap'n will be here soon, but in the meantime . . . I think I'll shoot myself a Pan."

My gut drops to my numb toes.

Tootles set me up.

I can hardly believe it.

I'm going to strangle that little wretch—

All my senses jolt alert as the pirate goes for the trigger of his gun.

I duck back under the water just before the first bullet cuts through the surface closest to me. Cursing, I desperately swim down, trying to get deep enough that the next spray of bullets that slices through the water doesn't end up lodged in my cranium.

I narrowly manage to get deep enough, swallowed in darkness but aware of the ripple of the bullets cutting through the water above. But I can't hold my breath forever. And I can't swim back out without coming up for air first. My limbs feel heavy, but I force myself to swim toward the corner of the cavern. My only chance is to find someplace shadowed enough that I can go up for air without getting a bullet to the face.

But the bag slung over my arm is pulling me down.

Wait! That's it!

Despite the cold and the barmy circumstances, I grin. I cut silently through the icy water and reach the edge of the cavern. The need for air is dire, but I ever so slowly raise my head above the surface. I inhale quickly, hands fumbling under the water with the bag.

It takes the pirate on the steps a moment to catch sight of me, and then he snarls, lifting the gun again.

I raise a hand, gripping one of Tootles's round explosives, and chuck the heavy little bundle at the pirate's blasted face.

Take that, you blithering cad!

He ducks, but the small sack slams into the rock behind him. A loud popping sound erupts, followed by a flash of light and heat. Scorch marks mar the rock.

That's more like it.

The cavern suddenly fills with the sound of footsteps clambering forward. A light appears at the tunnel opening behind the pirate, and within seconds a certain crimson-coated captain bursts into view, a dozen large goons on his heels.

But I've already got more of Tootles's explosives in my hands. I heft one after another, tossing them at the pirates. *Bam! Bam! Bam!*

One of the explosives hits a pirate's shoulder, snapping to life with a burst of heat, followed by the stench of singed flesh. Another slams into the curve of the rock above their heads, and they all duck at the flash that follows.

I keep tossing the homemade bombs, trying to keep enough coming that the pirates don't have time to aim their weapons. I skirt toward the side of the cavern closest to the underwater exit through the rock's gaping jaws. Tootles might have tossed me in here to be fish food, but at least he didn't leave me defenseless.

Hook is cursing up a storm, firing his pistol into the cavern, but he's unable to aim clearly from trying to avoid the explosives.

Ha!

I'm about to dive for the exit when a piercing scream cuts through the air. Followed by terrified voices and more screams.

I know those voices.

They're my Lost Boys.

My throat closes up.

At the screams, even the pirates stop. The bomb clutched in my hand drops away to sink into the water as all eyes are drawn toward the entrance to cavern.

Tootles stumbles forward, blood leaking from a nasty gash on the side of his face. Nibs—looking a bit older and more weathered than last time I saw him—is just behind Tootles, shoulders slumped. They're both shoved forward by a tall, gaunt figure dressed all in black.

"Give me space!" Connor hisses to the pirates, and the handful surrounding Hook immediately dart out of the way. Hook even steps back, posture going rigid as he watches Claire's brother kick Tootles to his knees and shove him toward the very edge of the step just above water. Salty spray kicks up and hits Tootles in the face, mixing with the blood dripping down his jawline.

My mind reels, trying to puzzle this out. What is happening?

Connor pushes Nibs forward also, although he manages to keep his footing.

Hook takes the lantern off the holder behind him and hands it to Connor. I can finally make out Claire's brother's features.

"Come out, come out, Peter . . ." He lifts the lantern in front of him, and the light thrown back brings his expression into focus. I cringe, sinking deeper into the water and pushing back against the cool wall.

I hardly recognize him.

Dark veins have taken over his skin, and they seem to be cutting into his flesh, making chunks of his skin appear broken apart and craggy. Like a shattered mirror reflection.

But it's his eyes that are the most haunting.

The blue color is almost indistinguishable. All I see is darkness there.

He holds the lantern out over the water, his gaze raking across the surface. "I know you are out there. In fact, I've known you were here from the minute you landed on this island yesterday."

He suddenly kicks at Tootles, and the boy gasps sharply. "I knew you'd have some kind of plan, but I never expected the Lost Boys would be daring enough to use you as bait for a distraction."

Ouch.

I would have thought I'd have at least been some better use than just bait.

Connor rounds on Nibs, who has sidled as close to the edge as he can without falling into the water.

Connor just shakes his head. "And they almost managed it too. Almost managed to unlock my sister's cell and smuggle her out." He scoffs, flicking a hand, and a spray of water rips up, smacking across Nibs's face like the crack of a whip. "Stupid. Although, I can understand it. That sister of mine is something special."

The splintered young man turns back toward the center of the cavern, and this time looks directly at where I'm doing my best to hide. "But you already know that, don't you, Peter? Why don't you come out so we can do this the easy way?"

Yeah, not blooming likely.

I cross my arms over my chest, gaze skittering toward the underwater exit again.

Connor shakes his head. Behind him, Hook's face pales. "All right. Harder way it is, then. I guess I'll just kill off each of your precious Lost Boys until you give me what I want."

Connor looks down at Tootles, still on his knees at the edge of the lowest step, and the water rises, snaking like thin tendrils up Tootles's arms and toward his neck. The threads of water wrap around his neck, and Tootles chokes, clawing at the water noose around his throat.

"*No!*" Nibs says it before I do. He launches forward, reaching for Tootles.

Connor's shadowed eyes narrow fiercely. He flicks his hand again, and the tendrils of water fall away from Tootles. The Lost Boy collapses, gasping. Then Connor turns on Nibs, and clamps a hand around the boy's neck. Nibs's eyes go wide.

"Fine. We'll start with you then, Nibs. The little goody-goody who somehow convinced Hook you were the most trustworthy of all of Peter's boys." He gives a humorless laugh. "The one who first got close to Claire."

His grip on Nibs tightens, and the water around me thrashes, thrown from side to side by an invisible hand. It spills up the steps, and the water climbs Nibs's legs.

How is Connor doing this?

This is something far different than just being connected to Neverland.

Tootles manages to scramble up a few steps as the water continues to rise around Nibs. Connor ignores him, leaning in closer to turn his razor-sharp glare on Nibs. "You were the last person I expected to turn on us. Even Hook was rather fond of you."

The captain lurking in the tunnel entrance opens his mouth but says nothing.

The water continues to climb up Nibs, creeping over his waist and up his chest.

Connor's shattered face leans in close, spittle flying as he hisses, "But no one likes a traitor, Nibs. I doubt even Peter is fond enough of you to risk his own neck."

A shiver carves down my spine. I've never seen Claire's brother this heartless—not even when he first snapped, lashing out at me for my careless words that seemed to start all this.

Nibs's brown eyes are bloodshot and panicked. I don't blame him. The Lost Boy manages to dart a desperate glance my direction.

"P-please, Peter."

Connor rolls his eyes. "Yes, *please,* Peter. Why don't you come stop me before I suffocate this little traitor. Oh—wait." He gives another hollow laugh. "That would mean you'd have to care about someone other than yourself."

The water is up to Nibs's shoulders now, and Connor releases his grip on the young man's neck, letting the water climb from there. Nibs's face pales and then turns blue, as the liquid slides over his skin, tightening. Cutting off his air, his circulation.

My whole body is shaking in the water, watching—not sure what to do.

If I get close, Connor will drown us all.

Tootles slumps against the curve of the cave, staring at me, face white with panic. "Peter," he pleads. "Do something."

Connor steps back in morbid fascination as the water reaches

Nibs's face and spills into his gasping mouth. "Yes, better do something quick, Pan. His lungs are filling."

I scramble for one of Tootles's bombs and chuck it as hard as I can, but Connor simply flicks a hand. A spray of water bats aside the charge. I try to find another, but the bag is empty. I watch Nibs helplessly hacking as the water forces its way down his throat. Watching him slowly drown.

I bob about, panic and desperation filling my chest. *Do something!* My head screams as I watch Nibs's eyes roll back in his head, body wracking.

Terror fills my pulse, I spread my hands out in the water, reaching out for that tether to Neverland that has always been there. Draw on my connection this island that still pulses faintly through the water. Pulses through my fingertips. Pulses with my desperation.

"Stop!"

My overwhelming panic poured into that single word.

The island screams with me.

The Neversea swells around us, the entire rock shuddering as a large wave bursts into the cavern. It slams into the room like a small monsoon, knocking me to the side and flooding over Connor, Hook, Tootles, and Nibs.

Everything is wiped away as the water tosses me about. I tumble, over and over, submerged, trying to right myself. I strike for the surface while the water continues to roil and swell. Rising. I catch sight of Tootles swimming toward me. He's holding onto Nibs.

Hook and Connor fight to keep their own heads above the surface. Connor leverages the water to push them up the steps and into the tunnel, out of reach of the main wave.

I get to Tootles and grab for Nibs. Everything spins and swirls, and Tootles's face is streaked with blood and sorrow.

I try to hold Nibs up, but his body seems impossibly heavy.

"I can get him out!" I scream at Tootles, but the Lost Boy reaches for Nibs wrist, then his neck, feeling for a pulse. And then Tootles's face goes very, very pale.

"Peter . . ."

No.

The water thrashes again, and I go under for a moment. Clinging onto Nibs, I force us both back above the surface, teeth chattering. "If he can hold his breath, we can get him out."

But Tootles shakes his head, white as a sheet and almond eyes drowning in grief. "Peter . . . we can't."

My eyes burn. "No—no, he's going to make it."

I stare down at Nibs's blue face. At how cold he is. How heavy. How I can't see any rise or fall of his chest.

Still, the water rages. I hear the crack of thunder.

I hear the thunder of my own pulse in my ears and Tootles's desperate pleas.

"Peter, if we don't go now, we're all going to drown. We have to let him go." Tootles is shaking me, voice cracking as he pleads. Tears drip down his face.

I choke on a sob.

I glance up, past the roiling water, to find Connor standing silhouetted by the tunnel entrance, lantern in hand again. The water begins to shift direction and drag us toward him.

Beside me, Tootles begins kicking and shouting, "Peter, you have to let him go! We have to get out of here!"

I stare down at Nibs's limp body, the weight that makes my arms ache. My fingers are frozen in place from clenching his shirt. He almost looks like he's asleep. He almost looks like he could blink at any moment. Blink those glazed eyes and challenge me like he always used to.

But Nibs isn't blinking. He isn't waking up.

Tootles is right. Connor is going to drown us all if we don't get away now.

I pry my fingers from the Lost Boy I'd brought to Neverland all those years ago. Nibs's body slides beneath the waves. Disappearing into the dark, churning water. Everything burns.

This has to be some kind of nightmare. I feel like a part of me is sinking with him.

Tootles grabs my arm, pulling me with him as he dives under the water. My body goes numb as we strike out for the edge of the cavern, toward the submerged portion that will lead us out.

The world is a blur, but I somehow manage to get past the pull trying to force us back to Connor. Tootles and I narrowly make it to shore and drag our shivering bodies across the harsh sand.

"We can't go back to the hideout," Tootles pants. "Too easy for Connor to find now."

Especially now that he knows I'm here. And that he is much stronger than I am.

We start to walk, but my legs just blooming stop moving as we pass the sand into the jungle. I don't even care as they give out and I collapse to the ground. Twigs crunching, packed dirt hard beneath.

I just stare at my shaking hands.

Hands that had held Nibs. Hands that had let him go. Let him slide back under that water. He wasn't breathing, no pulse. He was dead when I let go.

So why do I still feel like I drowned him?

I slam a fist into the dirt so hard that the skin on my knuckles shreds. But I don't feel the sting. Only the deep, piercing ache ripping open my chest.

This isn't make-believe.

Nibs is *dead.* And if I can't find some way to stop Connor and set Claire free, the death of Neverland will be on my hands too.

9

PETER

Neverland

I've never felt this cold.

Tootles and I hide within a deep thicket of skeleton trees hedging a rocky cliff face, and after I help him patch up the gash on his forehead the best I can, I wander away to sink down at the base of one of the ashen trees.

I pull my knees to my chest, leaning my head back against the rough bark of the tree trunk as a shudder sweeps my damp limbs.

My hands, the ground beneath my feet, the breeze needling across my skin. It's all so cold. As hauntingly chilled as Nibs was when I was holding him in that water.

My eyes fall closed and, for the first since I can remember, I just sit in shock.

I don't know what to do next.

While Nibs was never my closest mate, he was still one of my Lost Boys. He was family. He'd tried to help save Claire. And he saved Tootles.

And Connor killed him. Like *that*. Like it was nothing.

I press my fingers against my aching temples. I've seen death before. Seen Hook kill his own men in cold blood. But this time, the death rips through me like an arrow. Grief plunges in deep and fast—and takes a much bigger chunk when I try to pull it out.

This time it was someone I cared about.

And this time the island can't erase the loss from my memory.

I cave forward, curling into a ball, wanting to scream. Wanting to rage. Wondering if maybe this is how Connor feels. So filled with darkness and shattered thoughts that he can't escape. That not even this island can carve it away.

No wonder he's thrown this entire blasted place into chaos.

How am I supposed to change any of this? How can I rescue Claire when I can't even get close to her?

This is not a game . . . this is not a game . . . this is not a game . . .

The words chant through my head, mocking me, and swell into a mammoth headache. As I reach for a stray root, the trees shudder around me. A sharp intake of breath from the whole island.

And every time I close my eyes, I see Nibs's frozen expression staring up at me.

We didn't even get to say a proper goodbye.

I rake my hands through my hair and kick at the nearest rock. I hear Tootles grunt, and for a moment I think I might have hit him, but when I get to my feet, I realize he's just huddled by one of the trees, looking rather pale as he bandages up a nasty scrape on his lower leg.

Tootles always looks a bit like he could blow away in a strong wind, but now he seems even more fragile.

Stop just staring and help him!

Wiping at my dripping nose and aiming one more sound kick at that rock, I finish cursing out this whole island and this sadness that makes it hard for me to breathe. I kneel at Tootles's side. "Lemme help, mate."

He lifts his head slowly up to me. "I thought you'd be angry after I left you in that cavern. Why are you helping me?"

I tear a strip from my shirt and mop at the bruising cut on his leg. "Oh, I was mad," I told him. "Fumin' mad." I sit back. "But I get it. I know you and the rest of the boys don't trust me. You were doing what you could to try and rescue Claire."

A muscle tightens in his jaw, and I notice how red his eyes are. I'm not the only one who's been blubbering.

He gives a small nod. "It was the only shot we had. You were the best distraction we could come up with to get Connor away so we could go in. And we weren't going to actually let him capture you. We just needed to get her out. But it failed." His head droops. "Just like it always does."

He really is a decent chap. "You did the best you could, mate. This whole thing is blasted insane."

"That's for sure." His voice cracks, and I know he's thinking about Nibs. I doubt we'll be able to think of much else for a long while.

I wind the clean-ish material around the cut on his leg, when I hear a rustle in the brush behind us. I bristle and glance quickly over my shoulder, ready to reach for the nearest stray branch and go down swinging.

But instead I see a familiar silhouette sliding across the ground, pushing trees out of its way as Shadow joins us. I step toward him, and suddenly he's grabbing for my shins and playfully swinging around me.

I wince, my body more bruised than I'd care to admit, and his jovial behavior making me flinch. "Now's not the time, mate."

Shadow stares up at me for a moment, and I know he's understood, but suddenly he's darting past me toward Tootles. Tootles shoves to his feet, visibly groaning, but he's not fast enough. Shadow reaches him, and before Tootles can shake him off, the little creature is shoving a finger directly into one of the wounds slicing across Tootles's arm.

"Ouch!" the Lost Boy yelps, shaking off Shadow. The thin silhouette of a boy rolls across the ground, gripping his belly and shaking with laughter.

My anger flares. "Hey! Tootles is hurt—that's not funny."

But Shadow just keeps laughing.

I kick a shower of dirt at him. "Cut it out!" I lick my dry lips. "Nibs is dead. So now is not the blithering time."

That makes Shadow pause, head inclined to me, listening. And then he makes a movement of pulling back a bow, and I nod. "Yeah. Nibs. He taught me how to shoot."

He vaults up the tree and dissolves into more laughter.

It grates on my raw, nearly snapped nerves. Grates on the throbbing hole in my chest.

He's *laughing.*

Like all this means nothing.

"Stop it!" I shout up at Shadow.

Tootles has finished wrapping his own wound and has moved away, shooting a glance at Shadow. He doesn't trust the little bloke.

I'm not sure I should either.

There's something unhinged about him.

Maybe from the time he's spent here, cut off from me. Maybe he's affected by the island and Connor's impact on it.

Maybe my younger self always had this sense of disconnected

cruelty, and I couldn't see it.

Either way, his mimed laughter and poking at Tootles's wounds is the last thing I need.

"Stop laughing!" I shout up at Shadow, and he kicks a stray branch toward my head. I duck away from the projectile, but I've had it.

I scramble up the tree.

Before I can reach for Shadow's blasted ankle, the frightful little creature scrambles back down the bark and slithers across the ground. This time aiming for Tootles.

Not again.

Tootles is sitting propped against a tree and kicks back at Shadow, but that only seems to set him off more. Shadow darts around and kicks up a mound of dirt, flinging it into Tootles's face. The Lost Boy hacks and coughs, wiping dirt from his eyes.

"Hey!" His eyes water as he tries to blink the granules out. "That's not funny."

I've had it.

"Get out of here!" I bellow at Shadow, leaping out of the tree and storming toward him. Before he can slither away again, I aim a sharp kick at his side.

Shadow moves a few inches away and then reaches for a rock poking out of the ground. "No, you don't!" I leap over him and land on top of the rock, pinning the stone and Shadow's hand to the ground. I glare down at him.

"Unless you can behave, I want you gone."

I lift up my heel just enough for him to pull his hand out. "I'm done with your shenanigans. Either you stop or you leave."

Shadow hisses at me. *Hisses.* And there's something like a threat in his expression.

He slithers off through the jungle, pausing a few feet away from me to find a new rock and launch it at my head. It clips my shoulder as I duck, and then I'm about to race at him again when Shadow hisses a final time and disappears into the jungle.

Heaving a mammoth sigh, I go back over to Tootles and drop down beside him.

"Please tell me I wasn't as much of a blooming mess as that pipsqueak is."

He regards me solemnly. "Only sometimes. Usually you cared about us enough to not laugh at our pain. And he usually listens to me. He must just be in a mood."

If he's trying to make me feel better, it's not really working.

Suddenly his hand shakes on my shoulder.

"Peter . . . is that . . . ?" His voice trembles.

I launch to my feet, half expecting that Shadow has come back for a second round.

But my jaw drops when I catch sight of something small and glittering flying through the craggy jungle toward us. My eyes sting again. It's a pixie. The first pixie I've seen since arriving here. A wall of homesickness crashes into me.

She dips and bobs as she flies our direction. Is she sick?

I hurry through the trees toward the little pixie. Gray mist spirals around us, the trees like skeletal hands reaching for the overcast sky—but the tiny pixie is like a drop of sunlight piercing through the dreary wood. She ignites the tiniest spark of hope as my frozen, bare feet skim over the jungle floor. When I reach her, I realize the reason her flight path is wavering is because the tiny winged creature is carrying some kind of pouch.

"What is . . . ?"

She lifts her big eyes to me and whispers in a lilting tone,

"Are you safe?"

"I think so."

She drifts a little closer, holding the pouch tight. "Are you one of Claire's friends?"

That hits like a blow to my gut, but I jerk a nod.

"Glimmer? Is that you? I can't believe you're alive!" Tootles's faint voice drifts toward us, and the pixie brightens, giving an excited little cry. She jets around me, still hefting that pouch, and flies quickly to Tootles. A trail of faint pixie dust stretches across the mist behind her. The pixie drops the pouch into the Lost Boy's hands and then snuggles up to his face, peppering his cheek with tiny kisses.

Of course, Tootles is best friends with the first pixie we've seen yet. I'm not jealous.

Not much.

I slowly walk back toward them, watching as Tootles raises the small bundle in his hand. "What is this, Glim? What's going on?"

She settles down on his shoulder with the same casual comfortability the pixies used to have with me. I catch fragments of her tumbling of words as I reach them.

"Claire . . . sent some of her dust . . . fly back . . . get Tiger Lily . . ."

I plop down beside Tootles, gaping at the tiny pixie. Tootles shoots me a look and then turns to the tiny winged creature.

"Glimmer," he says carefully, "are you saying that this bag is filled with Claire's dust? And that she wants us to fly back to Earth and get Tiger Lily?"

She nods emphatically. "Lily. And the Guardian too."

Of course.

Of blooming course.

I can't help but shake my head and give a little smile. Brilliant, Claire. We need reinforcements, and her dust is the only magic potent enough to be able to carry someone all the way back to Earth, since most of the pixies are gone. The ones left, like Glimmer, are much too weakened.

But even as I nab the bag of dust, despite Glimmer glaring at me, and balance it in one hand, measuring how much dust is inside—I know something doesn't seem quite right. Filled with this much pixie dust, and Claire's potent magic at that, this bag should be floating off my hand. Instead, it seems weaker than usual. Exhausted, probably like Claire herself.

Without her connection to the island and with whatever else those blaggards have done to her that the Lost Boys didn't even know about to snitch to Tootles, even her magic has waned.

Which only means one thing . . .

"There's only enough dust for one of us to go."

Tootles stares at me. "Really? You're sure?"

I nod. "Aye. There might be enough to bring Lily and Jeremy back, but definitely not enough for two of us to go and return."

Tootles sits up straight. "You're Peter Pan. Of course you'll go." His tone is matter-of-fact. Then he gulps. "I can stay behind. I always do."

I close my eyes and knead my forehead. I'm seeing Nibs's shocked eyes again. Feeling him slip through my fingers and sink beneath that water.

There's no way I'm losing anyone else.

I lift my head and drop the bundle of pixie dust back into Tootles's hand. "No, you should go. I'm not leaving Claire—not ever again. Besides, I think it's high time you get off this island, mate."

His eyes well with surprised, relieved tears. "Really?"

I pat his shoulder. "Absolutely. Plus, once you get there, Lil can patch you up much better than I could."

At the mention of Tiger Lily, his face colors a shade, and I bite back a smile. Another good reason to send Tootles.

"Thank you, Peter. You have no idea how much this means to me."

Oh, I have an idea.

My face grows serious, and I look straight at him. "I should never have left you behind for so long, mate."

He gives me a slow smile.

We both know that it's best if Tootles leaves as soon as possible, before anything else can happen to mess this all up. We spend the next two hours trading information—Tootles showing me the ropes of everything he's learned to survive on the island and avoid Connor, and me laying out everything the lad needs for the flight. We quickly scrounge up berries and other food for him to eat now and take on the journey. Glimmer darts around us, adding in her thoughts as I walk Tootles through the star map he'll need to follow to get back to Earth.

Then he's ready.

He knows where he's going, and he's got enough food to last if it takes him a little longer than usual to make the flight.

As he stands next to me, about to open Claire's bag of dust, it hits me how real this is. Tootles is leaving, and then it's just going to be me. Hiding in any of the small nooks I have memorized in this island, trying not to step on Shadow's toes or tick him off any more, and seeing if I can convince Glim to help me get to Claire. Because those are my main goals:

Get Claire back.

Don't die.

I suck in a deep breath and reach out to lightly punch Tootles's shoulder.

He looks at me, surprised. "What was that for?"

"Nothin'," I say blithely. "I'm just gonna kind of miss havin' you around is all."

A smile stretches across his features. "Me too. I'll try to be fast, Peter. And I know you'll find some way to turn the tide even while I'm gone."

I huff out a breath. "I hope so." I pull my shoulders back and whack his shoulder again. "All right, y'gaffer. The longer you wait around, the more chance we have of Hook stumbling upon us. Get out of here, will you? The faster you leave, the faster you can bring the chums back."

He nods quickly and gently tugs the bundle of pixie dust open just enough so we can see the shimmer of gold dust inside. Glimmer leaps off her perch on the curve of Tootles's ear and flies over to gingerly land on my shoulder. She seems a tad uncertain but settles in, and even that simple movement sparks a bit of warmth in my chest.

Maybe we will be almost okay after all.

"You ready?" Tootles asks.

Shouldn't I be asking him that? "Ready."

He takes a few pinches of Claire's pixie dust from the small bundle and sprinkles them over himself. The thin, golden flecks cascade over him, and he rises off the ground. The dust catches the edge of Tootles's shirt and filters in his thick hair, lifting his worn shoes off the ground.

He sprinkles a little more over his body for good measure, then reties the pouch and slides it into his pocket. His eyes shoot wide as he stares down at the ground that he's quickly floating higher and higher away from.

"Whoa! I forgot how fun this was! "

His cautious expression has transformed into a grin, and I can't help but grin back at him. At the way flying, being weightless and spinning in the air, frees the perpetual weight Tootles usually carries. Even his scars and the bandages on the side of his head and leg seem to fade away in the light of this magic that defies gravity.

I wave at him. "You've got the hang of it, mate. Now, remember what I said about finding the second star—and go get Lily."

He flashes me a quick salute. "Aye, aye, Cap'n Pan."

At that moment I'm reminded of the other time Tootles and the rest of the Lost Boys flew. We'd stolen Hook's ship, and I'd announced that I was captain, and then we'd flown the Darling children home.

All of those carefree adventures feel like they were an eternity ago.

But maybe we can still be okay. Both island and boys.

"Safe travels, Tootles." I toss a salute back at him.

He gives me one last lingering look. "Thanks, Peter. You really have grown." Then he turns his gaze to the gray sky and shoots up through the wrinkled foliage. Tootles is a gleaming beacon for a brief moment, a flash across the overcast sky, and then he is out of view.

And the world feels cold again.

A single tear drips down my face.

The hair on my arms stands on end, my ribs constricting and pinching in at my lungs again.

Because I wish I could fly out of here too.

Instead, I reach a hand out to scoop up the little pixie perched on my shoulder. She stands in my palm, peering up at me expectantly.

"Guess it's just you and me now, Glimmer." I lift her closer so I can meet her shining, curious eyes. "Are you okay? I know it hasn't been easy and that most of your people are . . ." I'm not sure how to finish the sentence, and from the way her wings droop and she hangs her head, I decide maybe I don't need to.

So instead I cup her close, and she nuzzles my cheek. "Don't worry. You've got me now, for what that's worth."

Her color has gone a little blue, and her eyes glisten as she peers up at me and pecks a kiss at my cheek. "What now?" she asks in that lilting voice.

I glance at the gray sky where Tootles disappeared and the direction of Skull Rock.

"Are you ready to try something a little crazy?"

10

CLAIRE

Neverland

Sound echoes down the hallway as Paige leads the Lost Boys toward my cell. I lift lightly off the ground, the tips of my toes trailing across the rocky floor until I reach the door and can peer out between the bars.

Paige is on the rampage. A chill spirals over my shoulders.

Her eyes are filled with fury, hair spiraling around her like a dull red halo of fire. She has one pale hand clamped tightly on Slightly as she pulls him mercilessly after her. The twins and Cubby are right behind them.

The posture of their bodies and hunch of their shoulders spell defeat. I stare out at them. Just an hour earlier, Tootles and Nibs came racing down the same hallway, shouting for me to move aside so that they could get me out.

But then Connor appeared. I hadn't seen him in weeks, but suddenly he was there, eyes dark and expression fractured. He dragged Tootles and Nibs away, the whole cavern shuddering with his seething anger.

Now, Tootles and Nibs are nowhere to be seen, and it's Paige who is seething.

My grip tightens as Paige shoves Slightly toward my cell.

"Open it," she snaps.

I dart back from the door as Slightly fumbles with a key. "What's going on?" I mouth at him. But he doesn't see me.

He gets the door open, and Paige storms into the cell, forcing Slightly in front of her. The other Lost Boys stumble in too. The twins look so young as they cower against the wall, eyes frightened.

"What's happening?" I ask again, pulse kicking up.

"Ask them!" Paige shrieks, gesturing to the Lost Boys. "Ask them what happens when traitorous little boys try to betray us." She slaps Slightly hard across his face, spittle flying with every vindictive word she spews. "Ask them what happened to Nibs when he double-crossed us."

Her voice has taken on a taunting tone, and I go rigid as I stare at Slightly, freckles so pale they've practically vanished. "What about Nibs?" There is only silence, and my gaze flicks to Paige. "What did you do?"

"What had to be done. Punishment." Her words are icy. "And I'm not finished yet."

I back up, my heels hitting the edge of the rocky cell wall. "Where is Nibs?" I ask, voice shaking.

Paige's expression is cold. "He's dead."

My whole body crumbles. The weight of those words fills my lungs like burning seawater.

"You're lying!" I fling the words at her. But she just regards me with hollow eyes.

I turn in desperation from Paige to the Lost Boys. The twins cower against the wall, expressions misted with glittering tears that begin to streak down their faces. Cubby is biting his lip hard to hold back his own tears.

But it isn't until I look at Slightly, his face still red from where Paige struck him, and I see the nightmares reflected in his eyes that it really hits.

Grief is like a sledgehammer.

"*No!*" I cry out. A sob breaks out, and I begin to weep. "No, no! This isn't right!" This isn't how the story goes. Yes, the girl may be holed away in a tower for too long, but then the hero arrives and rescues her, and they're all okay in the end.

No one dies. Nibs doesn't die.

I can't stop crying. I never got to say goodbye.

I'd hardly spoken to him at all. I'd locked him out since I was thrown in here. But I could see how guilty he felt, how he didn't even know how to start a conversation.

Did I push him away?

Now he's gone forever.

"No!" I scream again. I beat my fists on the curving rock wall.

My whole body feels caught in a storm. Anger, hot and blazing, fills every aching place inside me, and I face Paige.

"What did you do to him?"

She's infuriatingly calm. "It was your brother, actually. Connor drowned him."

She says it so coolly. So matter-of-fact.

I try to strike out at her. But she just steps to the side, still watching me through those cool green eyes. I stumble, almost falling to the ground, but Slightly grabs my arm, steadying me.

I don't want to be steady. I want to wake up from this nightmare.

So I push away from Slightly and lock my burning eyes on

Paige. Glare at her as more tears spill down my face.

I can't wake up. This is real. But I want to wipe that insultingly unfeeling look off her face.

The ashen dust leaks from my skin instantly. Thin, burning flakes that singe the ground and drift like spots of pale ink through the air. The Lost Boys scurry away from me, toward the door, but before they can get out, Paige cuts them off. She quickly pulls the door closed and locks it, tossing the key through the bars. Locking us all inside with her.

She stands behind Slightly, using him as a shield, and I rail at myself for not moving faster.

Burning, aching dust continues to ripple out from me, and I come as close as I dare so as not in range to hurt the Lost Boys.

"Let them go," I snap at her. "This is between you and me."

"Actually, you are exactly where I want you," Paige says, lifting her pointed chin to smile at me. "I told you I wasn't done punishing the Lost Boys for their deceit. What better way to teach them a lesson than to use you?"

She grabs Slightly roughly by the shoulders and shoves him at me. He slams into me and howls as the acid pouring from my skin scorches him.

I scream too, sharp panic flaring through me.

Wrenching away from him, I fly across the cell to hover at the back of the room. Slightly has tossed off his shirt and is quickly patting out the other places where flakes of dust are burning him. One of the twins comes forward to help, but in the split second Slightly was near me, my dust has already peppered his body with burns.

My stomach contorts. I'm desperately trying to slow down my flood of dust, but the fear filling the room is suffocating the calm

I'm frantically trying to create.

"You're a monster!" I scream at Paige, my voice raw.

Her look is sardonic. "*You're* the monster, Claire. And now you're *my* monster. It's about time you served your purpose."

Fear creeps up my throat like bile, choking out my air.

Paige unsheathes an eerily familiar dagger, pressing the tip into Slightly's back and forcing him forward, toward me. He looks around for the twins and Cubby for help.

But their expressions are white with terror, and they look ready to crawl out of their skin. What has this woman done to them that they are so terrified to cross her?

"Where's the captain? Or my brother?"

Paige's cool expression is locked on me. "They're both otherwise occupied. It's just us. And I'm in no hurry."

I push against the wall, trying to become small, to put as much space between me and Slightly as possible. But his eyes are still filled with fear—the same fear reflected in the eyes of the twins and Cubby behind him, huddled by the locked cell door.

I shake my head stubbornly. "I won't do it. I refuse to hurt them."

My dust has already ebbed, and at those words, at the sincerity behind them, it completely vanishes, the air cooling. Slightly's shoulders visibly lower with relief.

But Paige shoves him closer, a foot away now. She narrows those chilling eyes on me. "You can try and hide it, but I know what you are . . ."

She leans in. "You're the kind who leaves a trail of fractured, broken people in her wake. You couldn't help Connor, so you just let him go on and become what he is now."

I swallow, crossing my arms over my chest, trying to build a wall around my heart to brace against her onslaught of words. "No. I searched for Connor for years. I never gave up on finding him."

She lets out a long, barked laugh. "He ran away from you, Claire! Not even your own brother wanted you." Her eyes narrow, and a shudder ripples over me. "He still doesn't want you. He can't even bear to look at you."

I press my arms tighter, nails digging into my biceps.

"That's not true . . ."

But the words falter.

Despite how desperately I'm trying to cling to all the truths I've branded into my thoughts over and over to stay alive in this hole of a rock. The things that kept me from dissolving in the darkness. Two months with my own voice in my head. The shadows lapping at my thoughts, hammering to get in.

But now the darkness is leaking from her lips.

And my walls are starting to tremble.

Paige can smell the blood in the water, eyes narrowing on me. "Your brother is falling apart, and you've done nothing."

I shake my head fiercely.

"He killed Nibs. Is that the Connor you remember?" She's grabbing my chin and forcing me to look at her. "Or what about Peter?"

My mouth goes dry. "Peter?"

"He was there when Nibs died. But not even the great Pan could save him." She waves a hand around the room. "And he's certainly not here to save you. Face it, Claire. Not even Peter wants to rescue you. He's left you here for weeks to rot."

Paige pulls away, letting go of my face, and kicks at Slightly who's sunk to the floor. He's gasping down chugs of air to cool the burns rippling his skin.

"He lied to you in London, and you were too weak to see the truth."

That hits like a slap to the face. The deep, seeping shadow that used to fill my veins begins to leak back to the surface.

Paige gestures for the twins and Cubby to move forward. At first they shake their heads, but then she points her blade toward them. "You know I could slit your throats and Connor would just thank me."

She says it so evenly. Calmly.

The Lost Boys lurch to stand beside Slightly. They're all far too close now.

"And you also betrayed Tiger Lily by joining Hook."

I think of Lily and the look on her face as I lifted the *Jolly Roger* into the air and toward the stars. The same desperate, pained look that had been on Peter's face.

Peter may have lied—but I abandoned them. Betrayed them.

I sink down to the floor of the cell, bury my face in my knees, and wrap my arms around my head. Trying to block out her voice.

She kneels in front of me, her cool voice penetrating even though my fingers plug my ears.

"And then you came here to Neverland only to find that you really knew nothing at all. You're not some beacon of pixie light— just a siren of darkness."

"Stop. Just stop," I whisper.

"And then there's Nibs." And at that, my whole body rocks. Chest growing so tight I can't breathe. My head spins.

I want to pass out. I want to stop feeling.

But I can only feel—and it's all too much. The nausea and the scream of my pulse in my ears. The way the room spins.

"Nibs, the boy who begged Hook and me so many times to let

you out of here." Paige's words cut through me like a blade. Twist. Sink in deep. "The boy who was your friend for years before you even knew who he truly was. Who was only doing what he thought he must to protect you."

My heart lurches in my chest, stutters.

"He died attempting to rescue you, and your own brother killed him for it."

I lift my burning eyes, and even as the swimming world dulls, I can still make out Paige's gaunt form towering over me.

"Stop."

It's the only fragile word I can utter. But it doesn't stop her from saying the final sentence that breaks me.

"You're a selfish child who only destroys others."

I can't lock it away then.

The world is consumed by the shadows and the wave of ashen dust that explodes out from me.

Paige jumps back, shielding herself by throwing Slightly toward me again, and then she's forcing the twins and Cubby in my direction. This time, they try to push back against her, more afraid of me now than they are her—but Paige has already reached the door. She draws a second key from her pocket and slips outside of the cell.

She locks them in. Locks all four boys in as they wrestle with the bars and scream at her to let them out.

I'm horrified as their cries for help turn to screams of pain as my dust reaches them.

Slightly throws his body over the twins as best he can, but he can't protect them.

Neither can I.

I desperately want to stop myself, but I don't even feel attached to my own body anymore. I can only watch my ashen, burning dust envelop their bodies and hear their screams.

I scream, too, and claw at my own body. The more I hammer myself into the floor, trying to quench the storm, the worse it gets.

The terror that throws me into a full-blown panic attack, shuddering and suffocating and heart skipping beats, also thickens the burning dust.

I can't make it stop.

I've never hated myself more than this moment. This moment as my fears and failings turn the air to fire and burn the Lost Boys who have kept me sane these several months and who just risked everything to try and rescue me.

I scratch at my own arms till I draw blood, trying to stop the thick, ashen flakes that lift over and over from my skin. I look up and see Paige watching through the bars.

My screams continue to merge with the Lost Boys'.

I'm about to do something desperate. I reach for a broken shard of glass to stop myself from ever hurting anyone again when suddenly there's a flash of crimson. "Stop!"

The cell door is wrenched open and boots storm across the floor. My vision is blurred and burning, and I reach a shaking hand out, thinking finally someone has come to help.

Instead of a hand finding mine, a heavy cane slams into my temples, and the world goes totally dark.

I come to sometime later, lying on the ground, a gloved hand moping my forehead. I shudder, and Hook turns me over on my side just in time for me to throw up all over the cell floor.

He wipes at my mouth with a handkerchief and then offers me some water. I awkwardly pull up to a sitting position, sagging against the cell wall. I manage to turn my head to him as he sits beside me, quietly watching.

There's something like sadness in his eyes.

I'm confused why he's here. Why he saved me.

This whole cell looks charred and dark. Blood splatters the floor, and Paige and the Lost Boys are nowhere to be seen.

"Are . . . they . . . ?" I croak out.

Hook offers me the cup of water again. "They're in the infirmary, getting their burns tended to. They'll survive."

Weak with relief, I sag back and let more tears roll down my face.

"Thank you," I whisper.

He just nods. His hook gently pats my knee. "I told Paige that your brother would not be pleased if he knew she was egging you into panic attacks. He doesn't want you broken." The captain shakes his head. "She says I have a soft spot for you." I look at him, taking in just how wrinkled and weary his features are beneath the gray-flecked beard. "I suppose that it is true. You remind me of her." He glances toward the closed cell door. "The way she used to be. When she was vibrant and filled with so much potential and spirit."

I must look skeptical because he drags his hook against the dirty floor and adds, "I can't say more, love. But she wasn't always like this. I hold out hope that one day things will return to how they once were."

He's in denial. I almost feel sad for James Hook. I know what that's like to be willing to do anything to chase something you hoped could still exist.

But the world I wanted is gone. The brother I searched for has vanished too.

And as I stare around this charred, darkened room, I realize if I stay here, Paige will continue to use me.

I can feel the core of iron, deep inside my heart, the foundation of metal that has always been there. I need it now for what I have to do.

Hook prepares to leave, now that he knows I'm coherent.

I manage to get to my feet and lift my hands, I take a breath and step toward the pirate captain.

Hook turns toward me. "Claire, I—"

But I've already grasped his hook, my hands around the curving metal prong. I look at him. "I'm sorry, but I can't let her make me into her weapon."

I unleash my dark dust, letting it fill my palms and pool over James's hook.

I'm my own weapon.

The dust mangles his hook, contorting the curve and sending a few sizzling hot pieces of metal dripping to his polished boots, but I'm not finished. I lift my hands, dark dust filling my palms, and blow it at his chest. It's not going to kill him, but it's enough to make his face go white with agony as he falls to his knees.

That moment is all I need. I quickly remove the cell key from the ring tied to his waist. This door is too thick for me to melt, but with the key, I unlock it in seconds, darting out, and lock it behind me.

I toss the key and start running.

The first window I can see is beyond a handful of unsuspecting pirates. I barrel through them before they can react and raise my hands to the thin bars securing it. It only takes a heartbeat to muster the burning dust this time. I spray a handful at the pirates to make them scatter and then coat the bars in the rest.

The metal turns to liquid and melts away. I hoist myself up and through the hole drilled in the rock before I can lose the rush of adrenaline. I fall through open air for a moment and desperation fills each heartbeat like a ticking clock.

But then I find one happy thought to latch onto, and my dust ignites to life. It's frail and uncertain, a hesitant golden color, but it's just enough to lift me before I crash into the water, and I soar through the humid air away from Skull Rock.

It's the first time I've felt fresh air and warm sunlight on my skin in what feels like an eternity.

As I fly, I glance over my shoulder at the towering crag, wrapped in climbing ivy and the chill of mist. The dense catacombs buried in that skeletal place that have been my prison for so long.

But my heart is still trapped by the brokenness that bars the restoration of this world.

There's so much more to be set free.

11

PETER

Neverland

This pixie is about to slap me.

"Hey! I just want to *talk* to them, okay? I'm not going to blooming steal their gold or whatever."

Her faint coloring grows scarlet as she flies at me, tugging on a strand of my hair and chattering wildly. "They don't want to talk to you! I already told you!"

I bat the little pixie away. "But why? Why are the pixies all in a snit?"

Glimmer does a little flip and jets back around to pause in the air inches from my nose. She sets her little fists on her hips, her dress made of a bedraggled daisy swishing as she glares at me. "You're the reason Tink is dead and that Connor is so upset!"

"Hey! That's not all true. I didn't realize Connor would—"

But she crashes into me, slapping a hand over my lips and kicking the bottom of my jaw to make my mouth snap shut. "If you hadn't taken them to Earth in the first place, if you'd left them here to be raised by Neverland herself, none of this would have ever happened. We could have taken care of our own."

Her raging fiery color begins to fade into a weeping orange. I cock my head at her. "How do you even remember when I did that?"

"We remember the important things," her little voice says.

So I let the ache settle, blink a few times and focus on the little pixie hovering in front of me. "Raised by their own? What does that mean?"

She hovers boldly in the air. "They're children of Neverland. They belong with us. Not locked away."

Watching her skin so pale and her light dimmer than ever, I realize just how much Claire and Connor mean to her. Mean to all of the pixies. When I took them to Earth all those years ago, I didn't just take the twins away from the island—I took Neverland away from the twins.

I reach out to her. She tries to dart away, but I gently lift a finger and pat Glimmer's little head. "You miss her too, don't you?"

She raises her blue eyes to stare at me, the sadness dissipating as her coloring returns to its usual sullen gold. "Yes, and we want her out."

"I'm working on it."

She flashes red again. "No! You leave it alone."

My brow ripples. "What? You don't want me to save her?"

The tiny pixie laughs at me. A flash of gold skimming the red color. "Everything is not always about you, Peter boy."

My jaw drops.

She flies a little higher, wings beating quickly, and waggles a finger. "You keep hurting Connor more—and the island." She darts closer, hovering at eye level, her tinkling light voice taking on a sense of gravity. "You won't save them with a blade. You can't heal a wound by making one."

I stare at her. "When did you get so smart?"

She gives a little twirl and tosses her hair over her shoulder with a snarky grin. But even as I enjoy the comradery, I can't ignore her words. It's not just the island and Connor I've hurt. I can see the same pain woven through this tiny winged creature. In the way her body is a little too thin, her dust too pale, her light too dull. The pixies have always been easily affected by the moods of those around them. Falling dead when a child refuses to believe in them. And with their connection to the island, I can only imagine the pain they've felt from Connor's desolation and the poison filling this place, pulsing beneath our feet.

No wonder none of the pixies want to see me.

Everything I've done so far has just made everything worse.

"All right, Glim." I rub at the back of my neck. "What *can* I do?"

She sits cross-legged in the air, tilting her little blonde head at me. Then she speaks in that windchime voice. "The warrior people are in the northern jungle—"

A massive crash of thunder cuts off her words. The ground shakes, the air rent by the sound.

Uh oh.

Glimmer and I both lift our eyes to the sky. The storm clouds are rolling in at an unnatural pace. The wind kicks up, driving away the sweep of mist and pelting my skin with rain. And then there is more thunder as the sky grows dark.

Someone is not happy.

Glimmer races off through the trees, spiraling upward, toward the sky. I race after her, clambering up the tallest spindly tree I can find. "Wait for me!"

My bare feet help propel me up the tree, bark rough beneath my touch as I pull myself up. I reach the top of the tree, crouching to perch and peer out over the sweeping storm. The wind howls around us, driving Glimmer to burrow in the collar of my hoodie. I squint, scanning the dark sky and the flash of lightning that rips through the cloud layer.

I see it at the same time Glimmer does. She launches out of my hoodie, screeching excitedly, gesturing toward the edge of the island that is barely visible from here. The curve of Blindman's Bluff—

And the gleaming figure standing at the very edge of the cliffs.

I can't quite make out her shape, but I'd know that glow anywhere.

"Claire."

How did she even get out?

I grip the frail tree, trying to stretch taller, trying to see her. What does it matter how she got out? She *did*. I have got to stop underestimating things about this girl.

But the way the whole island has been thrown into this crashing, screaming storm—I'm not the only one who knows. Connor is after her. I doubt she's been cornered on that cliff of her own volition.

"I have to go help her!" I tell Glimmer, and she looks at me questioningly. "Flying would be nice."

She darts back, wings beating fiercely against the storm. I turn on my puppy dog eyes, trying the charm that used to work on Tink. "Please? Claire needs my help! You don't want me to abandon her, do you?"

Her little mouth purses to the side, eyeing me for a long moment. Then she finally gestures to the pistol tucked in my belt. "Fine," her tiny voice rings. "But you can't use that! No more hurting, remember? Just help Claire."

I lift my smallest finger. "Pinkie promise, little mate. I'll just help Claire. Plus"—I wink at her—"the pistol is empty anyway."

She crosses her arms over her chest, staring at me again. I know that if she helps me, she'll be going against the many threats Hook and Connor have laid on the magical creatures of this island for doing so, let alone the fact that the other pixies hate me.

But her love of Claire seems to trump her fear, and Glimmer brightens with determination and then darts toward me. A pulse of excitement swells through me as Glimmer's pixie dust pours from her in a steady stream. I push to balance on the upper branch of the tree on one foot and spread out my arms.

Glimmer spins silken lines of pixie dust around me, circling in graceful swirls as she coats my body in the shimmering dust.

Cor, I've missed this. Missed having a little pixie companion.

I don't know if Tink knew Glimmer, but they would have gotten along.

Neither of them put up with my foolery.

I close my eyes for a moment, feeling the wind on my face and the pixie dust in my hair and the way my body lifts out of the tree. We are still just out of reach of the storm pooling over the bluff— but we'll have to be fast. The minute the rain soaks us, not even Glimmer's dust will hold us aloft.

Glimmer is not as strong as Tink was, since she is not as strong as she should be, but it's enough. We continue to fly higher and higher, until I can hover over the dark storm clouds, and I aim around a small mountain peak and toward the bluffs on the south side of the island.

The pixie burrows into the hood of my jacket, and her dust continues to drift over me as she hitches a ride. Below me, through gaps of the forming storm clouds, I can see the shriveled remnants of jungle, rivers turned to dark ink, and meadows now overcome by spindly veins. I catch sight of a small encampment within a thatch of trees and wonder for a moment why a portion of Lily's tribe has splintered off. I stop trying to puzzle it out when a flash of lightning splits the clouds far too close to us.

I swing to the left, calling for Glimmer to hang on tight, and watch the bluffs come fully into view. The storm is the worst here, but through the downpour of rain and rush of wind that severs some of the cloud layer, I can make out Claire's bedraggled form standing at the edge of the rocky cliff. Her dust flows in a steady glow, but even though it's brighter than Glimmer's magic, it still feels worn.

But it's the tall figure standing opposite her that roils my gut.

Connor has already reached her. And he looks about as chuffed as expected.

Although, he does seem to be holding himself back a bit. He hasn't grabbed at her yet. Desperation is written in every jerky move of his hands and the way he hunches and sways.

She keeps shaking her head, and that seems to only make him more frustrated.

This won't end well.

Ducking and preparing for a rocky landing, I tuck Glimmer tighter inside my hoodie and drop through the clouds, landing lower down on the bluff where Connor won't see. I scrape my knees as I tumble to the rough cliff. I check Glimmer and see she's still hiding inside my hood, peeking out at me and nodding.

I skirt around the opposite side of the bluff, creeping up behind Connor. Long ago, Lily taught me how to walk soundlessly. With the crash of thunder and the heavy downpour, I doubt Connor could hear me anyway.

I take a deep breath, creeping closer and closer until I'm only a few feet away from Connor.

Claire's attention is locked on her brother, and now I can make out her words: "I won't. You know I can't do that. Besides, you left me in that cell for two months! You didn't talk to me once all that time!"

Her gaze lifts past him as she lets out a frustrated breath—and snags on me. Surprise sparks in those blue eyes, but to Claire's credit she manages to suppress it as I lift a finger to my lips. She gives the slightest nod and is focused on her brother again.

"I wanted to talk to you," Connor says, raking a ghostly hand over one side of his face, fingernails catching in the scarred pieces of skin, "but I couldn't. There were other things we wanted. Other things to do."

Raindrops streak down his pale skin and trace along the dark, jagged lines. I'm only a foot away from him now, crouching, reaching for the weapon at my side—

Glimmer tenses, but I wink at her, nudging her to trust me.

But then I think I see something. Something in Connor.

Something shifts when he shudders. Like darkness that moves a split second before he does. It might be a trick of the storm, but darkness seems to seep from his skin, hovering around him one minute and then gone the next, dissolved into the inky veins carving out his body.

What was that?

It was almost like a shadow.

I don't have time to puzzle it out, because Connor is getting more anxious. I can hear the roar of the water on the other side of the bluff churning to life.

Time to get Claire to safety.

And see if old skills still hold.

Pulling the pistol out of my belt, I dart forward and push the barrel against the back of Connor's head. I imitate the deep, snarling voice I've been impersonating for years.

"I'm done with your stupidity, boy. I'm taking Claire, and you're letting me do it."

The deep, rich croon of the pirate captain rolls off my tongue like it was just yesterday I was hiding in the corner of Skull Rock using his voice to send Smee scrambling to free the Darling children.

And it's certainly worked many other times.

Of course, the gun helps with overall effect.

My mimic must be pretty good because Claire blinks and manages a "Captain!" that's half convincing.

Connor has frozen against the feel of my gun at his head, and I can sense him weighing the situation. Finally, he growls, "Hook?"

Got 'em.

"Aye." I push the muzzle of the empty gun a little closer into his dripping hair. Rain rolls off my nose and down my steady hand. "I'm done playing your filthy games and being one of your dogs. I'm taking the girl, and I'm going back to London—back to my mansion." I wince, thinking the mansion may have been a bit much. I muster a growl and say the most important bit. "And if you don't step out of our way, I'll blow out your brains."

I can practically feel Connor's snarl as his body shudders again. "You're threatening me, Hook?"

I stand my ground. "Not even you are faster than a bullet."

Claire gulps, staring past Connor at me. "He looks desperate, Connor. And those burns must still hurt."

Burns? What is she even talking about?

But a look of real fear fills Claire's eyes, and she reaches for her brother. "Please, Connor. I don't want him to hurt you. Just walk away."

Connor's fists tighten at his sides, but I don't address him this time. "Good advice, love."

That seems to sell it.

Connor tries to glance over his shoulder, but I stop him with a poke of the weapon. "Let her go first."

"I'll just kill you the minute I have a chance. You won't get far."

I set my jaw. "Let her go."

The moment stretches long, the rain thudding around us—and then Connor lets out a ragged breath and flicks his hand. The vines that were curling around Claire's feet, tethering her to the ground, slither away.

It's working!

Connor's shakes are more intense. The back of his head is reverberating against my gun. "I swear I'll kill you the minute I can, Hook."

But his threats don't matter now. Claire's dust ripples over her body, and she lifts off the ground, and we're seconds from being home free—

Then I hear the echo of footsteps behind me.

Oh, blarmy!

Before I can even turn around, or push Connor off this blasted cliff, I hear the click of a real gun pointed at me.

"Game's up, Peter."

It's Hook's voice. Hook's *real* voice.

Dangit.

Furious, Connor raises his hands and vines shoot out, grabbing Claire again and jerking her back to the ground.

Anger floods through me as I spin around, ready to pistol-whip the lout with my empty gun. But instead of the pirate captain, I come face-to-face with a pair of pale green eyes.

She almost seems like an apparition of the storm, the rain running down her deathly pale skin, and her soaking wet hair falling around her face and shoulders like snaky coils. Something about her just seems to fit here, on this stormy ledge. The instant I take her in, a mammoth headache slams into my temples, and I nearly fall to my knees.

"Who—are you?"

But she just shakes her head, icy glare cutting through me.

"You're so predictable."

12

CLAIRE

Neverland

*I*t's Peter.

Despite the rain thundering around us, and the crash of water slamming against the bluff behind me, and the lightning streaking the sky—Peter is here.

His thick curls are drenched, and those green eyes carry more gravity, wincing with how close he had been to pulling off this ruse.

But once again, he's too late.

Paige has appeared from the mist, and Hook on her heels. The pirate captain strides forward and loops his mangled hook around Peter's neck, but Peter doesn't even seem to notice. His brow is furrowed as he looks to Paige and me and back again.

Thunder booms across the sky. Connor's attention is locked on Peter, filled with an anger that ebbs and flows through the island, like the tide behind me.

"You always ruin everything!" Connor shouts at Peter. The island starts to shake again, and I'm strangely glad for the vines tethering me to the side of the cliff.

Peter's eyes widen as his knees go out, and he thuds to the rocky surface of the bluff. His body shudders in time to the fierce quaking of this cliff.

I try to reach for Peter. "You're hurting him! Whatever you're doing, Connor, stop it."

Connor just ignores me, body now rigid as he stands above Peter. "Give me the island. All of it."

Peter leaps to his feet at that, stumbling backward only to bump into the muzzle of Hook's pistol. Pan darts a fleeting glance around the small group circling him and then glares at Connor. "Never. There is no way I'm giving you more power."

Color and emotion drain out of my brother's face, and darkness seeps into his irises until his eyes are nothing but obsidian holes. "Wrong answer."

Water slams into the edge of the bluff behind me, growing in violence as it swells. At first, I could just see the whitecaps far below, but now the water is roiling and rocking. Another wave surges up, arching and pounding into the top of Blindman's Bluff. The spray of water drenches me, and I gasp, but my heart stops when I see the water keep going.

The wave that swept over me thins out into three streaks of water that hurtle forward and bury themselves in Peter's breast.

The world blurs. I blink rapidly, trying to clear my vision and process what I'm seeing. Peter is gasping, gurgling, as blood leaks down his green hoodie. I stare at the slivers of ice protruding from his chest.

I realize Connor is standing in front of Peter, his hand outstretched, and the three lances of ice shifting upward as if having just dripped from his fingertips. Like he commanded them there.

I'm suddenly so nauseous I have to clap a hand over my mouth.

Peter is doubled over on the ground, spitting blood, desperately grasping at the jagged spikes of ice protruding from his chest. He pulls one spike out and utters a ragged gasp through gritted teeth.

"Are you ready to give me the island now?" Connor asks, voice devoid of any feeling. His perpetual tremors have stopped. He's standing stiffly, but I see something shift beneath that pale skin. The veins that clamber up his face bulge and darken as something skims there. A dark shadow passing beneath a frozen lake, taking all possible warmth with it.

"C-Connor. Please—"

Connor just shakes his head, and another vine snakes up my neck, spinning around my mouth, silencing me. I gasp, trying to bite at the vine, but it's useless. But I'm not defenseless.

Angry, biting dust begins to lift from my skin, starting to soak into the vines—

Suddenly Connor flicks his hand. The raindrops splattering around us beat down harder, shifting direction—barreling straight into me with so much force they sweep away the dust as soon as it forms. They soak into my hair and through the vines.

The water cools my dust.

My eyes shoot wide, and Connor smirks.

"Pixies never could fly in the rain."

I'm left shaking, soaked through and incredulous as my brother's inky eyes narrow on Peter. "I need that connection."

Peter spits blood. "I said *no!*"

The rain has abated but thunder still rumbles above us. Connor stares at Peter for a moment. He lifts his hand toward the edge of the bluff. A spray of salt water hammers up its side, and a rod of water shoots toward Connor, crystallizing to ice as it pours into his hand. It elongates into a jagged, icy spear.

Even Hook takes a noticeable step back when Connor approaches Peter again. His face is still eerily, dangerously passive. He points the spear at Peter, and when he speaks, his tone is hollow. As if any shred of my real brother has dissolved away. "Give me your connection to the island."

Peter's eyes are bloodshot and filled with pain, but he still lifts his head and meets Connor's eyes. "Try your worst."

Connor doesn't even blink. "If that's what it takes."

Paige has faded to the background, watching like a hovering wraith, a sickening smile on her lips. But when Connor raises the spear, aiming it squarely at Peter's chest, she suddenly speaks.

"Wait."

The word stays Connor's hand. A muscle ticks in his jaw. "What?"

She takes slow, even strides forward, her long brown dress tattered and sweeping her ankles. "We don't want to kill him, and somehow I doubt torture will work." She slides a knowing glance Hook's way. "It certainly never did much for the pirates." She looks down at Peter. "To him, death is just another adventure. But"—she nudges aside Connor's spear, crouches beside Peter—"I can make him cooperate."

Something about the way she says those words makes me wince.

Still, I'm surprised when Connor merely nods. His spear dissolves into water again and splashes to the ground. The icy blades in Peter's chest dissolve as well, except for a few small bits of ice that skim over the slender wounds, stopping the blood flow.

Paige glares down at Peter Pan, arms crossed over her chest. "You really should give us what we want, or I will tell everyone here what you did. Including your precious Claire—and if she knew, you'd lose her forever. And if somehow you didn't, I'd throw her off that cliff, and you'd lose her just the same."

The threat hangs in the air like the tang of poison, but Peter just stares at her blankly. "Do I know you?"

Her eyes go wide—fractured and human for that single moment—and then she slaps him across the face. "Don't play games! I know that the island used to withhold things—but not this. Y-you have to remember this." Her voice strains, a thread of desperation.

He rubs at the stinging red spot. "'Ey? Sorry, but I don't . . ." He squeezes his eyes shut, fingertips at his temple, as if trying hard to resurrect some forlorn knowledge. I hold my breath. He just shakes his head, lifting those vibrant green eyes to meet her dull, wild ones. "I really have no idea who you are."

Paige's angry shriek rends through the air.

"No!" She shoves Peter over and over bringing them both dangerously close to the edge of the bluff. She kicks and pulls at his hair. Paige is frantic and fraying. Hook looks like he wants to jump in, but Connor shakes his head at the pirate.

Peter raises his hands to protect his face, but Paige's sharp nails claw his arms. "You don't get to just forget me!" Her voice is ragged, thick. "Not like everything else. Like you forgot Mother."

Peter's hands drop, and he stares at her, freckled features painted with perplexed shock and a wash of guilt. Paige leaves a nasty scratch on his cheek, and then with a wild gasp, she runs her thin hands through her mane of pale reddish hair and turns around.

She comes at me, grim, frantic determination in her eyes. "Well, maybe this will make you remember."

"No—*Claire*!" Despite the blood and pain, Peter rushes toward me. But Paige is already ripping at the vines anchoring me to the cliff and pushing me toward the edge of the bluff. I kick at her as one foot comes free but am aware if I fight too hard, I could wrench the rest of the vines for her.

I teeter, feeling the vines around my ankles beginning to snap one by one. I stare into the desperate eyes of this woman who claims to be Peter's sister.

She glances over her shoulder at Peter as he races for us, Connor and Hook just watching hollowly. Her lips curl. "Let's see if you remember *her* drowning."

Paige shoves me. The last vine snaps.

I tumble over the side of the cliff.

But my dust pours from my skin, a pale gold haze, catching me just in time. I soar away from the spray of white water, and for a second, I consider leaving. Just turning and flying as far away as I can.

But Peter is still up there. Stabbed and bleeding from trying to rescue me from my own brother.

That invisible tether of guilt or duty or whatever it is pulls me back toward the bluff.

My feet alight on the ground, and I stand opposite Peter. The wind tosses my pixie dust across Paige's weathered features, igniting her pale skin and green eyes and giving life to her wet hair.

And in that moment, with the shine of magic bringing a bit of warmth into her desperate expression, she almost looks a bit like the boy she claims is her brother.

My attention shoots to Peter, and I find him staring openmouthed at Paige. The relief that flooded his features when he saw me fly shifts into something else as he stares at her. A spark of something long lost, buried deep in those beautiful green eyes.

And then Peter screams. He crumples to the ground, writhing, in more pain than he'd even been in only minutes ago when Connor had stabbed him. He's clutching at his head, thrashing against the mottled ground.

"What's happening?" I run forward and drop to my knees beside him. I try to hold him still so he won't hurt himself further. "Someone help him!" But if this is anything like the strange headache attacks he'd get in London . . . I'm not sure anyone can.

Connor and Hook stand silent as the wind shrieks along with Peter. Pan's cries convulse the island. Peter and Neverland rock and shudder and howl.

"What is happening to him?" I gasp again, pleading with Peter's sister as his body wrenches so violently I can't even hold him down.

Paige is deathly still, her thin lips tipped up in that sickening smile.

"He's remembering."

13

PETER

Neverland

My head splits apart.

At first, darkness pools into my vision like the storm clouds Connor conjured, blocking everyone from view. I writhe against the ground as the pain carves out my temples. But then fractured images and scraps of moments appear through the blackness. Each memory burns into my mind like a comet, and the pain sends shockwaves throughout me.

I can't stop it. I can't hold it back anymore.

Just scream and tear at the coarse ground as memories sweep me backward into a black hole of things I'd never wanted to confront again. Places I never wanted to be.

But I'm back there again. In my own room, as a young child, curled in a corner next to my bed. Crying because Father was yelling again. But then, she's there. *Mother.* A young woman with soft red hair and vibrant blue eyes—and something almost magical about her. As magical as the stories she told me when she tucked me into bed, her lyrical voice whispering of whimsical, distant places. Of a world where shining sprites could peer through window frames, and where a pixie once fell in love with a human man. Where that pixie traded her wings to be with him, letting go of her pixie dust to instead eventually hold a little child in her arms. And tuck him into bed.

A little boy whose blood was mostly human, but with a trickle of magic still there.

When she was with him, all was right with the world. And then she became sick. Sunny smiles and whispered secrets and adventures in parks were traded for long hours at her bedside. The worse Mother grew, the darker the house became. Especially for the man she had traded her wings for.

The father who turned to a bottle and a harsh voice to cover his grief. Who screamed at his son for playing, for not just *growing up.*

I moan, curling into a tight ball, just thinking of it. Thinking of the day I snuck into her room to find her bed empty. She was gone.

She took all the light with her.

The time between is a blur. A blur of broken glass and even sharper words and tears and hours huddled in a dark corner of my room. With all the magic gone too.

Until one night when a spark of light perched on the windowsill. Peeked in at that little boy and began to tell him stories so very much like his mother's. Little voice tinkling of a place he could go if he wanted it. If he only wanted it—*needed* it enough. Needed an escape.

And I did. I was so desperate for an escape from that blasted world. I'd spent so much time lost in my own imagination, making up stories of being abandoned as a baby in a park or living with a flock of birds—but I could only lose myself in my own mind for so long. Until the angry footsteps and the scent of alcohol would thunder into my room and rip me back to the gray world I existed in.

And so one day, when I'd forgotten to finish a chore and my father had become so angry, so volatile that he had beaten that young Peter . . .

I was done.

So I waited for that pixie, that little Tinkerbell, to arrive at my window again. A pixie with magic that existed well outside of any worlds I could create. This time I told her I was ready to go. I opened the window, climbed up on the sill, my boyish heart beating fast as she drizzled me in pixie dust—and I *flew*. That sensation stirring up the whisper of magic in my blood. The whisper that said I was different. Special.

Most children can escape to their Never Never Land when they need it, usually at night when they dream. But it takes a boy with magic in his soul and freedom sparkling in his eyes to bring to life an entire world.

For an instant, that moment captures me so completely that the pain in my temples fades. I can see it—that first night when I flew away. Soaring over the rooftops of old London, past the chimney smoke and the ships docked on the Thames. Aiming for a certain star to the right and feeling closer to my mother than I had in ever so long.

But then, something skips. Something jars in my brain, and the pain comes flooding back in, as the memory sharpens into focus. My whole body seizes as I realize something I'd been missing . . .

As the memory of the night I escaped to Neverland fills into the hollows and secreted parts of my mind, I realize that I wasn't flying alone that night.

I can see that small reflection of myself, that young Peter

rolling and laughing in the air as he soars higher and higher.

And then he looks behind him and reaches out to grab the hand of the girl flying at his heels. The moment I picture him reach for her hand, watch their eyes meet, both the same ivy shade of green . . . it all clicks into place.

Memories start to rearrange like a puzzle putting itself together.

I wasn't the only one in that house who cried themselves to sleep. I wasn't the only child who grieved the loss of a mother.

Our mother.

My sister. Four years older than me.

Paige.

She helped create Neverland too.

The knowledge skims through me like a jolt of electricity—and then swells back, bowling me over like a clap of thunder.

And the world tilts and shifts on its axis, and suddenly everything is cast in a new shade of raw color that changes the foundations I've stood on for so long.

How did I forget my own sister?

The headache starts to fade, to settle in, and slowly my vision clears. As my eyes refocus and I pull myself up to sit and look past Claire hovering, worried, to the slip of a woman standing a few feet away. Her arms are crossed over her chest, green eyes dull and worn but regarding me carefully.

This time I recognize her.

She's a frail, faded version of my older sister, but it's undeniably Paige.

Which should be impossible.

I try to keep the tremble from my voice "Paige? But . . . how are you here?"

My sister's eyes flash. "That is the question, isn't it? Maybe I'm not really here. Maybe I never really came back."

A chill snakes over my arms. "How long have you been here? We were just children the last time I saw you . . ."

Paige glances at Hook.

"I found her," the pirate captain says. "I found her about two years ago."

"And then she found me." Connor twitches as he says it, those hollow, dark eyes lightening for a fraction of a second. "It turns out Paige and I have a lot in common."

I press a hand against the stinging wounds as I turn to Hook. "*Where* did you find her?"

"It's not important," Paige snaps. "What's important is what needs to happen next. You have to give Connor your connection to the island so we can undo everything you've done and fix this whole mess."

My brow creases. "But how will that shift what . . ." I'm not sure how to say it. "How will that fix what happened to you?"

Long, oily strands of pale hair fall across her eyes. "I will finally be able to leave this cursed island once and for all."

"Heh? Now, just 'ow does that work?"

Paige's expression has closed off again. "It doesn't matter. Just give him what he wants."

Yeah, not so fond of that plan.

I suddenly realize I haven't seen Glimmer since I came to. Hopefully she did the smart thing and got out of here. The burn of the cuts on my chest grows worse, but I tense my jaw and try to ignore it.

But Claire notices. "You're bleeding again, Peter."

I press the heel of my palm against the biggest of the cuts and toss her a lopsided smile. "I'll manage, Pixie-Girl." Then I look at my sister. "I'm sorry, Paige. I'm awful sorry that I forgot so much. But I'm still not giving you my connection. Torturing me won't change that."

Connor frowns at my words, and the churn of poison that seethes from him through the island makes me feel physically ill. But I dig deep, forcing myself to remain sitting upright, to not show them how affected I am.

Paige's lips purse together. "I knew you'd be this stubborn, which is why it's not you that we're concerning ourselves with right now." Her eyes flick to Claire. "Since Claire has already given up her connection to Connor, we really have no need for her besides using her burning dust for . . . other means."

Claire pales, and her eyes dart to me and then toward the edge of the bluff. She manages two quick steps toward the edge, but only lifts a few inches off the ground before Connor loops a thick vine once more around her ankle and slams her to the rocky surface. She gasps, wind knocked out of her, on her knees.

Desperation is in the look she gives.

I press an arm around my waist to hold back the pain and leaking wounds, and push myself to my feet. I cross over to Paige, shoving a finger at her. "You wouldn't dare use her like that. I doubt Connor would let you."

But Connor just looks away.

My sister's mouth cracks in a dry, humorless smile. "We already have, little brother."

Wha . . . ? I turn toward Claire, and at the look on her face, my heat plunges. She darts a telltale glance toward Hook, and then lowers her head. Morbid fascination gets the best of me as I watch the pirate captain roll back the cuff circling his hook. His eyes never leave mine. My mouth opens when I see the burn marks going all the way to his shoulder. The metal around his hook is contorted and digs into marred flesh. The burns marking Hook's neck and the side of his face now make sense.

"Claire did that?" I ask, incredulous.

Paige shrugs so casually it riles. "You should see the Lost Boys. They'll be in the infirmary for months."

Claire whimpers, backing up as close to the edge of Blindman's Bluff as Connor will let her. There is fear in her eyes, and the way she keeps glancing back over her shoulder at the churning water below her stills my breath.

Her eyes look at me, pleading. "I can't hurt anyone again."

I realize the corner they've backed her into. Backed both of us into.

My brain scrambles, trying to find a way out. Something. Anything.

Even if I could whisk Claire away, Connor would just find us again eventually. He has this entire island under his thumb. And once Connor found us again—well, I'm not strong enough to stop him. Not alone.

But I can't leave Claire here. If I leave her with them to use as such a vile weapon, it will break her.

Suddenly, a faint sound begins to echo through the noisy waves below. A hauntingly familiar sound . . .

Tick. Tock. Tick. Tock.

The ticking sound of a large clock, echoing from inside a certain aquatic creature.

Hook curses. "You've got to be kidding me."

But the sound just grows louder as the crocodile draws nearer and nearer. Even Paige seems a little unnerved and moves away from the corner of the cliff. Claire is too numb to react. Connor, on the other hand, ambles closer to peer out over the edge of the bluff.

"I thought you said you killed it!" Hook snarls at Connor, who just shrugs.

"I said I tried. But after I struck it, it disappeared for months. I guess Peter's brought it out again."

My mouth pinches into a little smirk.

I make my way to the edge of the bluff and look down at the gray water slamming against the sharp rocks rimming the bottom of the cliff. The churning ocean sprays up like foaming fingers. And then I see it. A large, dark shape slicing through the water, drawing closer and closer to the bottom of the cliffs. All jagged scales and huge snout. It angles its head toward the top of the bluff, somehow knowing we are here, and its dark green maw snaps at us.

Cor. I'd forgotten how massive that thing is.

I'm not even sure how the ticking clock can be heard as loudly as it is, ricocheting from somewhere deep inside the beast— another Neverland oddity? The croc swallowed the blasted ticker during the same sea battle where I lopped off a certain pirate's arm, and it's the only reason why it hasn't managed to devour the rest of the captain yet. Pity.

The crocodile snorts, swishing its long, mossy tail back and forth in the choppy water.

Claire seems fascinated by the ticking crocodile, but the sense of danger she should have is missing. Her eyes are glassed over. *Not good.*

I glance at my sister again. A hollow reflection of the girl who's just beginning to fit into place in my memories. My gaze skims Connor, standing just behind her, and Hook, ever at her side.

None of them used to be like this. Well, maybe Hook. But not this dark.

What pushed them so far?

Was I so desperate for things to remain how they were and to not lose this place that I shoved anyone out of the way because of it?

I survey the island sprawling around us. Soak in the overcast sky and the pounding rain and the rocky bluff. I don't know how to fix this. I don't know how to undo this.

But there are two things I do know.

My selfish desperation to keep this island is what lost my sister.

And if I give up Neverland, I may be able to save Claire.

If I don't? If I let them have her?

I'll lose Claire too. If the look in her eyes means anything, I realize that if Paige tries to turn Claire into any sort of weapon . . .

Claire will take herself out of the equation.

And when I'm faced with that reality, the answer seems simple.

"If I give you my connection will you let Claire go?"

Claire gives a disbelieving snort, but I'm watching each opportunity to shift this tide slipping through my fingers.

Paige nods. "As agreed."

I take a deep breath and go up to Connor, who is still standing at the edge of the bluff, a few feet away from his sister. He is facing me, dark irises burrowing into mine.

"What do you want to do with the island? With my bond?"

His gaze visibly clears, and for the first time since I arrived, I can actually see the color of his irises. Blue, like Claire's. "I want what you had. To forget all the shadows and undo all . . . *this*." He gestures to his face and then out at the island around us.

My brows rise. "That's actually not a terrible idea." But

something seems off. I try to read my sister's expression, to filter out if Connor is being truthful, but her face is only a cold, blank slate.

Well, I guess there's only one way to find out if things can get any worse.

You can't heal a wound with a blade. Glimmer's words surface. They sound like something my mother would have said—now that I remember her.

Mother would have liked Glimmer too. She always used to say that even when it may seem impossible, there's always a way out. That magic lurks in the unexpected places.

I hope she's right.

Turning back to Connor, I slowly reach out a hand to him. His eyes brighten as he grabs it.

I created this island.

And to rescue my Pixie-Girl, I may have to lose it.

But I do have a knack for bringing lost things home again.

I clasp Connor's hand hard and meet his hungry gaze. "This is not over," I inform him.

Before the surprise can flicker in his eyes, I give the storybook villain everything he wants.

I close my eyes, reaching deep for that connection to the island. For the hum of magic that has always pulsed in time to my heartbeat. *Hello, love,* I whisper to Neverland. *I know I haven't always cared for you like I should, and I promise this isn't the end. I've got at least one more trick up my sleeve. I'll be back. Just always be waiting.*

And with that, I let go. Let go of this place that has been my sanctuary forever. Let go of the island that was like my own reflection where I gave lost things a place to belong.

Because there's one Lost Girl I have to save.

My whole body goes icy cold as the connection wanes and snaps to an end. Part of me wants to go find a tree to hide behind and have a good cry.

But there's no time for that.

I wrench my hand out of Connor's. He glows with the injection of magic I just gave him. The pelter of rain vanishes, and a huge streak of lightning cuts across the sky.

I can no longer feel the hum of the island under my feet. But Neverland pitches and bows as Connor stares at his hands, as if seeing something new—and I know he's definitely feeling it.

I have a tinge of regret in missing every pulse of my body being a cacophony that this whole island is singing along to. But I shake it off and go quickly to Claire as the vines holding her down fall away. I grab her hand, a thrill racing through me as she looks at me, eyes wide.

"I can't believe you did that! But, Peter, they're not—"

"Not going to actually let us go?" I wink at her, pulling her close. "I know. That's why I've got another idea."

She bites her lip, glancing around me at her brother who has turned his attention on us. "He won't just let us fly away."

"Who said anything about flying?"

"If not flying—then what's your plan?"

"The unexpected." And with that, I toss Claire over the edge of the cliff. Her shocked cry echoes as she falls and crashes into the water below, avoiding the rocks, but landing a little too close to the croc for comfort.

I take a step back so that my heels are hanging off the edge of the bluff and mock salute Connor. "Take good care of my island, would you? I'll be back for her."

And with that, I leap backward and plummet after Claire.

I twist midair just before I hit the surface and sink in feet first. I slice through the water like a human-sized bullet, surrounded by bubbles and icy depths. I kick my feet, hands churning as I try to peer through the icy water as I swim away from the bluff.

Where's Claire?

Suddenly, I see her. She's a few feet ahead of me, suspended underwater, her hair floating around her. Staring at the face of the massive crocodile.

It's submerged just in front of her, large reptilian eyes watching her unblinking. I've never seen it so calm with anyone before. Even when I've interacted with the beast, I've had to remind it who's boss to keep it at bay. But it seems enamored with Claire as her golden dust ignites the water all around us.

She reaches out and gently places a hand against its muzzle. The same massive jaw that I'd fed Hook's hand to nuzzles closer to her hand, and the creature gives a little murmur.

Well, blarmy. Claire's got herself a pet croc.

Suddenly, a webbed hand grabs my wrist. I look down to see a familiar pair of round eyes and dark, seaweed-like hair crossing her face. A dozen other sirens suddenly come into view, filling the water around us with their obsidian scales and swishing tails. Several reach for Claire, and her expression fills with panic.

I wave, trying to gesture for her to calm down.

The crocodile eyes the sirens but gives them space. My lungs are beginning to scream, but suddenly the sirens are grabbing Claire and me and dragging us through the water. Deeper and deeper.

If I didn't know better, I'd think they were dragging us to our watery deaths.

Thankfully, the sirens are here for an entirely different reason.

Nyssa's grip on my arm grows tighter as she tilts her head to bare her sharp teeth at me. "You owe us, Pan."

That's where she's wrong. If I can actually pull this off, this whole bloomin' island is going to owe *me*.

14

CLAIRE

Neverland

At first I'm afraid the sirens are trying to drown us.

I shiver at their glassy, too-large eyes. There's something familiar about the depth in those round orbs. One of them drifts nearer, purses her lips together, and blows out an air bubble. It bobbles in the water, sort of bluish tinted—and then the siren gestures to my mouth with a webbed hand.

They want me to eat it?

I reach out and hesitantly plop the bubble inside my mouth. It immediately pops—and I can breathe. It's as if there's a strange coating that fills my mouth and crawls up my throat to my nose. When I inhale water, it's like breathing oxygen.

What kind of weird magic is this?

There are two sirens on either side of me, and they grab my arms once more, nodding at me, before they're swimming again. They pull me along at an amazing speed, ripples streaking past us through the onslaught of water. As I let them pull me, I take in these incredible creatures.

I thought seeing the pixies for the first time was incredible, but seeing the sirens is unreal.

Their bodies are covered in a graying skin, with slender, shimmering dark scales that skim over their forearms and up their shoulders. Gills are visible on their necks, when their long, wavy hair that moves with a life of its own shifts enough to see them.

These eerie creatures are breathtaking. Glossy dark scales ripple down the curves of their tails, rimmed with thin ridges and tapering into wide, flickering fins at the end. They swim with such languid, forceful movements that it's almost hypnotic.

They feel so familiar somehow.

My mind must be boggled to have not connected it immediately. *I'm half siren.*

I gasp underwater. The sirens glance back at me, and I muster a little smile. They whisk us through the depths, changing directions a few times through the seemingly never-ending expanse of dark Neversea, and finally we are near the island again.

They aim upward and toward the lightening water above. We break the surface, cresting with small waves that break over our heads. I wipe saltwater from my eyes and try to orient myself. One of the sirens lets go of me, the other has a webbed hand around my waist and is pulling me forward.

We're in some kind of small inlet. Steep cliffs circle around us, and we are hedged by tress and dangling vegetation that hides this little lagoon from sight of anyone traversing the island.

Little lagoon . . .

The siren pushes me toward one of the outcroppings of rock that juts from the sea floor, and I scramble up to sit on the flat plateau. While I take in a deep breath of pure air and feel that odd coating fading from my mouth, I finally survey the surroundings.

The mermaids' lagoon.

Or the sirens' hidden cavern.

The curve of the inlet is made from some kind of gleaming clay. Instead of the reddish color I expect, this has an opaline sheen and almost looks purple. The sirens have certainly made use of it.

They've carved small seats out of the towering face of clay, dozens of little nooks and crannies where they can sit with their tails dipping in the water as they sun themselves. But it's not just the little alcoves and small clay slides that are etched into the clay walls. There are also beautiful murals. Polished rocks and seashells and gleaming scales and fish bones have been pressed into the purple surface, making an expansive work of art that curves around us. I gaze at the shapes of curling tails, massive sea creatures I don't recognize, and various underwater seascapes.

The glint of the sun ricochets off the water, reflecting off the sheen of the scales and polished murals, and casts the entire lagoon in an array of dancing colors.

"Wow."

"Claire, are you all right?" At Peter's voice, I find him sitting on one of the little carved-out seats. He runs a finger over one of the shells pressed into the wall behind him. The movement is absent and familiar, like he's studied these murals and sat among the sirens dozens of times.

Hoping that the aquatic creatures maintain their streak of being peaceful, I slide off the rock. The sirens circle around, watching closely, but the hungry look I see in their eyes when they look at Peter seems to vanish when it is turned to me. All I see is curiosity and a sense of respect—as if they recognize I belong here too.

I give them a hesitant smile and strike through the chilly water toward Peter. He sits with his back pressed against the curve of the towering cliff, and from the way his jaw is clenched tight, I can tell the wounds have begun bleeding again. I spot four pools of crimson staining his hoodie. He must be in a lot of pain. Still, he reaches a hand down for me.

I take it, and he pulls me to sit beside him. I don't let go right away, though, and scoot a bit closer. We sit side by side on the carved ledge of clay.

I squeeze his hand. "Peter, I can't thank you enough for what you did. Giving up your connection to the island was not a small thing. I still can't believe you did it and"—my voice gets small—"did it for me."

He gives me that sideways grin. "I'm not sure I can believe it." He hangs his head a bit. "But I had to do something, especially after lying to you for so long . . . and everything with Connor . . ."

I nod, not sure what to say other than, "Thank you." I hold his chilled hand a little tighter. After a moment, he gently eases away and wraps both arms around his chest.

Peter has certainly looked better. His skin is far too ashen, and his hoodie is getting even more saturated with blood.

"Please," I ask the sirens that have swum up to us. "Can you help him?" This wound is too deep for even my dust to heal. We need to stop the bleeding and patch him up.

One of the sea creatures flicks her tail and lifts out of the water to rest her arms on the ledge where we sit. Her round eyes regard us.

"Because you asked—yes."

Peter's eyelids flutter, and he glances down at her. "Thank you, Nyssa."

She nods and makes some quick, high-pitched clicking noises

to the other sirens. A handful of them disappear beneath the waves, to return a few minutes later bearing some kind of gauzy mesh and a variety of strange underwater plant life.

"Shirt off," Nyssa orders Peter.

"Let me help you." I kneel on the hard-packed clay and help Peter out of his hoodie and the shirt beneath. His smooth, tanned skin has more scars than I remember. Several look very recent. Four jagged holes are raw and bleeding, most on his abdomen with one on his shoulder.

"Good. Now move. I'll do the rest," Nyssa tells me.

"You're sure I can't help?"

She shakes her head, dark hair swirling. I glance at Peter, and he nods.

I slide back into the cold water, teeth chattering, and find another nearby seat cut into the curving clay wall. I watch as Nyssa perches beside Peter and begins treating his wounds. Other sirens glide closer, handing her various things. Her tail swishes as it spills over the side of the ledge.

"Eat this," she tells Peter, putting a strange-looking, prickled underwater fruit of some kind in his mouth.

He bites into it, releasing juices that streak down his chin. He makes a face. "That's nasty!"

"It's for the pain." She quickly cleans each cut, wiping away blood, and I'm amazed at how fast her webbed fingers are. She fills each puncture with a mottled green mixture and then scrapes a chunk of clay from the wall and packs his wounds with that. The bleeding has been stopped, but Peter's face is white, body tight.

She finally wraps his whole chest with a seaweed-type bandage and then leans back to survey her work.

I lean forward for a better look. "You're done?"

Nyssa nods and launches herself off the ledge to disappear beneath the water. I swim over to climb up on the ledge beside Peter. I lean my back against the clay wall, my legs hanging off the end of the shelf.

Sirens still surround us, more than I can even make out from the overcast sky and the way they blend effortlessly into the water. But I can see their soaked, stringy dark hair and dark and reflective eyes as their webbed hands keep them afloat.

Peter rallies enough energy to pull his hoodie back on over the strange poultice and stretchy, mossy substance packing his wounds.

"Are you feeling any better?"

He rubs a hand over his cheek, wiping off some dried clay that has stuck there. "Still hurts like blazes, but yeah, it's a little better."

"Good." I lean in and look right into those green irises. "Because I have a lot of questions, and this time you are going to be completely honest with me."

There's a spark in his half smirk. "Yes *ma'am*."

The windchill has begun to get to me, so I pull my knees to my chest and muster a bit of pixie dust to warm myself. I can hear the swishing fins as the sirens drift in a little closer. Their eyes gleam as they're transfixed by my show of dust.

But it's Peter who has all my attention.

"First off, how did you get here? Secondly, is Paige really your sister? Why does she hate you so much?"

He winces, but not from his freshly treated wounds. "I was a blasted idiot for lying to you so bloomin' much in London. I honestly thought that if you knew the truth, you'd never help me. More than that"—his shoulders slump—"I couldn't bear to tell you about Connor. So, I lied." He squints at me, waiting for a response, but when I can't muster one, he sighs. "To answer your questions: Jeremy had some pixie dust—just enough to get me here. And Paige . . ." He takes a deep breath. "Paige is my sister."

I rub at my shoulders to generate some warmth. "I was stuck in that cell for a long time, Peter. And it gave me time to think." His eyes deepen and he starts to speak, but I hush him. "I don't entirely trust you, but I think I understand. I honestly don't think I can fix any of this without your help. I'm . . . out of my depth." I lift my hand out for him to shake. "So, if you promise no more secrets, I guess I'll consent to being partners."

That lights up his whole face. "Absolutely! Yes, yes." He practically shakes my arm off. "Tellin' truth—that's my new middle name."

I actually laugh at that. "All right, well, now's a good time to start."

And so he does. He quickly explains about the pixie dust from Jeremy, finding Tootles, and the insane series of events that led him to me. When he gets to Paige, his whole expression changes. I can't place it—it's like a mixture of bewilderment and pain and yearning.

"I honestly couldn't remember her before, but it's all trickling back now. Especially without my connection to the island—nothing to lock it all away anymore. And I have a blasted headache to prove it."

"So . . . what happened to her?"

He doesn't answer for a long time. Instead he rubs the back of his neck, glancing anywhere but at me, gaze skimming the lagoon filled with sirens still watching us, tails swishing beneath inky water.

"No secrets? Even the bad ones?"

I nod and take his hand, trying to pour some of my warmth into his clammy skin. "No secrets. I can handle it all."

When did I become so gentle with him? When did all the anger I'd been storing up for months suddenly disappear?

I know the answer. When Peter gave up his whole island for me.

He's growing. That realization sends shockwaves through me.

Peter takes in a deep breath, stares down at the water, and his voice is quiet but rough as he speaks. "Paige was my older sister. Four years difference. She came to Neverland with me the first time, all those years ago. She was the first Lost Girl. She helped me create the island and was connected to it too. Kinda like you and Connor."

"What happened?"

He rubs his temples. "She fell in love with Hook. Though he was just James back then, one of the first and oldest of the Lost Boys. She fell for him and started to grow up, and so did James. I hated that."

I sit completely still, watching his pale, freckled face intently. "I had a big argument with Paige and James. So I tossed James in the water and fed his arm to the croc." He blinks quickly, like he's fighting back tears. "Paige screamed at me to stop. Said he couldn't swim. But I was too brassed off to care. So I stormed away, and my anger sent the whole island into a monsoon. The waves from the Neversea were huge."

He takes a shuddering breath, and a tear trickles down his cheek. I suddenly realize that this is the first time he's ever admitted any of this. "I didn't know it, but Paige jumped in after Hook. She was able to get to him and help him crawl away from the slam of the water. But she—" His voice falters. "She couldn't get out. I made that storm, and I realized while I was off sulking . . . When I got back, the Lost Boys told me she drowned." He mops at his tears, and his face contorts. "I thought I had killed my own sister, Claire."

I shake my head. I have no words. The anguish of his voice, his face, turns my heart.

"But it's not the end of the story," I finally say.

He lifts red eyes to me. "What?"

"Peter." I touch his arm gently. "How did she survive?"

He blinks. "I don't know."

There's a shuffle in the water, and Nyssa appears out of the darkness, emerging up against our ledge. Her gaze is on Peter. "I know what happened."

"You do?"

She gives a single nod. "We found her. We knew you would be angry, and then you would forget. So, as a last show of respect, we thought we would bury her."

"You—*what*?"

"Bury her in our graveyards."

Peter's tears completely stop. "Your underwater graveyards? The caverns that are at the very edge of Neverland?"

Her round eyes study him. "Yes. Why?"

Peter pauses, lost in thought. "Maybe it's not actually about Connor after all. Maybe it's always been her . . ."

"What?" I ask quickly. "What are you thinking?"

He finally turns to me. "The siren graveyards are at the very edge of Neverland, and some of them are literally on the line. It's the space of magic that separates our island from everything else."

"Okay . . . so?"

He reaches down to fill his palm with water and lets it slide through his fingers. "I said that Paige was still connected to

Neverland when I thought she drowned. And that her connection was severed because I stopped being able to sense her, and her connection shifted to me. But what if that wasn't what happened? What if the remaining amount of residual magic from her being tethered to Neverland is what brought her back?" His skin is beginning to regain its color, his eyes are beginning to glint. "No longer connected to Neverland, but alive again?"

I gape. "Is that even possible?"

"I don't know. Maybe? But if so, it means that the island is what is keeping her alive. And if she tries to leave—she might really die this time."

I gnaw the inside of my cheek, trying to understand. "That's why she said that she wants Connor to have control of the island so she can leave," I say slowly. "She's been trapped here the whole time."

Peter nods quickly. "Yes, but in order to do that, to disconnect herself, she has to fundamentally change the way the island works. I'm not even sure it's possible."

"Okay, okay. But, Peter, how does the siren graveyard play into this? Aren't they underwater? Even if the island brought her back, wouldn't she just feel like she was drowning again?"

"I don't know. But somehow, she's back, and she needs Connor to help her escape the island."

Escape. The same thing Connor wants. No wonder she was able to wrap him around her finger.

A shiver crawls over my skin. Paige is desperate and angry. A dangerous combination. My mind goes back to Connor. "If Connor has full control of Neverland now, he should be able to do whatever he wants, right?"

Peter is staring across the water. "It's not a perfect science, and Connor is abnormal. He's let the shadows that possess him bleed into Neverland already. I hate to see what he might be like if he can actually erase his own memory. Like I've realized, you may be able to erase the things you've done"—his voice drops—"but they are still there, boiling beneath the surface."

A tremor moves through the ledge and skims across the water. The sirens start stirring and hissing.

"What's going on?" I grab onto Peter as the shaking begins again.

"Connor," he says grimly. "I think he's trying to erase his memories—transform it all."

"Do you think it will work?"

Another earthquake tears through the island, and I see chunks of the clay cliffs beginning to come loose. Peter is crouched, ready to spring into action, as he scans the curve of the lagoon.

"Neverland represses memories in order to keep children young. Innocent and childlike. But Connor"—his voice is terse—"Connor is none of those things. And I'm not sure even this island can fix that."

The water begins to toss and roil around us, and my heart collapses as I see bits of the sirens' beautiful lagoon starting to crumble. "What happens if it can't? What happens if Connor doesn't get what he wants?"

"I hate to say it"—Peter's glance at me is sober—"but I think we're about find out."

I'm beginning to wonder if it's safe to be still standing on this ledge, when the entire cliff face rocks. I instinctively dive into the water, and Peter jumps in after me. Nyssa grabs my arm and begins pulling me.

"What do we do?" I gasp at her, bobbing in the cool sea.

But before she can answer, a single scream cuts through the air, echoing through the whole island: "*Nooo!*"

My frantic gaze crashes with Peter's, and I see my own fears confirmed in his expression. Connor just realized the island won't do what he is so desperate for.

This won't end well.

"Claire!" Peter yells as he tries to push toward me through the crowd of sirens. "Claire, swim!"

Just then, another massive earthquake shunts through the entire lagoon. But this time, it gains momentum, getting worse and worse. I hear a massive cracking sound and look over my shoulder to see a huge crack cutting up the face of the curving wall of the lagoon.

And then the entire island begins to fracture apart. Half of the lagoon splits and begins to collapse into the water. Half of the cliff, just cut loose.

I try to swim away, but the water is thrashing too strongly, and its current tries to pull me back toward the collapsing cliff.

Nyssa and other sirens grab me, but even they are having trouble swimming. Another wall of water surges, and I'm wrenched out of their grasp.

I tumble over and over. The entire Neversea is as angry and violent as Connor. My lungs need air, but I can't find which way is up. I can't see Peter.

I can't see anything.

The world is beginning to go fuzzy. I struggle to swim against the pressure, but I can't.

If Connor can't control the island like he wants, and if Paige can't leave Neverland, what will they do?

And what will the casualties be?

If Peter and I die—who is left to care?

15

PETER

Neverland

The entire blithering island is falling apart.

I bellow at Claire, accidentally downing water as I try to shove through the roiling waves toward her. But then the blasted cliff is collapsing on top of us, and it's all I can do to duck my head under and swim like a madman. My hands tear through the water as I aim down, trying to plunge deeper and avoid the massive chunks of clay that are cannonballing down at us.

I twist as one piece nicks my heel. Trying to see through the dark depths, I can make out the swish of dozens of siren tails, the sheen of scales and webbed hands, which are all swimming much faster than I am.

But where is Claire?

Panic flares, and I scour the water for her—and another massive piece of clay slams into me from above. I try to push it away, but it's too large. It's the tip of a huge portion of the cliff.

And as the cliffside sinks into the water, the clay collapsing on top of me takes me with it. I'm forced downward, its impossible weight on my back. My lungs yearn for air as I'm shoved toward the seafloor, as if the mountain itself has hefted a mighty hand to slam me down.

I'm surrounded by darkness and the filter of bubbles across my face. Piercing pressure builds in my ears. I wonder if I'll sink so far I'll fall out of the underside of the Neversea and go spinning into space.

And then I hit the seabed so hard I swear I crack a few ribs. Pain spirals across my chest, careening through the bandages on my wounds. My grunt is muffled by the depths of liquid shoving in on me.

At least I didn't fall out the bottom.

My head pounds. My whole body feels like there is fire racing through my veins. My ears hurt.

So done with pain.

First, stabbed by Connor, and now the entire island is trying to break my back?

Frustration funnels behind the pain. I start to choke on water, and it's when the metallic taste crawls down my throat that I realize—something is very off with this salty sea. The metallic taste is bitter and thick. I can feel it sapping my strength even as I writhe here, trying to push out from under the portion of cliff.

I try to crane my head upward and hope desperately that perhaps the sirens will swim down here and rescue my sorry hide.

But no such luck. Not that they would anyway. I'm not their favorite chap.

Those slimy tails really can hold a grudge.

But I helped with Claire, so that has to be worth something.

A burning fills the back of my throat. I'm *so* tired. So tired of constantly being tossed about by these dark tides. I can't even hear the whisper of Neverland in my blood anymore. It may have been faint these past few months, but it was always there.

And now it's not. I can't hear my island anymore.

As that sinks in, really sinks in, I lose all the energy to fight and collapse against the icy seafloor. If I can't hear Neverland anymore and can't see Claire and can't stop Connor as his shadows leak like poison through the island, what is left?

I almost wish I could just pass out, but the pain is too sharp to let me let go just yet.

Groaning, I lift my head one more time, and my vision snags on *her*. A lithe form, sheathed in glimmering flecks of light, striking toward me with surprising speed and agility. She is part siren, after all.

I hardly have any energy remaining when Claire reaches me. Her eyes are worried, but she manages to conjure a bit of dust under water and uses it to push against the massive chunk of clay.

It actually starts to shift and is enough for her to reach down, grab me, and pull me out.

The world is a blur of water and pressure and pain ratcheting through my chest as I'm dragged upward. Just when my lungs feel like they can't take any more, I burst out into open, beautiful air.

Once air fills my stinging ribs, my head starts to clear. My eyes burn from the salt as Claire takes me through the water and pushes me up onto something round and coarse. I turn over on my side, coughing up water:

"I'm so done with almost drowning!" I finally splutter

Her hands are on my chest, gently checking the Nyssa's bandages. "Peter, are you all right? I thought—I was so worried."

I blink again and realize that we are sitting on a large tree floating in the water. I prop myself up against the rough bark of one of the branches and manage a groggy nod.

She returns my nod and spits out something—one of the siren's bubbles. Ah, that's how she held her breath so well.

"I couldn't just leave you there." She shoves her hair back and bites her lip. "And Nyssa said she wouldn't help. You were so limp when I got to you."

Before I can answer, there is a strange splash, and for the first time, I really take in my surroundings. We're bobbing in the Neversea a little ways out from a splintered Neverland that is almost unrecognizable. The lagoon has shifted, split right through the middle, and other cliffs that are visible also have been ravaged by the earthquake. The sea is taking up more ground than ever before, angrily hammering against the side of the island. I'm not sure I want to see what the rest of my dreamland looks like. If the lagoon is split open like this . . . has Connor torn a chasm through the center of Neverland too?

Just the thought makes me shiver, and I sag against the branch at my back, making the whole tree rock. There's another splash, reminding my distracted brain once again what caught my attention in the first place. Half-fish, half-man creatures circle us. The curve of human torsos taper into sleek tails, and when their heads emerge, big, dark eyes stare up at us.

Mainly at Claire. Any time the fishy blokes glance my way, they look like they want to take a bite out of me. They hiss and show their sharp teeth.

Charmers, the lot of 'em.

Claire seems to have noticed this reaction as well. Although she looks a mite intimidated, she leans over the edge of the floating tree. She's bold enough to ask the slithering creatures, "What's wrong?"

A few whispers skim through them, and one of them lifts a hand. Water drips through its webbed fingers, and I can make out something about the sea turning sour.

Claire's brow creases. "There's something wrong with the water?"

They bob their heads in confirmation. Nyssa swims forward through the group, diadem gleaming on her forehead. She addresses Claire. "When the island broke apart, something happened to the lifeblood of the sea and the land. Hard to breathe, swim. Like sickness filling our lungs."

Concern and alarm fill Claire's face. "Do you think Connor did that too?"

Nyssa shrugs, but I would bet Hook's treasure on it. Connor's shadows have always bled into the island, and this time they're poisoning it.

Claire looks down at Nyssa. "Is that why you wouldn't help Peter? Was it the water?"

At that, the sirens surrounding Nyssa hiss, and sharp words are tossed back and forth between them. Nyssa sidles a look my way, then turns back to Claire. Her ominously pointed teeth flash. "No. We are not on good terms with the Pan. We only helped him rescue you, but that is where our loyalties end."

"Why is that?"

Nyssa's dark eyes shift my way. "Because he stole you away from us."

Then she hisses at me.

Rude.

I grunt. "You should tell her the whole truth, y'big water lizard."

My chest is burning with each breath, but I refuse to let the sirens have any idea how much blasted pain I'm really in. Not about to show weakness when they're circling us like I'm their favorite snack.

Claire's glance darts between us. "What . . . truth?"

Nyssa's tail swishes, and she hisses at me again. I make a feeble attempt to pretend my body is not falling apart on me. "Just tell her, you coward."

Nyssa almost looks as if she'd like to drag me under the water and deal with me there.

She glances back at the other sirens. "We may not have been entirely without blame in the situation."

"Explain," Claire orders. She's obviously aware of their behavior regarding her.

Nyssa swims to Claire but doesn't look up at her. "Long ago, one of our kind fell in love with a pixie. This was very frowned upon, but they were desperate to be together, so he traded in his tail for legs, and she gave up her wings to match him in height." Nyssa pauses to pull back a long strand of her dark hair.

Claire braces her bare feet against the worn bark. "I know that much."

Nyssa nods. Her gills flex against her neck. "Yes, and, as I said, this was not well received. The pixies were shocked, and my people were . . . enraged."

Claire visibly gulps.

"Pixies are frail creatures, and my people were not pleased with what had happened. Especially when the pixie gave birth. Many said it was a breach of the natural order." Nyssa grows quiet, and in my mind's eye, the memory sparks to life.

I remember a woman with Claire's long golden hair and laugh lines that would crinkle whenever she looked down at the tiny babies in her arms. I hadn't known her well, Marigold, but she had seemed nice enough. And gutsy, to defy both cultures the way she had.

But it came back to bite her.

"Poison," I croak out.

"What?" Claire's voice is pitched high in surprise.

Nyssa moves with unease as she scrapes a clawed hand against the side of the tree bark. "We are not proud of it."

Claire goes very, very still. She narrows her gaze on Nyssa. When she speaks, her voice is icy. "What did you do?"

I've never seen a siren look so nervous as Nyssa does in that moment. She licks her gray lips. "We poisoned her. It was a small amount only meant to teach her a lesson, but she was too frail to fight it. She died when you were a few weeks old."

Claire's face is frozen. "And my father?"

Nyssa releases her hold on the tree, sliding silently back into the water, only her head visible. Her voice is almost inaudible. "He went nearly mad with grief. And he blamed us. Rightly."

There's so much guilt in her words it catches me off guard. "He tried to attack us, but he was without a tail and so no match for us. He drowned in the fight."

Claire goes white as a ghost. Stares at the sirens.

She jumps to her feet, rocking the tree. Dark, furious dust leaks from her skin. "You are all hypocrites! You blame Peter for taking us away, but all this time you knew that *you* took away the only family Connor and I had."

Nyssa shrinks back.

Claire seethes with devastation and rage. Her ashen dust continues to flow out from her, scattering across the water, pushing back the sirens. Although warranted, the quick shift from curious and awed to angry and raging just reminds me again that this girl has both the quickly consuming emotions of the pixies and the pool of rage that makes the sirens so dangerous.

Her eyes narrow on Nyssa. "I felt so horrible about Connor poisoning the water. I wanted to do something to help save you."

Angry tears streak down her face. "But you didn't save me! You didn't do *anything*. Not when my mother was poisoned, not when my father was broken, not when I was trapped in that rock for days. Weeks!" She throws the word at them. She's shaking now, trying to rein in her anger and dust. "I'm done with this whole island. It's nothing but a nightmare!"

"Claire—" Nyssa tries, but Claire cuts her off.

"No. No, you abandoned me." She looks at me. "Even before he did. I'm done with being abandoned."

I brace my hand against the bark, try to lean forward, try to reach for her—but that only makes my head pound harder. A flash of pain cuts through my chest, and I double over, groaning.

Claire takes a step toward me, balancing on the round trunk. I try to hold back the pain and look up at her. Her face is cast in shadow and hazy from the subsiding ashen dust. A few flakes land on me, adding to the overall torment.

"Pixie-Girl . . . they didn't mean to really harm—"

Claire kneels beside me, balancing on the rocking log. Her expression is quieted, tinged with a gentle sadness. "But you're wrong, Peter. They did mean it. Because it was what was best for them. Only not for anyone else. Sound like anyone?"

I can't even look at her.

"I thought I'd find something beautiful here." Claire's tone is distant, wistful. "But instead, this island is just a reflection of you." She strokes my cheek almost pityingly. "With all your wild boyishness. But still so very selfish."

I wince, because the truth hurts even more than the pain burning through my ribcage.

"I'm sorry." My voice cracks.

"I told you being trapped in that cell gave me a lot of time to think, Peter." She brushes a strand of hair from my forehead. "I forgive you for what you did, but I won't be manipulated anymore. Especially not by a selfish island."

Her eyes fill with a heavy sadness. She glances out at the sirens who have all swum a few lengths away, eyes poking above the water, dark hair splayed in halos around their heads, watching.

"I thought this place was my birthright, but maybe I don't want that after all." She turns back to me, and I'm taken aback when she leans forward to press a kiss to my forehead. "I promise to get you somewhere safe after I do this . . ."

I stare up at her. "What do you—?"

Dust lifts from her palms, swirling around me and coating my skin. It soaks in with the same warmth as the last time she healed me. Only this time, as the magic sinks in, Claire peers down at me and whispers, *"Rest."*

My muscles relax, eyes growing heavy as all the adrenaline that held me up dissipates. The fatigue knocking at the edge of my consciousness washes in like a flood. I try to stay awake, but my exhausted body can't manage it any longer.

Darkness curls in around the edge of my vision—and then I'm lost in the nothing.

16

CLAIRE

Neverland

A gray wind cuts through my hair as I fly over the charred, crippled remnants of Neverland. It's almost unrecognizable as massive chasms rip through the center of the island. Parts that have already broken off. Skull Rock is tipped on its side, the lagoon is practically gone, the lush jungle is nearly flattened, and the mountains are crumbling.

The island is coming apart at the seams, just like the last shreds of my hopes for this place.

I left Peter squirreled away in the nook of a tree after I'd healed his wounds as much as I could.

But I can't stay. I can't even look at him anymore. Can't look at this place.

This whole island is just a reminder of how everything is so horribly wrong.

Tears streak down my cheeks as I aim toward the half-dissolved remnants of Blindman's Bluff. I've gotten better at leveraging enough dust to fly, but it is still unsteady compared to how much I used to be able to conjure up.

The emotional weight of everything doesn't help.

I almost leave right then. I lift my face to the sky, prepared to give in to the heat that pours through my bones like lava. Skin crawling, every inch of this nightmare a reminder of just how broken all my hopes are.

But then I realize I'm not the only one here, balanced at the edge of Neverland.

A lonesome figure is sitting on the very edge of the bluff, staring down into the water, head bent and darkness literally dripping from him. I can see it pouring from his skin and soaking into the island.

I know he's dangerous, but . . .

Despite everything, he's still Connor. He's still my brother.

And I know, just as surely as I know the scars that trace my own skin, that I'll always regret it if I leave without trying one last time to wake him.

My feet skim above the ground as I fly nearer to Connor. Even from this vantage point, I can see that he's gotten worse. His whole face and the skin on his hands are now that odd, cracked texture. The dark veins pulse as they split apart his cold skin. Darkness leaks from those veins, thick like oozing blood. It runs in streams down his face, from his hands, dripping into the ground around him.

I can't imagine the pain he must be in. I approach him cautiously.

"Don't worry, no one else is lurking to grab you. It's just me."

His words catch me off guard. They're flat and colorless but seem true.

"Why are you doing all of this, Connor?"

He slowly turns his head toward me, eyes glassed over. "I have to. She says this is the only way to move forward."

"By destroying yourself and poisoning Neverland? What are you talking about?" I want to scream at his wrenching himself apart like this.

"Having sole control of Neverland doesn't work." He turns away from me, looking out to the angry Neversea. "Paige says there's one last option. Using me—using my shadow and going straight to the source." He lifts his hands, staring down at the inky liquid that slowly drips off his fingertips.

"Your shadow? What does that mean?"

He looks away. "I've already said too much."

No, he hasn't said nearly enough.

"Can't you see how messed up all this is? Paige is using you!"

Connor is in front of me in a flash. He takes hold of my arms, and the dark sludge coats my skin and makes me nauseous. Twin black irises stare at me. "She wants to fix me."

"But Connor"—tears sting my eyes, yearning for him to understand—"you're not broken. This place is." I sweep a hand out to Neverland. "Peter and Paige created it to hide from the reality of their world, not to face it, not to make it better."

"I don't *want* to see reality, Claire. I just want it gone. I want it all gone. I want *me* gone. If this doesn't work, I'll find another way."

He sounds so hollow. I know that sound, that look, that numbness that leads you to stop wanting to breathe, to exist. For the pain to just stop.

I grab him. "No! I won't let you do that."

His head whips back toward me, and for a moment, he doesn't say anything. A sickening slow smirk crosses his face. "Maybe I missed something after all. Maybe I was still holding on to one piece of reality."

His hand juts out and curls around my neck. His dark veins pulsing even stronger. "Maybe I need to cut all ties."

I push my hands against his chest, as he continues to tighten his hold. I choke.

"That's Paige talking—not you."

His eyes narrow.

I take as much of a breath as I can manage, close my eyes, and focus on the stars that wink just above.

I reopen my eyes and utter each word with a steely force. *"Let. Me. Go."*

A wave of brightening, golden dust slams out from my palms and blasts Connor backward. He lands at the edge of the bluff, coated in a shimmering haze of gleaming pixie dust.

I rub at my throat, tensed, ready to fly away if need be, but the strangest thing begins to happen. The shimmering dust starts to soak into Connor's cracked skin. Soaking in deep like it did when I healed Peter—but with Connor, it has a different effect.

I take a hesitant step closer and watch his skin begin to slowly soften. It starts to gain just a bit more color, the thick veins cutting across his body shriveling a bit. As if the light itself is pushing back the shadows seeping out of him. He lifts his head to me.

And the real Connor's eyes meet my gaze. Bright, vibrant blue and no longer cold and distant.

He looks weak, shuddering, but gestures for me to come closer. "I told you to pay attention."

With a disbelieving, shocked little cry—I trip forward, grabbing him, pulling him into the tightest hug. "What is going on?" Not quite believing my eyes.

"It's complicated, and I don't know how long your dust will help, but . . ." He struggles to focus and form coherent words, sloppily draping his arms around me. "Paige did something to me. Years ago, when we first met. She found me after Peter said those terrible things, and claimed she understood. She told me that she could help. Make me stronger. So I let her."

"What did she do?" I can still feel a pulse of anger, of betrayal, flowing beneath my thoughts, but seeing Connor like this actually seems hopeful.

"I'm not entirely myself. Paige cut away my shadow, but it turns out that in this world, a shadow is not just a trick of the light." He gently lets go of me and glances down at the shadow behind me. "Here, shadows are more than that. They are reflections of us—darker, angrier reflections. The fears and uncontrolled sides. The other voice in your head. And mine is worse than most. She told me that by cutting off my shadow, it would help with the voices and the pain."

He gives a raw, humorless laugh. "But she didn't tell me she was going to inject it back inside me." Connor lifts a hand, examining his pale skin ripped through by the dark veins. "My shadow is not very happy about that. And it's pretty overpowering. Especially since Paige injected it with dark magic. She thinks because my connection to Neverland isn't enough that I could use my shadow to corrupt the star and to tether it to me and make this whole island into my shadow reflection."

I stare at him, and slowly his appearance begins to make a bit more sense. The way his own skin splinters apart, the dark veins, the way his eyes go dark.

His own shadow is trying to rip him apart from the inside out.

And they want to inject that shadow into the heart of Neverland?

"Can't you stop it?"

"You saw how powerful it was. It feeds off this." He gestures to the broken, cracked island. "It feeds off the desolation of this island and the power that hums in my connection to it. But I think that once I can inject it into the star at the center of Neverland, I'll be able to breathe again."

A shudder sweeps over him, and he grabs at his face, expression contorted in pain, trying to hold the shadow at bay. I see his eyes start to darken, but they flicker back to blue again.

I pour as much pixie dust out of my skin and across his as I can. "Connor, do you really think injecting Neverland with your pain is going to help you? There has to be another way. If my dust can give you relief . . ."

The ripples in his brow smooth out as my dust slides across his pale skin. He smiles weakly. "But it can't help forever."

I hate to admit it, but he's probably right. His shadow is feeding off the magical connection to this whole island, and the more broken Neverland becomes, the stronger the dark magic grows. My dust isn't even as bright as it should be, let alone enough to fully chase out his shadows.

Connor suddenly gasps in pain, wrapping his arms around himself, shaking as another shudder ripples over him. Those dark veins start to pulse again, and each word is painstaking. "You're different, Claire. There is something about you . . . and about who I am, who Peter is . . . how this whole island breathes . . . when you're here. You bring out a spark of light in others."

He slams a fist against his forehead, jaw tight, rocking back and forth. Fighting those shadows again. For a moment, his eyes are consumed by darkness again, so I thicken my steady stream of pixie dust, and it manages to pull him back one last time.

Just long enough for Connor, my Connor, to look into my eyes and say, "If you abandon us, Claire, the shadows win."

He convulses.

I create a pool of shimmering golden dust in my hands and try to pour it into the chiseled cracks in his skin, but it just slides away as the veins grow darker, cutting deeper. The shadow rising.

Suddenly Connor's head snaps up, and he yells at me, *"Run!"*

Connor's expression goes cold and hard. I see the Shadow Connor reach out a hand, and I hear the rustle of vines, his way of manipulating Neverland, but I'm not sticking around long enough for him to ground me again.

I launch myself into the air, pouring out as much dust as I can, and shoot upward. I plow through the thick, heavy cloud layer, higher and higher.

My vision blurs as angry, frustrated, desolate tears once more flood down my cheeks. They remind me of the tears I used to cry when I was trapped in that cell, hoping every night that Connor would come for me. That he would magically become the brother I'd remembered him to be.

All along, he was held as captive as I was, trapped by shadows that are shredding him.

I don't realize I've left the atmosphere until the air suddenly feels different. Gone. Floating, but still able to breathe somehow. It's part of the magic of this place.

I'm coated in a haze of dust and turn to float slowly in this far-reaching sky of shining stars and stare down at Neverland below. It seems so small from up here, the galaxy so vast. The island is resting in a sea that somehow floats effortlessly in the sky too. The whole thing defies explanation. There are snatches of clouds, but no clear atmosphere.

Magic.

A world created by a child's dreams.

And I cry for it. For what Neverland should have been, and for what it has become instead. All the ways that Peter's selfishness, Paige's pain, and Connor's shadows have twisted it.

But as I stare at this world where I was born, I realize I am not without blame. Although this Neverland is not what I wanted—definitely not what I expected—my first instinct of running away is more of my own selfishness.

Just because this world is broken and uncertain and may have abandoned me in some way . . . does that mean I should abandon it?

Or does loving someone, loving a place, go beyond what it deserves?

If I desert this place, how am I any better than the Peter of old or the creatures who turned their backs on Connor and me when we needed them most? I cringe as the memory of Peter and Tiger Lily's shocked expressions when I left them behind to travel with Hook sear through my mind.

My resolution doesn't happen all at once. It sort of flickers in slowly, as I let the tears flow, let the grief and the sobs and the hopes I'd had for a different world and a different journey drain away from me.

Once those tears are spent and I've cried for everything that is lost . . .

At the core of that, I find the realization that I am staying.

I may not have chosen Neverland, but in a way, it chose me. This world, these people, are a part of who I am. Even more than that, they're a reminder of what I was meant to be.

Light.

The only thing that can chase back the shadows.

I don't know what that will look like. I don't know if I can help Peter or save Connor or the island, but I have to try. Because this twisted, fractured, beautiful place is my home.

A new kind of determination deepens within, and the dust filling the space around me glows a little brighter. I pull my shoulders back, ready to fly back down to that world and go find Pan, when out of the corner of my eye I see a speck of light.

Two faint shapes are bobbing against the never-ending echo of space. Drawing closer and closer, aiming for Neverland.

I blink. I can't think of what they could possibly be.

And then I can make out the distinctive shape of a certain tribal warrior with gorgeous ebony skin and a soul like fire.

Fresh tears spill down my cheeks, caught by the dust and floating in the air. But these are tears of sweet, precious relief.

Tiger Lily is here.

17

PETER

Neverland

I can't find the willpower to move.

Old Peter would have. Old Peter would have shoved out of this twisted tree and stumbled across the ground. The minute he woke, Old Peter would have thrown caution to the wind and gone charging after Claire, wherever she is.

But I'm not that Peter. Not anymore.

That Peter's Neverland has been ripped apart beyond recognition—and I can't seem to find that little boy anywhere.

So, I stay here, knees pulled to my chest, head buried in them, just waiting. Hoping that somehow Claire hasn't left. Hasn't walked away like I probably would have if I was in her shoes.

That's what I deserve. What this whole blooming island deserves.

The minutes stretch and stretch, and I lift my head to the jungle churning around me. The ground is splintered by the thick, dark veins that cut across it, and the palm trees and tropical brush that used to fill this place with color and life are now shriveled and twisted.

Just like my mind. Just like the memories that skitter and click into place throughout my thoughts. The things I've done.

Good gad. How did I ever think I was an innocent child?

I stare distractedly at the limp, crinkled remains of palm fronds littering the ground.

What if I can't fix this?

My island was obviously never the carefree, boyish escape I thought it was.

Maybe Claire's right. Maybe it's only ever been a selfish game.

My eyes fall closed again, and the only sound I can make out is the hollow chatter of wind cutting across the cracked ground and whistling through the felled, hollow trees. Suddenly I hear footsteps.

I immediately jolt upright, peering through the mist. Three figures draw near me, and when I catch a gleam of silver tattoos, my first thought is that Lily's tribe has found me. And they're about to take their retribution.

But then I see the gentle glow of gold dust shining through the mist, and the curl of blonde hair. My heart stutters.

Trusting I haven't gone totally bonkers, I hit the cracked ground running. As I tear through the mist, the tall, slender tribal princess races toward me. She's wearing dark camo pants and a teal cutoff shirt that reveals the spiral of tattoos curling up her midriff. Her staff is in one hand, but she now drops it as she barrels toward me.

She knocks the wind out of my lungs when we collide and hugs me tightly.

"Peter." Tiger Lily pulls back, eyes gleaming with tears. "I heard about Nibs and your sister and . . . everything. I can't imagine. I'm so sorry."

I blink back the burn in my eyes. She's been back in Neverland for what, five seconds? And her first thought is for how hard life must be for me?

Good ol' Tiger Lily. "Lil. I can't believe you're here."

She fondly flicks the side of my face. "Of course I came. But it's not just me . . ."

She takes a step back, picks up her staff, and gestures behind her—and slowly two more figures step out of the mist.

Claire is first. Relief washes over me when she gives me a smile. I pull up short and quirk a brow at her. "Glad you came back."

She comes right up to me and looks me full in the face. "Neverland may have chosen me to begin with—but I'm choosing it back."

I restrain the urge to grab her and give her a hearty kiss but instead grin at her foolishly. Then I notice the lanky young man walking up behind her. Tootles is looking healthier than the last time I saw him—his eyes brighter, skin showing more color, and thick hair curling around his ears. He's wearing a pair of dark jeans with scuffed knees and a long-sleeved dark blue shirt that highlights his sort of scrappy strength. As I greet him, he glances past me to Lily, and his face flushes a shade.

And from the way the princess looks away, she's not missing it either.

I toss a smirk at Claire.

She gives a little smile. "Lily, why don't you tell Peter what you told me about Jeremy?"

Lily's fingers tap against her staff. "Oh yes! Of course." She turns to me. "When Tootles found me, I was staying with the Darlings. Jeremy considered coming, too, but with Tansy having just given birth, he didn't feel he could leave. Especially not if everything happening here"—she motions with her staff at the warped landscape around us—"somehow filters to Earth. They did give me some info, however."

I squint at her. "Yeah? What kind of info?"

"Because Tansy was training to be one of our healers, she has read a lot of our people's histories, especially those relating to the island. She said that if Connor is trying to gain control of Neverland, most likely he'll eventually need access to the star. So, we have to make sure we do everything in our power to hold him back from it."

I nod slowly, digesting her words. "Keep Connor away from the star. Check. Anything else?"

Tiger Lily fidgets a bit, tugging on her ear and sidling a glance at Tootles. "Sort of. It was more like a scrap of information. Tansy said that the ancient histories talk about three ways to form a connection to a Never Never Land." Lily numbers them off. "One, by being the creator of that island."

I tap my chest. "Like me."

"Right." Lily continues, holding up two fingers. "Secondly, by being born connected to the island by blood. A Blood Bond, of sorts."

"Like Connor and me," Claire says.

Lily nods, "Exactly. But Tansy also said there could be a third option called a Soul Bond."

My eyebrows rise, and simultaneously Claire and I move closer to Tiger Lily. "Soul Bond? What does that mean?"

Lily dips a shoulder. "That's where it gets tricky. Tansy said they're very obscure and not much is known other than they come from some deep sacrifice that is intrinsically connected to an island and forms a deep tether. No one really knows how they're made, or if the concept is even real."

I purse my lips. "So . . . an elusive maybe-Bond. Not super helpful. I guess for now we just make sure that Connor doesn't get anywhere near that star."

We stand in that small huddle a few minutes in silence, then Claire speaks. "So, where to, next?"

"The one place where Paige and Connor haven't gone yet but will eventually need to," Tootles pipes up. "The hanging villages."

Claire's eyes widen. "*Hanging* villages?"

I toss a cheeky smirk at her. "You'll see. And it's a good thing we have Lily with us, otherwise they'd probably shoot us on sight."

Lily nods and grasps her staff. "Yes, it's about time I go home."

18

PETER

Neverland

Despite the fact that the island has been torn into pieces, Tootles somehow still has the best sense of where we need to be going. He quickly slips to the front of our little gang, Lily close on his heels. Claire is beside me as we plod across the rugged landscape and toward the center of the island.

There's an eerie kind of silence as we all trudge forward. We trek deeper and deeper into the jungle, toward the very center of the island. I notice the trees that were splintered and shriveled everywhere else get a little thicker and sturdier as we draw closer and closer to the heart of Neverland.

Maybe Lily's village wasn't hit as bad as the rest of the island.

"Wow," Claire says in a hushed whisper, and I glance to see her looking up at the trees that rise on every side. If she thinks these trees are large, her eyes are going to pop out when she sees the mammoth trees where Lily's people make their homes.

I speed up a bit to fall into stride with Lily and Tootles. They're both scanning the jungle, ears perked.

"I haven't been able to get this close in a long time," I quib, "The last time I tried dodging in for a visit, Crescent almost shot m—"

Lily's hand snaps out, slamming across my mouth. Her eyes narrow. "If you don't want to get another arrow in your chest, I'd suggest you keep your voice down. They probably already know we're here, and the only reason you're still alive is because of me."

Her calloused hand is still over my mouth, and I look at Tootles. His voice is quiet but firm as he nods toward Lily. "The princess knows what she's talking about."

Of course he'd take her side. Twitterpated chap.

Tiger Lily drops her hand, gives me one last look, and then continues forward.

Claire is walking next to me again, and she cautiously whispers, "I'm all for meeting Lily's people, but how exactly will this help us stop my brother from injecting his shadow into the star?"

I glance down at her. "Their village is actually built around the star, Pixie-Girl. Lily's people have a sworn duty of protecting it, and if anyone will be able to rally to our aid, it will be them."

Claire's eyes go round. "So, we're close to the star?"

I dip a nod. "Fairly. I'll show it to you once we get there."

Tootles's and Lily's footsteps are eerily quiet. Suddenly, Tootles stiffens.

He moves closer to Lily, and I can just make out his whisper as he leans in. "Five to the right. Six behind us."

She gives the faintest nod. "A handful in the trees too. A dozen bows at least."

My heart thuds to my feet, and I lift my gaze to take in our surroundings. I can make out the flash of silver in the trees and maybe a dark silhouette or two, but I can't find anywhere near the number that Lily and Tootles apparently have sighted.

Still, I'll take their instincts over mine on this.

I shove my hands in my pockets, trying to appear nonchalant, but my hair is suddenly on end thinking of how easy it would be for an arrow to zing through the air and hit Claire as she walks beside me.

Steadying my breath, I move ahead of her and gently nudge Lily with a knuckle. "What do we do?"

Her voice is low. "Nothing. We let them come to us."

She darts a glance at Tootles, and understanding flashes between them. The Lost Boy drifts back to fall in step with Claire, and he and I trade partners in this silent dance across the jungle floor. He whispers to Claire, and she pales.

Trying not to think about this whole blooming mess that I've brought Claire into, I turn to Lily.

"All right, what's really going on here?"

The tribal princess continues to scan the foliage caving over us. "Something feels off. They would usually have approached by now. I know they're nervous but . . ."

Her voice trails off as there is a rustling in the foliage overhead. I gape as someone drops out of the trees, landing in a crouch directly in front of us. Lily stops abruptly, and I almost bump into her. The princess's mouth rounds as the figure in front of us slowly straightens.

The younger woman throws her head back, long dark plaited hair clattering against her back, and forehead circled with a thin ringlet of silver. She's taller than Lily, with muscular limbs and the same onyx skin and sharp cheekbones. Her eyes are almost the same shade as Lily's, but instead of being smooth as a polished river stone, there is something commanding and fierce about the strength in the brown irises.

She crosses her arms over the woven, silver plates of armor

covering her torso and clinging to her hips, leaving portions of her dark thighs exposed for better maneuverability.

I'm unnerved just staring at her, but Lily doesn't flinch.

"Took you long enough," she says.

The other lets out a laugh. "Says the one who hasn't even been on the island since the last starfall."

I don't like the edge beneath this warrior's laughter. But there's something familiar about her. I know most of Lily's people, so why—

There's a blur of movement, and the woman drops low to try and kick Tiger Lily's feet out from under her. But somehow, the princess was already expecting this. Lily leverages her staff to jump over the warrior's sweeping leg, and instead twists into a kick of her own. The tribal woman is knocked into a half flip from the blow and lands on her back, huffing for air.

"You're still too predictable." Lily stands over the woman and then reaches down a hand for her to grab. But the warrior ignores the hand and leaps back to her feet on her own. Instead of a scowl, I'm stunned when she reveals a row of white teeth in a broad smile.

"And I see your time off the island hasn't made you any slower."

They stand staring at each other, then Lily pulls the warrior into a hug. Only then does it suddenly click, just a second before Lily says it.

"I've missed you, Crescent."

The young woman's voice is muffled. "I guess I don't hate seeing you, either."

"Crescent? Little Crescent?" I stare at Tiger Lily's younger sister, jaw dropped. "How did you get so tall?"

She pushes back from Lily and sends me a scathing glance. "Some of us actually enjoy growing, Peter."

Crescent's dark eyes drift past me toward the others. Her eyes narrow, and she turns back to Lily. "You're really pushing it, bringing outsiders."

"We don't have the luxury of being choosy," Lily tells her. "The island is dying, Cres. You can see that."

Crescent sweeps a glance across the surrounding jungle, probably knowing where every warrior is hidden. "I'm just saying that it's going to take a lot for them to let you back, let alone an otherworlder, a Lost Boy, and the Pan. Mother won't be happy about this."

Blast it. I was really hoping the old cow would have knocked off by this point. Guess not.

Tiger Lily's mother, the previous leader of the tribe. She's a piece o' work.

Tiger Lily lifts her head, trying to regain a bit of confidence. This can't be easy for her, coming back to this place.

But she reaches out and locks forearms with Crescent. The silvery constellation tattoos that spill down their skin seem almost interconnected. "I'll make Mother understand. These people are here to help us, and they may be our last chance. The island is dying, so much of it is already laid waste. Our villages may be the last to go, but they won't survive forever. And it is our sacred duty to protect the star, no matter who tries to corrupt it."

Crescent nods. "If anyone could stand up to our people and make them listen, it would be you. But be warned, sister. The villages aren't as you remember them. Our trees may still stand, but our people have splintered."

Lily's brow furrows, but before she can speak, Cres glances toward Claire and Tootles. "I'm not sure what use the rest of the humans will be, but you might as well bring them. They could be good sport if nothing else. Follow me."

With that, she spins on her heel and puts two fingers to her mouth and lets out a shrill whistle. Immediately, the jungle begins to move, coming alive as lithe bodies detach from the trees. Over a dozen warriors spill out and stalk toward us, all wearing silver plated armor that matches the rhythmic flow of the silver tattoos over their skin.

They close in on us, surrounding us in such a way I gulp. "What do we do?" I ask Lily. She motions to Crescent, who now marches quickly through the jungle.

"We follow her."

We quicken our pace, and when I reach Cres, I ask, "So, what's with the royal guard? Whose orders are they under?"

"Mine," she instantly replies. "I'm the queen of our quarter now. They're under my orders."

I almost choke on my own tongue. "What? So just like that you replaced Lily?"

Cres darts a look at me. "What did you expect? Lily forfeited her right to lead, and Mother had led far longer than most of our queens are meant to. It was only a matter of time. You both knew that when you left."

I hear Tootles scoff behind me and share the sentiment.

"More like your mother wanted any excuse to cut her out," I mutter, and for a moment, I think I see Crescent's expression soften, a glint of regret. But then it's gone, and she's back to being a stoic warrior princess.

I've been to the hanging villages countless times, especially when Lily and I were younger, but as we finally enter the village, I still can't help an appreciative little smile. I quickly swivel to catch Claire's reaction—and am rewarded by specks of golden dust drifting from her skin, lighting up those blue eyes as she gapes up at the village appearing among the trees.

The houses come into view like a collection of stars winking into the night sky, dozens of lights sprinkled through the trees. Here, at the very heart of Neverland, the trees reach for the sky like giants waking from sleep. Massive and bronzed and unwavering. Despite the fact that the bark is splintering in places and massive roots are upturned from the upheaval that has shaken this island, this portion of the jungle refuses to fall.

Probably because of what is at the very center of this place. The very thing that Lily's people have protected for centuries. The reason why their houses dangle in the trees, set up in a specific array to mimic the constellations above their heads.

Crescent continues to lead us on, now toward the base of one of the trees where a dangling platform lifts up into the foliage.

As Tootles steps onto it, his steady movements remind me of all the times he used to visit here to see Tiger Lily.

I jump on to the lift and lean on one of the ropes, gesturing to Claire. "Your chariot, my queen?"

Claire joins me on the wooden platform and tips her head again, staring up at the intricate craftsmanship of the houses nestled in the trees above us. Small walkways run to and from verandas and thatch villas strung from the trees.

"Wait till you see it up close," I tell her.

Lily jumps onto the lift, and Crescent takes her place at the front of the square platform. Crescent lets out a long whistle and glances at Tiger Lily. "All ready?"

She gives a quick nod, and with that, Cres flips the switch on the large crank attached to the front corner of the platform. It creaks and whines but begins to turn, wheels spinning, sucking in rope and slowly lifting the platform.

The lift rises at a good pace, and there's something thrilling about leaving the gang of tribal warriors far below.

"This is gorgeous," Claire murmurs, light reflecting in her blue eyes.

My hands shift on the rope so my arms encircle her. "Sure is."

She leans into me, and I close my eyes. I can almost imagine that this is all there is. Just her and me, suspended above the ground, the world right for once and nothing to tether us but each other.

Then I open my eyes, and the moment is over. But, just maybe, if we can actually pull this off—there will be other moments. If I can just manage to not lose the stardust girl again.

"How long have these been here?"

Claire's words draw my attention back to the treehouses overhead. I can't help but feel a wave of admiration as I take in the incredible architecture that went into creating this hanging village.

The houses are either nestled against tree trunks or suspended between particularly large branches. All shapes and sizes, no two buildings crafted exactly alike. Some have circular porches that rim the outside of the house and curl around the tree. Others are stacked several stories high. Some have flat, open roofs where tribal members can be seen cooking or patching up armor, while other houses are more like small, cozy cottages nestled among the leaves.

Hanging bridges swing from one house to another, intersecting and creating passageways between portions of the village. Children run and play across the swinging bridges, while other bridges host cranks and large mechanical devices which connect to lift platforms for vertical travel. Smoke spirals up from many of the houses, these villagers having learned long ago how to cook safely inside the wooden houses using handcrafted stoves.

But it's the light that fills these dangling structures that truly brings the place to life.

The sky is overcast, the sun gone down hours ago, but the village is filled with thousands of hanging lanterns that are set on hooks on every porch, dangle at intervals across every bridge, and are carried in the hands of children or on the warriors' staffs. The lanterns are studded into the rooftops or strung out like fairy lights across some of the doorways.

It's not fire glowing and gleaming inside the lanterns.

It's something far brighter.

There's a vibrant, silver hue that shines from each one, and as our lift clicks into place at the top of a large landing platform attached to one of the trees, Claire leans out to take one of the lanterns dangling at the edge nearby.

She tips it, bringing it closer, and curiosity fills her face as she watches the gleaming silver liquid inside splash about playfully. It doesn't quite float inside the lantern, but it's not weighted either.

"What is it?"

Before I can answer, Crescent nudges Claire's hand away, and the lantern swings back into its usual position. "Starlight."

Claire lets out a nervous laugh. "No, really. What is it?"

Crescent's eyes narrow as she towers over Claire. "I told you. It's starlight from the heart of the island." She glares at me. "You apparently haven't told her much."

With that, Cres steps off the lift and onto the main docking platform. She doesn't even beckon for us to follow, just strides quickly toward the dangling bridge hooked to the far end.

"Guess that's our cue." Lily touches Claire on the shoulder and hurries after her sister.

I take Claire's hand, and we quickly follow.

"What did she mean?" Claire asks. "How is it starlight?"

I lead her onto the hanging bridge. It sways beneath our feet, but I step across the interwoven, smooth planks of wood with assurance. There's a hanging rope banister to hold on to, but I ignore it.

"Remember how I said that I created Neverland as a place to escape? A hidden world in the stars?"

She nods, her hand squeezing mine a bit hard while she clutches the rope banister with the other. Tootles eases past us to catch up with Lily.

"Well," I continue, "Neverland is actually a star herself. It's not just an island—it's an actual star. Just like all the others you see. A magical one, but still a star. If you look close enough, you can see that the heart of the island still hasn't forgotten that."

I chance a glance down, unsurprised to find that it's too dark to see all the way to the jungle floor below.

"So, they are able to use some of the starlight from the star at the heart of Neverland to light their village?" Claire asks. "Where is the star?"

We've reached the other end of the bridge and skirt the wide porch attached to a towering, four-story treehouse. Crescent leads us quickly around it, only pausing to wave and shout a few words at a couple peeking out their window at us, and then she takes us across another bridge which angles steeply upward.

Still holding Claire's hand, I help her with the incline. "The heart of the star is actually smack dab in the middle of this village. It's one of the reasons Lily's people are so obsessed with stars. They believe that the same deity who created the star at the heart of Neverland also hung the others in the sky. They call him the Ever One. And they think he speaks to them through the movement of the constellations. It's why they tattoo the star maps across their skin."

Claire soaks in my words and every sight around her, at the ladders that lead from one roof to another's doorstep and the children climbing through tree branches and playing tag. "It's fascinating. Beautiful."

We pass another wide, circular ledge that rims a row of houses and see Crescent climb up a hanging ladder. Lily has tucked her staff through the back of her shirt and is right behind her.

We all reach the top of the ladder to find another wide platform as Lily exclaims, "Oh! That's right. Asher's house should be—"

Her words are cut off as she freezes at the edge of the balcony, staring at a severed piece of rope hanging from the end. Across from her, over an eerily empty space of air, I can just make out a bridge that has been cut and is drooping limply off another porch.

She steps back. "What happened? Why is their bridge cut?"

"I told you the village was fragmented, Tiger Lily," Crescent says. "Much has changed since you've been gone."

"What?" Lily's voice is shocked. "Asher and his clan just cut themselves off?"

"It was their choice," her sister states. "And it was not just Asher's clan. Several of the other families chose to as well. There was a lot of infighting when you left. Several of the leaders tried to challenge my claim to rule, and when I refused to play their games, they decided they would leave."

Not even Tootles's hand on Lily's shoulder is able to calm the seething anger that fills her expression.

"And you *let* them? You let our clansmen just cut themselves off? Are they hunting alone now too? Rebuilding their portions of the villages alone? Do you know how dangerous that is?"

Crescent throws up her hands. "I didn't say I liked it! They won't let us get close anymore. They shot Darien for just—"

Lily practically screeches. "Now they're warring? Our own people fighting each other?"

I've never seen Lily lose control like this.

Tootles tries to intervene, "Lily? Maybe we should—"

But she shrugs him off, storming after Crescent and shoving her backward. "Do you even see what is happening to this island? It's *dying*, Cres!" Her voice is raw and choked with emotion. "This island is dying, and if we don't do something, if we don't band together, we're all dead with it!"

Crescent stiffens. "Mother says we can't get involved. We have a plan. If we just hunker down, we can weather it. The island will settle, or if we build boats, we can always sail—"

"So the plan is to bury your head and hope it gets better? Do you even hear how ridiculous that sounds? If we don't do something this island is *dead,* Cres."

Lily motions to the children playing tag through the branches, small lanterns attached to their belts. "Those children will be dead. And Asher and our family and the old woman who taught you to sew and Darien and—everyone." Tears are streaming down her cheeks now. "Our people are dead if we cannot fight for each other."

Crescent is ashen. Her bravado gone. She once again looks like the little girl with long dark hair who would scamper at her older sister's heels, begging to be part of the adventure.

Suddenly, another voice cuts through the air. "How dare you speak to your queen that way? You have forfeited any kind of voice here, Tiger Lily."

My stomach twists. I lift my eyes to see a familiar formidable figure coming across the other bridge connected to the platform. She's leaning heavily on a staff, her hair streaked with more gray than I remember, but her eyes are still every bit as cold and biting as always. Luna.

Lily moves away from Crescent, life draining from her.

"Well?" The woman steps onto the platform, only a few feet from Lily. "What do you have to say?"

Lily lowers her head. "I'm sorry, Mother."

Everyone is silent. Beside me, I can feel Claire go rigid. My mind is racing, trying to find some way to help Lily, to stand up to her beastly mother, but I never really managed to before. Kind of at a loss now.

But Tootles isn't.

He strides forward, past Lily, placing himself in front of her and meeting Tiger Lily's mother's eyes with a look of iron all his own.

"Actually, she's not sorry. Your daughter is one of the strongest people I know, and we all had to fight through things you could never imagine to get here. All because she wants to save you and the rest of her people. So, no, she's not sorry."

At Tootles's words, Lily lifts her head a few inches.

But her mother just gives a dry laugh. "And why should I care what you say? You're just a lost little boy."

Ouch.

You can't talk to one of my Lost Boys like that.

Blood heating, I step firmly up beside Tootles, reaching back to grab Lily's hand and pull her forward to stand between us. I glare at her mother. "You can't scare us like you used to, Luna. Lily just wants to help. Why do you have to be so stubborn?"

Her eyes flash, and she lets out a few choice curses beneath her breath. Her gaze slides over Lily. "I see no daughter. Just a weak child who deserted her people to follow an overgrown boy who abandoned her when he found a new shiny toy. Without us, she has nothing—*is* nothing."

I just laugh, shaking my head. I loop an arm around Lily's shoulders and quirk a brow at Luna. "See, that's where you're wrong. Tiger Lily is not alone. Not by a long shot. She is more of a queen than you will ever be."

Luna sucks in a deep breath, and if looks could kill, she'd have murdered the lot of us. "How *dare* you. I could have each of you shot in an instant."

She raises a hand, and even in the dark I can see the gleam of bows drawn suddenly glint through the trees around us.

Crescent creeps toward Luna, speaking low. "Mother, maybe we should let it go for now . . ."

But Luna just shakes her head and whips her carved staff around, aiming the point at Lily. "How dare you and the scum you've brought with you speak this way? You have no authority here. You are not on the counsel, not queen, not—"

And then Lily moves.

She lets go of our hands and steps forward, head up. "Then I will fight for my right to speak. I challenge Crescent and anyone else claiming a position of authority to a match for rank. If I win, I am queen."

Luna splutters, "You can't do that!"

But Lily doesn't waver this time. "It's ritual, isn't it? I am doing it." She whips around to meet her sister's eyes. "If you won't protect our people, then I will. Either fight me and win, or get out of my way."

19

CLAIRE

Neverland

Taking in the breathtaking village dangling from the treetops around me, and the dancing silver light filling the lanterns, and the hanging bridges that sway underfoot . . . it's almost too much. My eyes can hardly soak it all in.

But watching Lily with her family? The way her mother treats her?

That I understand.

I also resonate with the determination that fills every plane of Lily's body as she turns away from her mother and toward Crescent.

Lily lifts her staff in one hand, overhead, aiming the point at her sister. "I challenge you, Crescent Star. If I win, I get my title back."

For a long moment, there's nothing but silence as the sisters stare at each other.

Luna is practically seething. "Destroy her!"

Instead, the younger girl slowly reaches up for the shimmering band woven through her hair. She unclasps one side and slides the diadem free. She extends it out in front of her and bows, presenting the diadem to Tiger Lily.

"I never really wanted this the way you did. And if you're right and hiding here is going to only make things worse . . ." She looks earnestly at her sister. "You're the warrior queen we need, Lily."

Tiger Lily's mouth has dropped open. After a moment, she reaches out and takes the diadem from her sister. She lifts the ceremonial band and clasps it into her own hair, across her forehead.

The sisters are in each other's arms, a hushed exchange whispered between them. Lily looks at her sister with nothing but softness, and there is a shimmer of tears in Crescent's eyes.

Luna is glaring daggers at her two daughters, but there's a lightness in the way Crescent holds her shoulders now. Lily lets go of Cres and shifts her attention to the rest of us.

She picks up her staff and raises it high. There's a new sense of authority in her tone. "Because Crescent Star has surrendered her position to me, I am now the reigning leader of our clan." She gestures to the trees around us. "I'm also vying for the right to command our entire village. If there is anyone else who wishes to challenge that right and fight to maintain their portion of the clans, let them make themselves known."

At that, there's a rustle in the trees. Several warriors detach from the foliage. At first, I wonder if they're here to challenge Lily, but instead she is nodding to them.

"Go! Carry the news!"

They take off through the woods, racing across bridges and scaling branches, weapons clattering at their sides. The official command has obviously shifted.

This whole thing makes my head spin. I stifle a yawn and

realize just how late it's gotten. Beside me, Peter leans in and playfully pulls at my hair. "Tired, Pixie-Girl?"

I bat his hand away. "It's got to be past midnight by now."

"It *is* late." Lily's voice carries toward me. "And it will take some time for the news to spread across the village and for anyone to make their challenge known."

She glances over her shoulder at her sister. "Cres, is there someplace safe we can stay?"

Cres slides a look toward their mother. "Our villa is spacious and has several empty rooms."

At that, Luna lets out a small shriek. "There is no way I am letting—"

"Your *queen* requests it," Lily cuts her off.

Luna gives a ragged shrug. "Do whatever you want with your half-breed ruffians. You will not find me there." With that, she storms off down the nearest bridge, disappearing into the shadows.

Lily's shoulders drop the minute her mother is gone, and she sags back against the tree. "I'm sorry about all of that. I know we've had the longest day." She straightens and heads for a smaller, wraparound bridge that leads in the opposite direction her mother went. "C'mon. Cres and I will take you to our home."

"Claire? Are you awake?" The hushed voice is followed by a gentle knock. I pry myself out of the comfortable, thick hammock and quickly open the door. Lily is standing on the other side with a tray.

"Mind if I come in? I have some food for you, if you're hungry."

She and Crescent had gotten us all settled in the large, several-story villa where Tiger Lily once lived. There are multiple rooms, enough that each of us have our own.

I step back to let Lily in, and we sit together on the lush rug carpeting the floor. Broad windows surround us, but airy curtains somehow manage to make the space feel private. Instead of a bed, there is the hammock strung in one corner and a large silver art piece scripted across one wall, copying a collection of constellations that Lily said represent courage and strength.

I yawn, but there's a comfortable sort of tiredness, sitting here next to Tiger Lily. The newly crowned queen sets the tray of food on my lap.

I drink a cup of water and take an assortment of berries and some kind of smoky bread and then lean my head back against the woven wall behind me.

"Are you all right?" I ask Lily.

She arches a brow at me. "I should ask you the same. Tootles said you've been here for almost three months?"

I fiddle with the bread and nod.

Lily doesn't speak for a long moment. "I really am sorry, Claire. For Connor. And Nibs." Her eyes glisten just saying his name.

"I'm sorry that this is the Neverland you had to see. Not the beautiful, vivid place it should be." She reaches out and places a hand on my arm.

A sob creeps up my throat and my mouth goes cottony. Trying to maintain my composure, I pop a berry into my mouth and focus on the tangy flavor.

I gaze at the tattoos swirling down Lily's forearms and across her wrists like a starry map printed on her skin. I'm reminded of our conversation that feels like an eternity ago, on the steps of that London flat.

I clear my throat. "I'm sorry about your mother. I know a little bit of what it's like to have family members that are . . . not as you wished them to be."

She nods slowly. "It's difficult when there are people that you love so much."

I take a bite of the bread on the tray, surprised to find that it has a sort of warm, fizzy flavor. "I feel like sometimes I'm not even sure where the lies begin and end. Sometimes I wonder if I've lost my brother completely."

Just saying it out loud makes my chest tighten.

Tiger Lily moves over to sit beside me and wraps an arm around my shoulders. She leans her head against mine, the texture of her braids pushing against my thick curls.

"You haven't lost him quite yet. And if anyone could bring him back and help this island, it's you."

I gulp back the tightness filling my throat. "Peter said something similar. But do you really believe in me that much?"

Lily's lips quirk to the side. "You have more heart than anyone I know, Claire. Heart that has even brought Peter to life in a new way. You've never given up on Connor, and, despite everything he's done, he needs someone to remind him that there's another choice."

A few specks of shimmering gold float into my field of vision. "To remind him that there's still light?"

"Exactly." She gives me a squeeze. "We all need that reminder."

I smile at her. "Of course. You've done the same for me."

Lily's eyes twinkle, and she whispers conspiratorially, "Don't tell Cres I said this, but I sometimes feel like you're more of a sister to me than she is."

I give her a shaky grin. "It's an honor to be like a sister to a warrior queen."

Lily's eyes grow serious. "I really hope this works and that I actually can win if they challenge me." She stops short. "Speaking of which . . . can I ask a favor?"

"Sure. Anything."

Her eyes gleam a bit more. "Can I borrow some of your dust?"

I get probably the best night of sleep I've had in . . . well, a very long time. Once I finish eating and Lily leaves, I curl up in the hammock in the thatch room like a little cocooned butterfly and fall fast asleep.

Even though Connor—or Shadow Connor—is still out there claiming more and more control, and even though Lily has not fully taken command of this village, I haven't felt this safe in months.

I finally wake, hours later, to sunlight streaming through the windows, casting dappled shadows across the floor. There's a knock on my door, but this one is much more forceful. Peter's voice echoes through the walls.

"Claire? Are you up? You have to come outside and see this!"

I swing out of the hammock, shove my hair out of my eyes, scrub the saliva off my face, and race to throw the door open. "What's going on?" Has Connor attacked? What if Luna made good on her threats?

Peter is standing there, barefoot and grinning. "Lily is outside fighting one of the other village blokes, and she's making him look like a fool!"

Relief slows my hammering heartbeat. "Right now? Where?"

He grabs my hand, and we race out of the villa. I have no idea how Peter knows how to navigate these hanging villages, but somehow he does, leading me to the same section of the village we saw last night, where the bridge was cut off.

In the broad daylight, the hanging villages are still enchanting, but in more of a rustic way. I hadn't realized just how massive this network of treehouses and bridges and platforms was. It spans on for miles in every direction. But as the sunlight brings clarity, it also sharpens into focus the fact that many of the trees are beginning to splinter. A few dark veins have crept even this high.

But it's the single thick line of rope that has been thrown from one platform to another, spanning where the chopped bridge had once been, that really steals my attention. There are two people standing out in the middle of the long span, only a foot or two from each other.

One is Tiger Lily, her back to us, staff in hand and held horizontally for balance. The other stands opposite her, facing us. He's a tall warrior, with skin a little bit lighter than Lily's and hair cut closer to his scalp. His glittering brown eyes are locked on Tiger Lily, watching her closely, calculating. He's wearing a pair of plain brown shorts and a tank top, no armor, but he's spinning two batons in his hands.

Their ability to balance on the single rope is impressive, and something about the way they tentatively bat at each other, his baton clanging against her staff, and making the rope sway, but both holding their balance, makes me think they've known each other a long time. Neither really wants to hurt the other.

"Who is he?" I ask, moving forward to join the cluster of people standing at the edge of the platform. I catch sight of Tootles at the front of the crowd. There are dozens of villagers crowding the platform, and when I scan the surrounding houses and porches, I realize that hundreds of Lily's people have come out of their houses, legs dangling off the edges of porches or sitting in branches or on rooftops, to watch.

"That's Asher," Peter answers my earlier question as he elbows our way to the front.

Tootles greets us and points to Lily. "She's pretty amazing, huh? Asher is the only one who dared to challenge her. If she beats him, she'll be entitled to have the respect of the whole village." Pride fills every word, and it makes me smile softly at him. This Lost Boy is a good man, and I hope Tiger Lily gives him a chance, when the time is right.

"How does she win?" I ask him.

He shoves a shock of floppy brown hair away from his eyes as Lily spins her staff, striking at Asher again, this time a little harder but still holding back. "Whoever gets knocked off loses. That's it. No other rules."

I lean forward just enough to glance down. Even in broad daylight I can't see all the way to the jungle floor. My stomach twists. I turn to Peter. "Shouldn't they be wearing harnesses or something? If one of them falls won't they—"

"Die?" Peter finishes. There's a strange glint in his eye. "That's why no one else has dared to challenge her claim to lead."

I watch the warrior with the batons spin one of them and dart forward just enough to swing at Lily's side. She jumps back, out of the way, and I'm amazed at how quickly her feet move, staff braced and toes gripping the rope to hold her in place.

"They don't really seem like they're trying to hurt each other. Why did Asher challenge her?"

Tootles coughs. "Stubborn rivalry? He's been vying for her throne for years. If they weren't rivals, they'd probably be good pals. But he told Lily that he felt like since she left Neverland, someone who stayed should rule."

"Why didn't he challenge Crescent months ago?"

Tootles shrugs. "Lily seems to always bring a bit of daring out of others."

I glance around at the crowd that is filling the trees around us. "I'll say."

Tiger Lily swings at Asher again, and he leaps back to avoid the sweep of her staff and almost loses his balance, but teeters on the rope and narrowly manages to catch it again.

"We can't keep going like this!" Lily's voice rises through the ring of treehouses. Sweat glistens on her smooth skin. "Why don't you just surrender?"

Asher flashes her a snarky grin. "I could say the same to you, Princess." And then he charges at her. He swings one baton at her legs and tosses the other one at her head.

I can't breathe as Lily vaults into the air, jumping over the lower baton. But the second one hits the side of her face. I watch her head snap back, her weight shifting midair. She lands on her side and scrambles for a hold. But the rope is swinging dangerously, and she loses her stability.

And falls off.

"No!" I scream as Lily's lithe body slips away.

Asher himself still is fighting for purchase as the rope swings and twists, but he, too, loses his fragile footing and falls off.

But then I see two slender fingers still holding on. Three

fingers. Then five. Then Lily is grasping the rope with both hands and pulling herself back up.

My mouth falls open as I watch her. She must have kept a grip even when she slid off. That's impossible.

The rope wobbles beneath her as she crouches, but she holds on tightly with her toes and slowly rises back to her feet. She lifts her hands over her head in triumph.

The woods around me erupt into loud cheers and screams. Feet thudding into the porches and hands slapping tree trunks.

The entire village is applauding her. She won.

But then Lily does the last thing I'd expect. She takes a moment to survey the uproarious applause around her, making eye contact with the crowds, capturing their attention—and then she dives off the rope.

She drops like a rock.

I grab at Peter. "What's going on?"

His face is white. "I have no idea!"

Please tell me Lily did not just plunge to her death?

My heart is beating wildly. Suddenly a faint glow shines far below us. It rises through the cluster of branches and leaves crisscrossing across the trunks that feed to the floor. The light grows as it gets closer, until I can make out the tribal princess, coated in pixie dust, shooting back up through the trees.

And bringing Asher with her.

The treehouses explode with more cheering, this time even louder.

My pixie dust coats Tiger Lily's lithe form, its gold clinging to her enchanting skin and flecking her long eyelashes. She shoots upward, flying toward us.

We all scoot back, making space for her. She lands in the

middle of the platform, surrounded by a circle of whooping warriors and a grinning Tootles. Beside me, Peter just shakes his head. "Blooming heck, Lil. Why do you have to give me a heart attack?"

But I can't stop smiling. She looks like a queen with the gold dust studding her features and the proud lift of her chin. The roar of her people drowns out the ghost of her mother's harsh words last night.

Beside her, Asher looks a little sheepish but undoubtedly grateful to be alive.

Raising her voice, Tiger Lily addresses her people. "I am not here to fight you or force you into submission. I want to be here to catch you if you fall. To protect you. I believe that if we stand together . . ." She turns toward Asher, reaching out a hand. He hesitates. But finally, with a dimpled grin, he grips her hand. Lily raises their clasped hands above their heads for all to see. "If we stand together, we will be stronger!"

More cheers ricochet around us, and the platform shakes underfoot from the amount of stomping and clapping that echoes through the space. Tiger Lily beams.

The crowd closes in. Tall warriors with fierce, silver tattoos scramble down from the trees, filling our porch and pressing in around hers. Peter and I drift to the back as Lily is swallowed up by her people. This whole village has definitely accepted her as their leader.

I bump into the tree trunk behind me as I reach the back of the circular porch. I smile at the glimpse of Lily through the crowd. "Pretty amazing, huh?"

Peter has stayed especially close to my side, and he presses his shoulder against mine. "Yes. And you know what? This is how we win." His eyes shine, and he looks more Peter Pan than he has in a good while. "Not by trying to beat Connor with force—but by saving those we can and not letting him get his blasted shadow anywhere near that star."

I put my hand in his and entwine with his fingers. He's come so far from that selfish boy who tried to push me off the roof of his flat in London. While I wish I could wipe away the grief that tints his gaze, I'm also pretty insanely proud of the leader this Peter is growing into.

"Do you really think we can do this?"

He leans enough to whisper in my ear, warm breath skimming my neck. "I think with a bit of faith, trust, and magic . . . anything is possible."

I give a little laugh. "I've missed your optimism."

Peter gives a lopsided grin. "Me too."

I had no idea just how much he needed this. To not be alone. To find a part of Neverland that isn't destroyed. It has certainly buoyed his spirits.

A part of me wants give him a tight hug and kiss that freckled nose, but before I can debate the idea, I hear Lily calling my name.

"Claire! Claire!" She's pushing through the crowd toward us, dragging Crescent behind her. Lily's face is absolutely beaming, and it's not just the afterglow of dust. She pushes Crescent forward, words tripping over themselves. "Tell her what you told me, Cres!"

I look puzzled at Tiger Lily's sister. "What's going on?"

A slow smile spreads across Crescent's face. "Well, now that Lily is the leader of our village, I guess it's safe to let you in on the secret we have been holding. If it ever got out and the pirates found out, we would be—"

"What secret?" Peter cuts in, practically on his tiptoes.

Crescent tosses her braids over her shoulder. "When we saw that Connor was tearing apart the island and just how sickly it was becoming, we knew the pixies would be the most at risk. Especially after Tink was—" She pauses, glancing at Peter. "Well, the pixies are also very susceptible to any kind of emotional upheaval. Connor's mood swings could have been enough to cripple most of them. So we decided the only thing to do was . . ." She pauses.

I can't breathe, eyes riveted on her. "Yes?"

"Hide them. Connor thinks they've all died and that the hollow was destroyed, but actually"—Crescent turns away from us, glancing up at the thick foliage of leaves overhead—" they've been hiding among us in the hanging villages for months. We share our food and keep them safe from the pirates."

I gasp. "Are you saying they're *here*?"

Crescent just tips her head and lets out a long, shrill whistle. "All safe!"

And just like that, the entire jungle lights up like a grove of Christmas trees. Hundreds of gleaming, golden lights ignite the foliage and begin to rise, bobbing and floating and drifting down toward us.

They draw closer, and there are more pixies than I can count. I soak in the sight of their tiny bodies and their iridescent wings and the windchime sound of their voices and I just . . .

Melt.

My knees go weak, and I collapse to the floor, tears of utter relief and joy streaming down my cheeks. *They're alive, they're alive, they're alive.*

I don't even have to reach out for them because the pixies all flock to me. They land on my arms and shoulders and burrow into my hair. Warmth and light and familiarity.

Hope.

Peter is sitting beside me, pixies all over him. He's calling them by name and grinning from ear to ear, and all I can do is weep.

Because for the first time, for the first time since I saw Neverland . . .

The world actually feels whole.

And it pours into my soul and chases out the cold that has become such a part of my chest. The cold that has soaked into my lungs and weighed my breathing for so long.

I nuzzle the pixies and cry big happy, heaving sobs all over them. Several of them chide at me and the crowd of Lily's people move back to give us space.

The tears just keep coming, and I don't try to stop them. Instead I just give a sort of hiccupped, shaky laugh. Because if my family is alive, if Lily's people are still safe, if these trees still stand, if Peter can still throw his head back and laugh like a little child . . .

Maybe we can be okay after all.

20

PETER

Neverland

"Let's all take Claire to go see the star!" I propose.

Lily's people have finally dispersed to go prepare weapons and discuss strategy for guarding it. Claire and I will take the first post after I introduce her to the spinning ball of silver heat that beats like a pulse in the center of Neverland. Tootles wandered off several minutes ago, leaving just Claire, Lily, and me on this wraparound porch. As soon as I announce my plan, I catch Tiger Lily's wince.

I sigh. "You're not coming with Claire and me, are you?"

She shuffles her feet. "Uh—I was going to go meet up with Tootles and the rest of the clan leaders. I should actually be there already, but I wanted to make sure you both were settled."

I waggle my brows and flick her on the nose. "Oh, meeting with Tootles, eh?"

Lily colors, smacking me. "Not like *that*! After we discuss the best way to protect the star, we're going to do a sweep of the outer perimeter of the villages and make sure everything is properly fortified. I also want to see what shape the trees at the edges are in."

I snort, giving her a grin. "Sure, sure." I wave her off. "Go find your Lost Boy. I'll show Claire the star myself."

Lily rolls her eyes but gives Claire a quick hug and then takes off down a swinging bridge. She climbs up a dangling ladder, which carries her out of view.

I turn toward Claire, rather enjoying the fact that we are finally alone. "So, what do you say?" I lay a hand beside hers on the rail, letting my fingertips brush hers and enjoying the way her face goes pink. "Want to see the star at the core of Neverland?"

Flakes of dust drift from her cheeks and catch in her thick golden curls. "I'd love to, especially since this star is apparently the only thing between Connor and total control of this island. But first the pixies said they have something for me. Do you think it's a gift of some kind?"

As if on cue, a dozen of the little gleaming, glowing figures appear. They flit down through the overhang of branches lighting on Claire's shoulders and tugging on the hem of her shirt.

"Okay! I'm coming, I'm coming!" She lets them pull her away from me, around the porch and toward another intersecting bridge. Claire's eyes find mine. "I'll meet you back here in ten minutes? Does that work?"

I watch the pixies continue to tug her away. "Okay! But you better not be gone long!"

Even though she's several feet away now, I can hear her silvery laugh. "Don't worry! I'll come back to you."

There's something raw and deeper in those words, and I can't tear my gaze away from her until she has ducked around another tree trunk and is out of view. I heave another sigh, drifting a little further along the circular porch to sink down on a swinging bridge that connects to another treehouse opposite us. Sitting with my legs hanging off the edge of the curve of woven-together slats, I let the bridge sway like a large swing.

She'd better come back to me. Can't lose that girl again.

I close my eyes and let out a long groan. "I've become such a bloomin' softy!"

But part of me—most of me—doesn't hate it.

In fact, part of me is hoping that if we can manage this, manage to hang on to the last shreds of this island that we have, maybe I can carve out a better life for myself in the end. A world where Claire is still there, bringing light into an island that is no longer tangled up in my mistakes but blooms into something new. Something more whole.

I sit on that bridge, swinging lazily, humming pirate shanties to myself, until Claire returns. It's the sound of the pixies that alerts me first. The tinkle of their voices, like chimes echoing through the sun-dappled day. When I see her, I realize that she's covered in a mini-parade of pixies. Dozens of them, spinning threads of gold around her, pulling her along in a haze of pixie dust. Her feet aren't even touching the ground as she glides toward me, gleaming and laughing.

I clamber to my feet as she pauses a short distance away. My eyes practically bug out as I gape at her. Blast! I'm pretty sure my heart is trying to hammer out of my chest.

She's dressed like a fierce fairy princess, and I've never wanted to kiss her so badly.

The pixies have made her a dress of woven silky green leaves, small flowers, and thin golden thread. It's perfectly fitted to her curves, spilling over one shoulder, leaving the other shoulder bare, and then cascading down her hips to stop above her knees in a swaying skirt. It has all the elegance of one of Tink's dresses, just more grown-up-sized.

She is alight with pixie dust that studs her dress like a cascade of rippling gold, specks of her dust filling her hair and lifting her golden curls to float around her head like a crown.

Claire is enchanting as she glides toward me, some pixies hanging off the leaves of her dress, others grasping her hands or peeking out of the hair they've braided into a crown atop her head.

I stumble to the edge of the bridge, just staring at her. "You look . . ."

Her cheeks color. The pixies dip and fly around her, gleaming and dancing on air.

"A little wild?"

I lick my lips. "Breathtaking, more like."

Claire's eyes shine, and her golden dust spirals toward me and catches in my worn green hoodie that thankfully Lily managed to briefly wash while we slept. I feel my feet lift off the wooden deck, and I float toward Claire. We're only a breath apart.

She blinks those big blue eyes a few times, regarding me closely. "You've changed, Peter."

Not what I expected to hear.

I thud back to the deck with a half shrug. "Yeah."

Claire gently strokes the wings of a fairy sitting on her shoulder as she looks down at me. "You're more weighted than the Peter I first met. The Ben I first met."

I don't speak for a long moment. I want to brush her comment away.

But I can't. I can't keep putting this off.

Not with her.

I take a deep breath. "Seeing my island like this, seeing what happened with Connor and . . . Nibs and how I hurt them all in so many ways . . ." The pixies drift around Claire to float in the air beside me, enveloping us both in a haze of golden dust. But despite that, a chill races over my skin, and I force the words out. "I'm definitely not the same boy I was. That boy has blood on his hands." My voice breaks on that last word, just thinking of it all.

Of Tink and Nibs, their lifeless bodies and the coldness that even now haunts my sleep.

"I'm not quite sure who I am anymore," I tell her, voice cracked. "I just know that I can't let this place become any more fractured than it is. I'd give anything to try and piece it all back together."

Only then do I lift my eyes to her, to this enchanting Pixie-Girl floating off the ground, swathed in light and magic and all the things I'd held her and her brother back from for so long.

My eyes burn as I shove out the final apology that has been burning me up inside. "I'm so sorry for Connor, Claire. I hurt him worse than I ever thought I was capable of."

I blink fiercely and reach for the rail to steady myself. "I know I'll never be able to fully repay you for everything I've done, all the ways I've hurt you and your brother and this whole island." My vision blurs as stupid, salty tears streak down my face. I rub them away with a shaking fist. I look at her through the blur. "But I'll do everything I can, every day, to try and make up for it."

Claire has been silent in midair, just listening. Suddenly, her arms are around my neck, body pressed so close to mine, face buried in my shoulder. She holds me so tight it's almost hard to breathe, but the words she whispers in my ear somehow fill my chest more than oxygen ever could.

"I love you, Peter Pan." Her soft lips skim my neck. "Despite everything, I love you." The words cut through the concrete that has encased my chest.

She pulls back and gazes into my eyes. "Maybe I love you

because of those things. Because you're not perfect, but you are doing everything you can to make it right."

Her dress rustles against me as I circle my arms around her waist, gazing at her in disbelief as she continues. "You say you don't know who you are anymore?" She reaches up to gently wipe the tears from my jawline. "Well, *I* do. You may be the boy who lost nearly everything because of his mistakes and the brokenness of other people that he couldn't control . . . but you are also the boy who chose not to run. Who returned to his broken Never Never Land and has fought to bring light to this place, even when the shadows have nearly drowned it all. You love Neverland more than anyone could—and I love you for it." She brushes her fingers against the fringes of my curls and lays her forehead against mine. My eyes fall closed, listening to every word Claire utters like each one is filled with magic.

"You have always believed in the impossible, Peter. Don't give up yet."

We're breathing in unison, and she's wrapped in my arms, face pressed so close. This girl who said she loves me. I'm not sure entirely what to do with that. But I know one thing: I'm never letting her go.

"Can I kiss you?" I whisper. I can feel her smile from where her mouth is pressed against my cheek.

"You better."

With a light chuckle, I lean in, tipping my chin and capturing that enchanting little mouth. She's warm and soft and wrapping one arm around my neck, the other hand sneaking deeper into my hair, fingers in my curls. Her dust fills the air, and we rise off the ground. We float backward, until the backs of my knees hit the railing behind me. I perch on the edge, still holding Claire, pulling her in closer. Thumb rubbing small circles on her spine as I deepen the kiss.

I only pull away when we're both gasping for breath. I take in her mussed, dazed expression. And the glint in those big blue eyes. She pushes off my chest to sit up a little straighter, and I manage a sloppy grin. "You have no idea how long I've wanted to do that."

But her mischievous smirk catches me off guard. "You have no idea how long I've wanted you to do that."

I grin. "Touché."

Reaching out, I gather her into my arms again, pulling her closer until our noses are pressed against each other.

"You know what, Pixie-Girl?"

Her eyes spark. "What?"

"I think I've fallen for you."

And I kiss her again, tipping us backward, off the railing, and over the edge of the platform. We drop away from the treehouses, slowly falling through empty space toward the jungle floor far below.

We're wrapped in each other as we fall, Claire's pixie dust coating us, igniting the air and slowing our descent, as we gently drift downward.

I have no idea what's below us, but at the moment, with this beautiful lass securely in my arms, all warmth and life and shining magic, I don't care what we're falling toward.

Only that we're going together.

Our feet finally touch mossy jungle floor. I gently loosen my hold. Claire is laughing. She melts against me, burying her heated face in my chest.

"I can't believe I just did that."

I drop a kiss on the top of her head. "*We* just did that."

She playfully hits my shoulder. "Yes, we did."

Claire takes a deep breath of humid air. "Where are we now?" She takes a step back, but I capture one of her hands, refusing to fully let her go. Not sure I can ever do that now.

She lifts her face up at the massive trees towering above us, the treehouses that are an interwoven wooden patchwork far above our heads. I follow her gaze to the trees and then I look down at the mossy jungle floor. I let out a long whistle when I realize where we are.

"Isn't that handy." Without bothering to explain, I start running forward, feet lifting off the ground, pulling her with me as I fly quickly through the weave of tree trunks.

"Where are we going, Peter?" Claire pours on a little more dust, flying level with me.

"You'll see." I wink. She rolls her eyes, but she can't hide the glow.

And then I can see it just ahead of us. A sphere of silver rising out of the jungle floor. We fly to its very edge, and I take in the wide, curved star that protrudes like some kind of massive, shining geyser. Half of the circular star is buried beneath the ground, but the top half of the sphere crackles and pops, shooting silver sparks through the air.

Claire's hand covers her mouth in disbelief. "It's a . . . star. It's really a star."

I nod, watching it sway and spark. I hold my breath and listen and hear the soft melody. The faintest magical hum that flows from the silver liquid that dances and spills and turns over and over.

Claire kneels beside it. "Can I touch it?"

Ordinarily I wouldn't recommend touching the heart of a living star, but the silver sphere no longer seems as bright or burning as it used to be.

Swallowing at the sudden pang in my chest, I nod. "I think so."

She reaches out, and a few drops of shining silver starlight land on her palm. The silvery liquid slides across her skin, and flecks of golden dust stand out against it.

"This is what Paige wants to corrupt?" Claire's voice is trembling. "She wants to insert Connor's shadow into this?"

I crouch beside her and reach out to dip in a finger. The silver light isn't as hot as it should be, but it still traces thin streams down my fingertip. "Aye. I'm not sure exactly how they plan on doing that. Not that I intend to let them get close enough to try."

I examine the star more intently. My chest tightens when I see dark veins are crisscrossing the dusty ground leading right up to it. Some of the dark lines have even crept up the shimmering silver face. That would explain why it is less bright, less hot than usual.

Claire is watching the star quietly, intently. Watching the silver sweep and dance and arc with texture of its own. "Does she have a name?"

My brow furrows. "The star? Not that I know."

Claire gently lays her hand against the curved, rippling edge of the sphere. "I think she'd like one. She's a little sick like the rest of the island, isn't she?"

I nod, pinching my lips to the side. "Yeah."

The haze of golden dust that has been surrounding Claire sweeps out, skims down her arm, and soaks into the portion of the silver star around her palm. "Don't worry," she says in an assuring voice to the star. "We're going to find a way to heal everything. I promise."

I blink, staring at her. She speaks to stars?

I just hope we can keep that promise.

21

CLAIRE

Neverland

I kneel beside the star, watching her dance and sway, listening to the gentle rhythm of her heartbeat. *Silveria.* The name just pops into my head and somehow seems right. Peter moves a little closer and drapes an arm around my shoulders as we watch the star breathe and whisper to us. The moment is more peaceful than I thought I'd ever have again when trapped inside that cell for so long.

The tinkle of bells greets my ears, and I glance at Peter, wondering for a moment if I'd imagined it. His face breaks into a wide smile, and he whispers, "Look up."

I tip my head back and find that the trees have come alive. Thousands of bright, bobbing pixies have filled the canopy, streaks of golden light that are descending toward us. A blanket of light and golden threads of pixie dust and glittering wings.

The pixies hid among Lily's people for months, but something about our arrival has coaxed them out.

I stand and lift my hands toward them as the array of pixies flutters toward us. Grateful tears well, reminding me just how thankful I am that they are all alive. I'd been terrified when Connor claimed all their lights had gone out.

Even in the midst of all the shadows that claw across this island, a bit of light has still managed to survive.

Peter laughs as the pixies fly down to spin threads of gleaming dust around us. They laugh and chatter in those singsong voices, the entire grove filling with the music of my people. These small, glowing creatures whose magic also runs in my veins.

The pixies circle me, perching on the fluttering leaves of my dress, nuzzling my shoulder and braiding portions of my hair that pulled free from my tumble with Peter. Their song grows louder, windchimes that fill the air in time to the gentle whish of the star.

Peter nudges me. "They're saying, *Welcome home.*"

I smile. "I know."

The pixies burrow into Peter's threadbare green hoodie, tugging him toward me and tittering at him in their high-pitched voices. He lifts up his palm and a few land there. I recognize one of them, and Peter cocks his head and grins down at her.

"Glimmer! I wondered what had happened to you. Good to see you, little lass."

She stands on the tips of his fingers, little fists planted on her hips, growing red as she chatters at him. Peter's brows arch. "Oh, right. Well, you're the one who left when we went to Blindman's Bluff to help Claire. I would have searched for you if I'd had a blasted idea where you'd gone."

Her coloring fades to orange, and she shakes a small finger at him. Peter snorts. "Well we were being dragged away by a bunch of sirens! What did you want me to do? Pop my 'ead out of the water and be like, 'Hoy, Glimmer, meet us at the lagoon!'"

Glimmer rolls her eyes and gives a little sigh, but she seems pacified. I put my face down to her little figure. "Oh, Glimmer! I'm so glad you're all right! And thank you so much for taking the pouch of dust to Peter. You were very brave." I gently stroke her small cheek with a finger. "We wouldn't have gotten this far without you."

Glimmer beams, her coloring growing bright and golden again. The other pixies continue to fly around us, chattering gaily. A little male pixie, wearing a leafy top hat and pair of suspenders made out of tiny vines, lands on Peter's hand, shoving Glimmer out of the way, who is outraged at the treatment.

He crosses his little arms and stares up at Peter, chattering something at him. Peter shrugs. "Sorry, mate. I didn't bring my pipes with me and can't play them. Maybe later I can make some."

The poor little gentleman seems so dejected his wings droop. I bite back a smile and hesitantly offer, "I could always sing a bit, if that would help?"

The pixies explode with bright, vibrant gold hues, overjoyed at the idea. What have I gotten myself into?

I glance at the treehouses far above our heads. Somewhere up there, Tootles and Lily and her people are rallying to join us to create a barrier of protection from my own brother. It seems odd to think of singing at a time like this . . .

I look at the pixies surrounding me with their excited faces and their even more vibrant golden color.

Maybe this is exactly what they need.

Sometime soon, Connor will arrive, and the world will become tense and violent again. A bit of joy in the midst of the chaos is what we *all* need.

"If you sing," Peter cajoles me, "I'll teach you a fairy jig."

I have missed dancing. "Deal."

"All right, then. Jig first!"

Peter slips his hands into mine, helps me to my feet, and pulls me close for the first few steps. The pixies are giddy with excitement, flying in little dizzying loops around us.

"Move your foot here . . . like this . . . and then like this . . ."

He's a surprisingly good teacher, and our bare feet dip and dance across the jungle floor as he sweeps me in toward him and then pushes me out again.

The pixies have partnered off and are replicating the same dance, only through the air and without my chronic fumbling.

After a while, I get the basic steps down, and I begin to sing. Peter's eyes are dancing too, and the spray of silver from the star sparkles behind him.

"Dancing in the moonlight . . ."

My steps interlace with Peter's, and he pulls me in.

"Singing with the stars . . ."

He spins me out, and my toes tap on the mossy ground to the same rhythm of the floating pixies.

"Every note a promise . . ."

The pixies quicken their pace, swirling and leaping and spinning in unison. There are dozens of small couples hand in hand, wings brushing and glittering.

"That the night is darkest before the dawn . . ."

Peter has pulled me in again, and as he quickens his own pace, my feet dance around his, a patchwork of movements and fluid steps. The pixies have begun to harmonize with my singing with their own airy voices, like the melodic symphony of a hundred chimes ringing through the grove.

"Whispering an enchanted—"

Suddenly, a faint sound echoes through the woods, and the

pixies all freeze at once, suspended midair. Glimmer hurls herself at my mouth, cutting off the song.

I pry Glimmer away as I turn to Peter. "What's going on?"

He places a finger on his lips and bends toward the nearest pixie. The little creature is trembling, wings humming as it floats.

"What's wrong?" Peter mouths.

But it's Glimmer who answers, hovering just between Peter and me. Her big eyes are filled with dread, and her color has faded to an almost gray. "They're here. The bad ones."

My chest grows tight and I look toward the darker, sprawling portion of the jungle.

That's when I see them. Thick, coiling veins snaking across the ground toward us. And just beyond them, tramping silently through the woods, shouldering weapons and burn scars are the Lost Boys. Slightly at the head of the pack, the twins and Cubby just behind him.

My heart twinges, seeing the place where Nibs normally would have been.

If the Lost Boys are already—

"Connor and Paige must be close too," Peter finishes my thought aloud and then springs into action.

He sweeps his hands upward as he addresses the pixies in a hurried whisper. "You need to hide! Go back up to the village and wait there."

The pixies thaw out of their frozen state. But Glimmer looks at me, as do many of the pixies, as if waiting for my command.

I incline my head, keeping my voice low. "Yes, you'd better hide."

At that, the pixies all shoot back up toward the distant foliage. They streak like little stars, falling back up into the sky, heading for the security of the hanging village.

"I never expected them this soon . . ." I whisper to Peter as we watch the Lost Boys draw nearer and nearer. They haven't spotted us yet, but they will soon. "Should we hide too?"

Peter seems to consider it but then shakes his head, reddish hair falling into his eyes. "I think we've hidden long enough. If they're here, it's because Connor has decided he's ready to corrupt the star. I didn't think he'd try so soon. I'm not even sure how the scouts haven't spotted them yet. Maybe Connor is somehow shielding them—although sending the Lost Boys ahead was probably so that they would hit any traps the warriors had set up."

He doesn't take his eyes from the Lost Boys as he says to me, "I need to stay and protect the star. Fly back up and find Lily. Tell her that Connor is almost here and that we're going to need every warrior she has."

I glance behind me at the beautiful sphere of silver starlight. The thin veins that had started creeping over its corner thicken and begin to seep over the star. If Connor's nearness alone can seep darkness into the heart of Neverland, I don't want to know what will happen if he can actually poison the star with his shadow.

Heart sinking, I take Peter's hand. "You'll be okay?"

He nods, giving my hand a squeeze. "They're my Lost Boys. I need to do this either way."

I realize how much this boy truly has grown.

The Lost Boys catch sight of us. They pause as Slightly's gaze darts from Peter to me. Even from this distance I can see the bubbled burn scars that I am responsible for, and my stomach lurches.

The Lost Boys heft their weapons and run toward us. Peter raises his fists like that's somehow going to be a match against their blades. I quickly cup my hands, willing them to fill with pixie dust. Additional gold flakes drift from the rest of my skin, and I rise off the ground. I empty the handful of pixie dust all over Peter, which coats his worn hoodie and his curls.

He tosses me a quirked smile. "I can handle them, Pixie-Girl. Go get help."

I nod and drift higher. The Lost Boys are only a few feet away, and despite the way their bodies are tensed, weapons raised, I can't miss the glint of awe in their expressions as they watch me fly.

I just hope Peter really can hold them off.

But Slightly runs forward a few steps, staring up at me, his expression ominous as he shouts. "It won't be enough, Claire!" I pause, surprised at the rawness in his voice. I draw closer to him.

"What?" I stare at the freckled features of this Lost Boy who helped keep me sane the weeks I was trapped deep inside Skull Rock.

"No matter what you do, it won't be enough," Slightly repeats. "Paige used knowledge of dark magic she got from the healer they kidnapped and has contorted Connor's shadow even more. All they need to do is access Neverland's core, and she wins."

"Not if we have anything to say about it!" Peter's voice is filled with that familiar bravado as he steps in.

But Slightly just shakes his head. "They'll be here any minute, and when they come . . ." I notice how haggard and pale the other Lost Boys are. They're terrified. "They'll rip apart anything in their way."

Peter Pan perches his fists on his hips and faces the Lost Boys. "Let them come." He lifts off the ground. "You could fight with me, if you wanted . . ."

But Slightly shakes his head again. "They'll kill us instantly if they don't think we tried to stop you."

A muscle in Peter's jaw twitches. "Slightly, it doesn't have to be this way."

The Lost Boy doesn't answer. He lifts the musket slung over his shoulder.

Peter glances up at me and mouths *Go!* I see the sadness in the depths of those green eyes. And the spark of determination. If anyone could get through to these boys, it would be Peter.

But I can't stay.

I pour on as much speed as I can to shoot up into the foliage. Cool air and a few gunshots that zing a little too close for comfort whip past me as I fly through tangles of branches, past thick leaves, and up into the patchwork of treehouses.

I quickly spot Tiger Lily and Crescent racing down one of the hanging pathways toward the round building where we'd slept. Before they can go in I catch them, pixie dust practically spiraling from my body. The sisters pull up short.

"Claire?" Lily's voice is anxious "What's wrong?"

"The Lost Boys are here," I pant, trying to catch my breath. "Down by the star. Peter is trying to fend them off, but I think Connor and Paige are close by too. If Connor gets to the star before we do—"

Tiger Lily nods quickly and turns to her sister. "Cres, go to the clans' meeting hall and tell them we need as many warriors as are ready. It will give us a start, and the rest can join as soon as they're able. I'll get Asher and the others who are already outfitted, and we'll go to the star immediately."

I suddenly realize someone is missing.

"Wait! Where's Tootles?"

Lily startles. "What? Tootles went to find you and Peter at the star. You didn't see him?"

"No." My whole body goes cold. *Please let him be okay.*

Tiger Lily inhales a deep breath. "Well, we'd better get those warriors down there as fast as we can."

She's right. But somehow, there's a cold feeling in the pit of my stomach saying that no matter how many of us may stand between Paige and that star, it won't be enough. Connor and his shadow will toss us aside like kindling.

22

PETER

Neverland

The Lost Boys look blooming terrified—and I'm not sure I blame them.

The whole jungle has dropped several degrees as a chilled wind snakes through, rustling the mossy floor and revealing more of those thick, dark veins that claw across the ground.

"They're close now," Slightly says tersely. They start forward again, and I skim back to hover just in front of the star.

"You know you don't have to do this." I pause. They've heard all this before. And from the way that the twins both cower behind Slightly, and the way Cubby's eyes are bloodshot and wide, I know they don't believe me. They don't believe I can protect them.

I didn't before.

My heart drops, and my feet thud to the jungle floor. I force myself to look at the Lost Boys. "I'm sorry, lads." The words are like drops of rain, thick and heavy, building into a storm. "I never should have left. I should have stood up to Connor a long time ago and not abandoned you here."

The musket on Slightly's shoulder slowly drops.

"You should have taken us with you." It's only a whisper, but his pain is vivid.

My eyes plead with him. "I know. I *know*. I was blinkin' selfish." My voice breaks. "It's stinkin' awful, and I am terribly sorry."

"But you're here now." The new voice comes from somewhere behind me. I recognize it immediately.

I turn to see Tootles coming toward us from around the star. The Lost Boys seem to relax.

A familiar nod flashes between the gaunt Lost Boy who hid here for months to the freckled youth who became a leader in my stead. Tootles tosses his gentle smile toward the twins, one now a little taller than the other, but both wearing the same dirty, worn trousers and dark blue jackets. They cautiously stow their knives back in their belts, and Cubby shoves overgrown hair out of his eyes and raises his club in a little wave.

Tootles is still limping a bit as he joins us, but his gaze is crystal clear. "'Ello, mates. I guess it's come to this, huh?"

He looks at Slightly. "I know you're afraid. Trust me, I know. I hid for months, too scared to even show my head. But this is it. This is the moment where we either stand for our own freedom— or we lose it forever."

He puts a hand on Slightly's shoulder. "You're not alone this time, mate. And if this selfish gaffer can change"—he jerks a thumb over his shoulder toward me—"then maybe we can be a little braver too. What'd you say?"

I hold my breath as Tootles and Slightly study each other for a long moment. And then Slightly turns to the twins and Cubby. "Well? What do you—"

Boom!

His words are cut off by a massive clap of thunder. Seconds

later, the foliage is lit up by a bolt of lightning slashing across the sky. Massive storm clouds roll in faster than should be possible, booming and dark and bringing with them a deep, eerie mist.

Like a scared rabbit, Slightly launches away from Tootles. "They're here!" Cubby screeches, and the Lost Boys scatter, racing to hide behind the shelter of larger tree trunks.

Tootles lopes back, eyes concerned. "Peter, I'm not so sure about this."

But he withdraws something from his belt and tosses me a small knife, keeping one for himself. He must have brought the weapons from the village. I lift the knife, testing the weight of it. I nod at Tootles, and we take our places, braced in front of the star, waiting as another billow of fog sweeps through the jungle.

Three figures approach, striding out through the heavy gray fog. Connor is at the head, but as he draws nearer, I hardly recognize him. His eyes are nothing but twin sockets of black ink, and his raw skin has been filleted, flaking away from the thick, dark veins that claw across his face. Thick veins that are dripping, dripping, dripping . . . like thick, obsidian blood down his body.

He's hardly a boy or even a young man now. Just a shadow of himself.

The two others emerge. Paige's red hair wafts around her head like a pool of pale blood, and her eyes are bloodshot and wild. Hook is a few steps behind. I can't make out his expression, but he seems to be hanging back a bit. Interesting.

"Out of my way!" Connor's voice rasps. I know they're close enough to see us.

Beside me, Tootles flinches. "Shouldn't backup have arrived by now?"

I quickly glance around. "I guess it's just us."

Tootles locks his shoulders in place, nodding. "I'm not leaving."

Connor doesn't seem amused by our little show. He tips his head to the side, eyes narrowing on Tootles. "You should have run."

A vine launches from the jungle behind Connor, cutting through the underbrush and immediately tossing Tootles out of the way. I watch his body go flying and see him land with a heavy thud. My body tenses, unsure whether I should run toward him or stay poised in front of the star.

But then I see his chest rise and fall. A shuddering breath. A few Lost Boys inch toward him.

I need to stay here. If I can't somehow hold Connor back, it's all futile.

Protecting this star is my best chance at protecting these Lost Boys.

I firmly place myself in front of the flickering star and hold my ground. Connor storms toward me as more thin vines snake across the ground, writhing on either side of him, ready to attack.

I hold up my hand.

"Connor, stop. Think about this—"

Paige's shriek interrupts, her bloodshot, erratic eyes on me.

"Don't kill him," she tells Connor. "He's mine."

Connor throws out his left hand, and a vine swivels, whipping forward. I brace for it to wrap around me, but instead it lurches toward the trees where the Lost Boys are hiding.

I watch the vine wrench one of the twins out from his hiding place, wrapping around his ankle as he kicks and tries to get away. Connor doesn't even turn to look at the boy as he speaks, voice gravelly. Hollow. Shadowed. "What about these cowards? They couldn't even face Pan."

The twin is gasping and struggling, trying to rip the vine from where it's wrapped so tightly that he's bleeding. He's blubbering, both apologies and pleas, so scared stiff that the words don't make much sense.

I tighten my grip on the knife, about to launch toward them, but Captain Hook moves swiftly to the twin. He towers over him, unsheathes the sword from his cane. He lifts the glint of metal, and a scream builds in my throat.

But Hook brings his sword down and cuts away the length of vine below the captured leg.

"Leave the boys alone," Hook says, and I stifle my surprise. The pirate captain gestures for the lad to leave, and the twin scrambles to his feet and races away as quickly as he can.

Paige narrows her eyes at him. "What was that?"

Hook sheathes his sword, and for the first time, I get a good look at his face. Shock hits me when I see the still-healing bubbling burn scars across his jaw. Even his metal hook looks warped. Claire did that?

Hook stares straight at me, and there's something weighing in those eyes as he answers. "Your quarrel is with Pan, not the boys. They've done everything you've asked."

The pirate captain is actually defending the Lost Boys?

He turns to Connor. "Or do you get pleasure from torturing terrified children now?"

You're one to talk.

Connor winces. His head jerks to the side like he was struck. I didn't even think he could feel anymore.

I rise a little higher, flakes of Claire's gold dust coating the air.

Maybe the old Connor is still in there somewhere.

I don't have time to reflect on that as Connor's full focus is now just on me.

Those shadow eyes lock in. "Move."

I squeeze the blade in my right hand. "No."

A vine launches from the jungle floor and wraps around my waist so tight my ribs instantly bruise.

I am tossed away from the star with such force that I slam into a nearby tree trunk. I fall to the ground, head spinning, fighting to remain conscious. My entire body throbs, the stitches in my side pulling open. Blood begins to ooze down my forehead and out of my side. I'm seeing stars.

I groan and try to lift my head. I'm barely able to raise my eyes.

Paige is watching me with that sickly smile. My broken, bent sister enjoying my pain.

This is so messed up.

My heart stops as Connor strides over to the star. His shadow begins to leak out from around his feet and stretch forward, like black ice reaching for the silver orb.

I try to push myself off the ground to go after him, but I don't have the strength. And now my ankle is beginning to throb so badly I wonder if I've broken it.

I stretch one hand out helplessly toward the star. This is it.

I can't stand. I'm too broken.

Connor has reached the edge of the dancing, arcing life force of Neverland. I watch him lift one hand, over the star, his shadow dripping and crawling toward it.

"Nooo!"

A gaunt form hurtles from the trees, straight at Connor, and bowls into him with enough force to knock him to the side. They both go flying. Connor lets out a guttural scream, but Tootles is already back on his feet in front of the star. He spreads his arms out, facing down both Connor and Paige.

"Get out of our way," Paige snaps.

Tootles shakes his head. "I won't let you hurt anyone else."

Her eyes seethe. "You'd risk your own life? For him?" Paige points a spindly finger at me.

But Tootles just lifts his chin. "It doesn't matter what Peter once did. We can do better now."

She steps forward, lifting a slender dagger to strike at Tootles.

But then several more forms hurtle out of the trees and race toward Tootles, coming to either side of him. Paige halts, knife midair, and stares at the ragtag gang of Lost Boys who lock arms with each other, dirt-streaked faces meeting her eyes.

She takes a small step backward.

Cubby breaks away from the group and swiftly races over to me. Before I can croak out any questions, he lifts me into his hefty arms, and hauls me back to the others. Shock sears Paige's expression. Connor's shadow flares across the ground at his feet.

Behind them, Hook is watching with cool amusement.

The Lost Boys all pull me forward, positioning me at the middle of their group. Slightly loops one of my arms over his shoulder, while Tootles takes the other arm, both of them standing on either side, holding me up.

"What are you doing?" Paige demands.

Slightly lifts his chin, freckles growing a little bolder as his face flushes. "Standing with our brother. Standing with Peter."

I almost break down right then.

Connor's eyes narrow, slits of black in his cracked skin. "Then you'll fall with him."

His hands dart out, and a dozen vines cut across the floor and wrap around arms and legs. One clamps around my throbbing ankle.

All six of us are tossed away from the star. We slam into branches and thud to the icy ground. The wind is knocked from my lungs, and tears mix with the crusty blood and dirt on my cheeks. My ankle hurts so blooming much, as do the slices across my side, but I force myself onto my elbows to try to find where the other Lost Boys landed.

The twins are gasping and groaning, Cubby's arm is at an odd angle, and he's writhing. Slightly must have hit his head on a rock, he's lying motionless but still breathing. Tootles has curled into a little ball, nursing a nasty gash on his arm.

At least they're all still alive.

For now.

I manage to look at Connor just in time to see him lean over the star. It spits and kicks up streams of silver that sizzle against his charred skin, but he doesn't even flinch. He hunches his contorted body over the star, eyes black chasms and skin splitting apart from the pulsing dark veins. He opens his mouth.

Dark liquid begins to seep out. Drip from his lips. It thickens and stretches and oozes as his shadow spills onto the star.

"Stop!" The cry is followed by a massive funnel of gleaming golden dust that slams into Connor, knocking him backward just before the shadow can touch the silver orb.

He hits the ground hard and rolls. The silhouette of his shadow arches over him, screeching and hissing.

Paige trembles with fury. "Not now!"

The tinkle of bells drifts down toward us. I turn over and look up at the canopy of leaves. A smile breaks over my face

The pixies are on the move again, and they're not alone.

Hundreds of the little creatures are pouring down through the branches and foliage. At their center is a Pixie-Girl soaked in so much pixie dust she could help all of Lily's village to fly.

Which is pretty much what she's doing.

All around Claire and the pixies, I see tribal warriors soaring through the air, weapons aimed at Paige and Connor and Hook. Tiger Lily is leading them, bringing her army to stand with us.

The blood drains from Paige's face as she watches the jungle come alive around her. More of Lily's people climb down from the trees. Warrior after warrior. Pixie after pixie.

They're boxing Connor in.

Claire hovers out of Paige's reach. "This island was built on faith and trust. Those things can't be broken down."

Paige moves closer to Connor, as if her pet weapon could protect her.

Claire touches ground, and she rushes toward me. She takes in the damage and, making a pool of dust, she blows it across my body. More drizzles over my ankle and torn side. "I'm sorry we're late, Peter," she says quickly. "It took Lily some time to convince the rest of the tribe to rally. They were still uncertain." Her dust is soaking in, taking away the edge of pain and starting to mend the wounds.

I push myself to my feet, and she puts an arm around my waist. I lean on her and gently kiss her temple. "I'm glad you made it."

Crescent and Asher and several of the warriors tend to the Lost Boys, while Tiger Lily kneels by Tootles, gently wrapping up his arm in a makeshift bandage.

The remaining warriors circle the star, lifting glinting silver weapons and decked out in full armor made of that silver metal tempered with the very heat of what they now protect. Their glistening tattoos and silver armor makes them appear like a living, breathing army of stars.

Connor and Paige and Hook stand at a distance, opposite those of us who now stand in front of the star. Lost Boys side by side with village warriors.

Claire's hand slips into mine, and she calls out to her brother. "Don't you see, Connor? You've lost. Please. Just stop all this. Let us help you." Her hand quivers in mine, and I tighten my hold.

"This is the only way to help him," Paige retorts, lifting her slender knife.

There's the faintest spark of something that flickers in Connor's hollow expression. He starts to turn toward Claire, but as he does, Paige brings her arm quickly forward, metal glinting in her fist, as she aims toward Claire. I watch, helpless.

But the knife clashes against a curved metal prong that swings forward to intercept it.

Claire jumps away, and I lurch forward to pull her back to the safety of our little army.

Paige's eyes narrow, a quiver in her thin lips as Hook come from behind her, his hook still looped around the knife in her quivering fist. "Sorry, love," he tells her, holding his sword-cane in his other hand as he stands in front of her, crimson coat skimming the back of his polished boots. "Even I can tell when we've lost." His voice drops low, leaning in, nudging her knife down. "Come away with me, Paige. We'll take the *Roger* and never look back."

Watching how sincere Hook is, I actually feel bad for him. He's sacrificed so much for this woman who loves her own pain more than she loves him.

Still holding her knife, Paige rips away from Hook and ducks around him.

Her half-crazed eyes glare at us. "You might have brought the whole island against us, but it won't be enough."

Tootles jumps in front of me. "If you want to hurt Peter, or this island, you'll have to go through all of us."

A volley of "*Aye!*" and "*Yes!*" catapults through the crowd wrapping around the star—and around me. I'm wondering how on earth I got this blooming lucky to have a bunch of mates like this. Lily comes to stand beside Tootles. She raises her staff and lets out a battle cry that is echoed by her people, and a barricade of weapons is raised.

"I have to go through *you*?" Paige eyes Tootles maliciously. "All right then."

In a flash, she throws her dagger. It sinks into Tootles's throat, up to the hilt, and a spray of blood floods down his neck and begins to soak his shirt.

"Tootles!" I yell. I try to grab him, but his backward motion pulls him out of my grasp, and he falls onto the silver sphere behind us.

I reach for him again, aghast by the sight of his blood dripping from his skin and sinking into the star.

Blinding heat from the star scalds my arm as I try to pull Tootles back. I don't realize Connor has become active until an earthquake churns the ground beneath our feet. All around me, warriors and Lost Boys try to regain their footing.

But vines are now slithering across the ground and tossing people aside like kindling. No matter how much courage Tootles inspired, there's no way it can't stand up to Connor's brute power.

I hold on to Tootles's limp hand, even as the earth rolls under my heels, but he's already being swallowed by the orb, his blood in crimson streaks across the silver.

Suddenly I realize something else is leaking over the star. Something thick and dark. My head snaps up to see Connor standing a few feet away from us. His body is once again hunched over, skin cut apart by the pulsing veins, his mouth open as he chokes out his own shadow.

It slithers out of his mouth like the vines that snap around his feet. The pool of darkness oozes down his chin, thickening and writhing and dipping toward the star.

I can't stop Connor. Not this time.

His shadow licks at the edge of the star, then starts to dissolve into it. Claire must now see, because she screams and races for her brother, but he just flicks a hand, and a vine wraps around her ankle, holding her back. She's held suspended, able to do nothing but scream her brother's name over and over as she watches his contortions.

The silver sphere writhes and shrieks as the thick, dark silhouette pours out of Connor. The shadow's greedy hands reach as if to plunge in. The waterfall of darkness finishes, and the silhouette of Connor's shadow dissolves into the star just like Tootles almost has. The Lost Boy's fingers clenched in mine, and his head gasping for air, are the only things remaining above the surface that is quickly turning dark.

Suddenly Connor jerks backward, and the star at the heart of Neverland starts to shriek.

Blinding heat spirals out, and everyone near jumps back. I reluctantly let go of Tootles's hand, barely throwing myself away before the star scathes me.

I crawl across the mossy floor, glancing over my shoulder as I watch the star thrashing and sparking. Watch Tootles as the last part of him disappears.

A thick, dark spot blooms in the middle of the sphere where Connor's shadow had sunk in, like a pool of spilled ink. It swiftly spreads, dark spindly fingers overtaking the star like the veins that have overtaken my island. The ground rocks and heaves as the star falls into shadow.

In utter panic, I shove to my feet. The jungle erupts into chaos as warriors and pixies try to get as far from the transforming sphere as they can. Claire is only a few feet away, and I quickly go to her. She's holding her head, crimson flowing from her temple, matting her thick curls. Crouching beside Claire, I glare at my sister. At the terrifying too-wide smile on Paige's face.

She and Connor are reeling toward the shadow star. Sucked in. They're pulled closer until Paige is behind Connor, watching as he reaches out and lays his hands flat on the star that has become a writhing ball of darkness. Ashen threads climb up his hands, up his chest, up his neck. I watch in horror as Connor tilts his head back, and the darkness pours down his throat.

When Connor finally pulls away, his eyes are so filled with black ink I can't even make out the curve of his iris anymore. Shadowed fire burns beneath his skin.

I reach for Claire, grab her hand, hold on tight. Wanting to say something, anything, but I have nothing.

Connor's hollow eyes are on me. "I win."

The star explodes. A massive wave of darkness vaults toward us, and in an instant, our world is lost in the shadow that swallows us whole.

23

CLAIRE

Neverland

I blink several times, assaulted by blazing light, but as my vision clears, I realize it's sunlight. Bright sunlight filtering through heavy, vibrant foliage over my head, warming my face as I lie on my back.

I haven't felt warm sunlight like this since—

Well, I haven't felt it at all since arriving here in Neverland.

This is not what I expected my brother's shadowed star to create.

My head only spins more as I push off the silky grass, curling into a sitting position, and slowly take in the world spread before me. *This has to be a dream . . .*

Vibrant trees swell around me, large flowers blossoming to life in colors I've never seen. A gentle breeze cools my skin. The air is filled with the soft tinkle of bells. I leap to my feet and spin in a circle, just trying to soak it in. My heart soars when I take in the parade of pixies flittering about the trees and perching on leaves or dancing through the air.

They shine brighter than I'd realized they could, like enchanting golden stars fallen from the heavens to fill the air. Their melodic chimes are interrupted by boisterous, echoing laughter that cuts through the jungle. The laughter is like a siren's song that catches my bare feet and has me running over the grass, past towering palm trees, and toward the source of the noise. I burst out of the jungle, pulling to a stop at the edge of a curving lagoon.

Below where I stand, the island swells into a crescent cove, the crystal clear water filled with splishing, splashing creatures. It's the sirens' lagoon, but it's whole.

This entire island is whole again.

I inch closer for a better look. The sirens' scales are a beautiful, shining navy color, catching the sunlight and playing across the water. Their hair whips in the wind as they dive and jump and kick up spews of water at the boy swimming with them.

He's laughing and kicking back, his reddish hair soaked through, and his dimples in clear view as he tips his head back and lets out a long crow.

My knees nearly go out. I race forward, down one of the little sloping trails carved in the warm clay wall of the lagoon. I pause just before my toes touch water and stare out at him.

At the boy who looks about twelve, with big green eyes and a mischievous grin as he tries to clamber onto one of the siren's backs.

I blink furiously, but he's still there. But so small.

I find my voice. "Peter?"

At his name, he glances up and is suddenly motionless in the water. Droplets roll down his forehead as he regards me. Then he cocks head, and a wide grin spreads across his boyish features. "Isn't it all amazing? It's how it used to be!"

There's a part of me that wants to agree. Wants all of this to truly be as whole as it appears, but deep inside something churns. A distant memory of Connor's voice whispers, *"Pay attention!"*

Before I can say anything, I hear footsteps above me, and I look up just in time to see several boys launch themselves over the top of the cliffside into the lagoon. The half dozen of them cannonball into the water, sending up splashes of foam.

I count heads as they pop back up. Slightly is laughing and wrestling Cubby as they kick to the surface and grab onto one of the sloping rocks in the middle of the lagoon. They're younger and healthier, skin tanned and expressions shining with joy. It almost makes me want to cry. The twins pop up in tandem, and their big eyes and childlike expressions actually suit their age.

Tiger Lily is here too, sitting on the top of a protruding rock and kicking water playfully at the others. She also is younger. Softer, and a little less battle hardened.

But when Tootles's head breaks the surface, and he shoves hair out of his eyes, and he calls "Ho, Peter!" and greets the sirens, I really begin to feel unnerved.

There's another boyish form here, too, swimming under the water, aiming toward the portion of the cliff where I'm standing. He fluidly glides along as sirens dart and slide through the depths beneath him.

When he reaches the edge of the lagoon, his head and shoulders emerge above water.

My knees do go out then. I sink down, staring down at those brown eyes and the thick, curly dark hair. He's younger than I've ever seen him, but he still has that gentle light in his eyes. Gone are the lines of guilt and pain that lined Nibs's features the last few times I'd seen him.

"Hey, Claire. Welcome to Neverland," he says with a grin.

I slowly shake my head. Tears prick at my eyes, and I shake my head harder, as I rise to my feet and take a few steps back and hurriedly climb back up the curve of the lagoon.

I glance down at Nibs, who is treading water, staring up at me with confusion.

Something isn't right.

I run.

I run back up the carved-out slope and across the sprawling grassy lawn that dips toward the lush jungle. I'm not quite sure what I'm running toward or what I'm doing, but there's something wrong in all this.

Then I hear the weeping.

Weeping I recognize.

I make my way through the jungle, passing a haze of pixies gaily swirling about. I go through the hedge of large, tropical leaves and the bursting flowers of enormous size, and then I see him.

A little blond boy against one of the tall palm trees, knees pulled to his chin, quiet tears rolling down his cheeks.

Connor.

I walk toward him, letting my fingers trail along the edge of one of the nearby flowers, a large thing with iridescent petals that shimmer rose gold, but something pricks my finger. I glance down at the flower, expecting to see if I missed a thorn. It's much worse than a thorn.

The entire inside of the flower is rotten. Charred black and oozing and smelling of death. I spring back from the flower and race to my brother. He doesn't look up. Just keeps staring at the ground, misty tears dropping from his hollow expression.

"Connor, can you hear me?" Something is definitely not okay. He's the one who should be tethered to this place.

"Connor? What's happening?" I kneel beside him and notice he's wearing that faded Captain America T-shirt. The one he wore when Hook put him on that plane, all those years ago, heading to London.

He doesn't respond, so I shake him by the shoulders. Finally, his head comes up, and his dull eyes meet mine. He swallows a sob. "Who are you?"

My whole body goes cold.

Suddenly I realize something. I let go of Connor and look carefully around. *This isn't Peter's dream world.* I glance back at my brother, sitting against the tree. He's no longer crying, just talking to himself as he plays with a long, slender stick, swishing it through the air like a sword.

This is Connor's version of Neverland. The one he first saw when Peter stole him. The one he wanted to escape to.

But in this Neverland, he doesn't remember his life on Earth.

Doesn't remember me.

I bite the inside of my cheek, mind whirring. I grab his shoulders again and shake him lightly. "Connor, it's me! It's Claire."

He ducks his head and tries to pull away. "Leave me alone."

I can't do that. "I'm your sister, Connor. You can remember me—just try." I hold tight until he's forced to look at my face.

He snaps the stick toward me. It stings a bit, but I don't let go. "Connor, look at me. It's your Claire!"

His body goes rigid, and then, like a flash of lightning, something massive and towering is suddenly there. It billows out of Connor, caving over him, an oozing, shadowed presence. It turns its massive head, hollow eyes glaring at me, and when it snarls, its deep, gravelly sounds come out of the little boy sitting in front of me:

"Leave us alone!"

I scream and scramble backward. But just as quickly as it had appeared, the shadow creature disappears, soaking back into Connor. He once again mutters softly to himself.

My whole body has begun to shake as I try to put as much distance between me and that thing as I can. I force my breathing to even out and walk back toward the lagoon, and there I collapse at the edge of the cliff, where I can see Peter and Lily and the Lost Boys playing below.

From this higher vantage point, I see something deep beneath the water. Spindly veins crawl across the seafloor. A little sob fills my throat, and I run my fingers through the grass. Thick, oozing liquid squishes into my fingernails.

I jerk my hand away and find dark goo dripping from my fingertips. Spreading the vibrant green blades to get a better look, I realize there is no dirt beneath the grass, only the dark, oozing sludge.

The same kind of darkness that leaked from Connor as his shadow absorbed into the star.

I want to cry just looking at this beautiful place. I wish I could just close my eyes and let them all have the world they want.

But Neverland is rotting. Whatever Paige did to Connor's shadow, and whatever it has become as part of the star, it's eating away at him. At this island.

Just sitting here, I can feel it. The hollowness seeping into my limbs, the nausea in my chest. Neverland is rotting, and we'll be poisoned along with it.

I pull my knees to my chest, bury my head between them, try to block out the happy sounds of little boys playing below.

Will we lose Nibs all over again? Tootles too? And where is Paige in all this?

A warm hand suddenly steals over my shoulder, and I muffle a surprised shriek, jerking away. I spin around, expecting to find a Lost Boy had crept up.

"What are—" I freeze, eyes going wide. I thought I'd seen everything, but the ethereal creature standing in front of me completely steals my breath.

She's glorious. Tall and willowy with blonde curls that fall over her shoulders and a long, dripping gold dress. Something about her feels almost frail and delicate, but there's determined strength there too. Her eyes are blue, a reflection of mine, and for a moment I almost wonder if this is . . . me. The me I will grow to be. She's gently bending down to reach out and stroke my cheek, and instantly I know.

"Mother?"

Her full lips part into a gentle smile. "I'm here, my sweet Claire. I'm so glad to finally meet you."

Before I know it, I'm in her arms. She wraps me in a hug, and I'm burying my face in her chest.

"Oh . . . *mama* . . ."

My voice breaks, all my determination breaks. How long have I wanted this? All those years telling Connor bedtime stories because there was no one to tuck us in, no one to care. Discovering who I was and never quite belonging to the world I was in and wondering what she would think of me. Would she be proud? Would she be able to explain my dust?

Would she blame me for what Connor has become?

Her arms wrap a little tighter, and she whispers gently, "Your brother's choices are his own. But Claire"—she cups my chin, lifting my face—"I am so proud of you. Proud of the woman you've grown to be. You have fought so hard." She leans forward

and gently presses a kiss to my forehead. "But, finally, you can rest
. . ." She gently smooths out my tangled curls, a tender smile on her
lips. "You can stop fighting, Claire. You can just enjoy all of this."

She sweeps a graceful hand at the vibrant Neverland spreading
around us. A few tears do leak down my cheeks, and I hug her again.

We've lost so much. Me, Connor, Peter, the whole island.

There, in her secure arms, I desperately wish I could do what
she says. I want to become small like the others and be a little girl
playing carefree with Peter and Tiger Lily and . . . everyone. To stop
fighting and lose myself in this world. The real world is so ugly and
filled with so much pain.

But there still is something off. Even about her. I can't stay here.
It can't stay this way.

"I'll miss you more than air, Mama," I whisper, kissing her
cheek before I pull away. I study her for a long moment. Imprinting
her image into my mind.

And then I let her go. I stand up and slowly turn toward the
lagoon. Toward Peter.

When I glance over my shoulder again, she's gone. I wipe away
the salty streaks that still trail down my cheeks. I inhale a deep
breath and step to the very edge of the lagoon. I can see Peter
playing tag in the water with the Lost Boys and sirens far below.

I close my eyes for one moment, soaking in the sound of their
laughter. Imprinting one more thing in my memory—that big,
innocent smile on Peter's face.

I open my eyes and call down to him. "Peter? Peter, I need to
talk to you."

The boys still instantly, turning to look up at me. Something
about their expressions tells me that they know their game is almost
over. Lily is almost sorrowful as she peers up, not quite seeming to

recognize me. Peter is the last one to finally lift his head and meet my eyes, but when he does, he nods. He swims to the shore of the lagoon and begins to climb up the same way I had. A small, golden blur darts past me and spirals down toward him, swirling around him as he climbs. He laughs and throws out his arms as he begins to lift into the air, pixie dust coating his body.

The little pixie lands on his shoulder as Peter flies up toward me. He grins down at her. "Thanks, Tink!"

My stomach plummets. If I can get through to him, Peter is going to have to lose so much all over again.

Peter's calloused feet have landed. He stands as close to the edge of the cliff fading into the lagoon as he can without falling in. He plants his hands on his hips, bare chest glistening with water droplets and pixie dust. "You wanted to talk?"

Even his voice is younger. His dimples quicker to appear. His eyes are filled with more mischief.

Add to that the little pixie standing on his shoulder, making faces at me and smoothing out her little green dress . . .

He's about as Peter Pan as it gets.

It kills me, but I have to take that away from him.

"Peter, we can't stay here."

He quirks a brow. "What do you mean? It's Neverland. Of course we can stay."

I take a small step toward him. "But that's just it. This isn't Neverland." Oh, Peter you have to listen. "Peter, this isn't real."

He scoffs. "That's codswallop, and you know it."

I throw a hand out at the sprawling green jungle around us. "Everything we're seeing—the trees and flowers and even the Lost Boys—nothing is real, Peter." I stumble through words, trying to find a way to explain. "This is like a film covering what Neverland really looks like. It's masking the rot that's underneath." I kick at the grass underfoot, dislodging some of that oozing, dark gunk. "Neverland is rotting, and if we don't do something, its poison is going to destroy us all before we realize it."

He shakes his head so hard that water sprays from his drenched curls. "This is how I remember it. Why do you want to ruin that?"

His voice is high-pitched, accusing. A little boy confused why I would take away his favorite toys.

I bite my lip. "I wish I could give you the world you want, Peter. But it doesn't work this way." At a glimmer on his shoulder, I put a gentle hand out to Tink, but the minute my finger glazes over her little wings, she disappears. Blinks out of existence.

Peter's face pales, and he spins, searching for the pixie. That's when I notice the shadow spreading out from his feet. I step forward onto it, and the instant my toes touch the silhouette, it disappears too.

"See?" I look at him, but he's crossed his arms over his chest, and his bottom lip is shoved out in a pout.

"Neverland, life, it wasn't meant to be a freezeframe, Peter. It can't stay suspended forever. As much as it may hurt, we have to grow." I take a deep breath. I know how much the little boy Peter hates that word. "If we don't grow, we don't live. We just stagnate and begin to rot from the inside out."

Peter gives a sigh and a little sniffle. Then he glances up at me. "I guess living is quite an adventure."

A corner of my lips starts to tug into a smile. "Exactly. And that's what we have to get Connor to see."

Because if we can't find a way to help Connor face himself, face his own shadows, then we will all shrivel inside this shell of a world he's lost in.

24

PETER

Neverland

I take in the pleading expression on Claire's face and the way she stands out so distinctly in this world. Neverland swirls around her in vibrant colors, lit by streams of pixie dust as the little winged creatures dart and dance about. But even though Claire's own dust is filling the air around her, she's different than this place. There is certainty in her gaze cutting through the playfulness that consumed my world just moments ago.

My instinct is to push away the blarmy she's spilling. I'm tempted to recede back into the world I created, where Peter Pan doesn't have to think about anything but the next adventure. The world where there is no weight pinning my heart to the earth.

I lift my hands, looking at their small size, scars and thick calloused from years of romps and scrapes. My Neverland is so tangible, so within reach. It would only take an instant to escape here. And how desperately I want to.

But just looking at Claire reminds me of what got us into this whole mess in the first place. I'm not that Peter anymore. I can't be.

"All right," I finally say. "Where's that brother of yours?"

That instant, something starts to shift. Warmth hums through my body, and I glance down to see a flicker around me. When I look back up, I'm at eye level with Claire. No, taller than her, even. The height I'm supposed to be.

Almost pretty much grown up.

I chuff down a deep breath, but while the knowledge smarts, it doesn't hurt as much as it used to. I look into Claire's blue eyes. "Thanks for finding me, Pixie-Girl."

Her smile is wide. "Thanks for growing. I like you better this way!"

We wind through the thick jungle filled with the high-pitched songs of tropical birds and the chime-like voices of flitting pixies.

"What do you think happened to Paige?" Claire asks after a while.

I kick at a little lump of brightly colored flowers. "Probably trying to get as far from here as she can. If Connor did what he intended, he probably cut her out of this place. Erased her memory from the island so that she can try to leave."

Claire glances up at the clear blue sky patchworked through the thick foliage. "You think she might be flying somewhere up there?"

"I honestly have no idea," I admit. "For now, let's just hope she's far enough away that we have enough time to get through to Connor before she realizes what's going on."

We continue through the lush greenery, and then I spot the little blond boy huddled by a particularly large palm tree.

I shouldn't be surprised that he looks so blasted young, but still, I am. This young Connor is the one originally whisked away to Neverland. He'd been on edge even then, something uneasy lurking beneath the surface, but at first, he got along swimmingly with the other lads. Adventuring and joining in on the treasure hunts and spinning tales of his own about all the superhero comics he'd read back in America.

And then things had started to shift. He'd gotten hurt in one of the games with the Lost Boys, and it all went wrong.

Claire and I cautiously approach Connor. She reaches him first and settles into the grass beside him. I squat down behind her. Connor doesn't look so great. His skin is pale, cheeks sallow and sagging, and his expression is blank. He's staring at his hands, muttering quietly to himself.

"Connor? I need to talk to you," Claire tries gently.

"You okay, mate?" I reach out to shake him, but Connor jerks away. A flash of a large silhouette towers behind him. Monstrous and hulking one minute and gone the next.

Claire clutches my arm. "That happened before too. Do you know what it is?"

Curiosity draws me closer to Connor. He may look like an innocent child, but underneath, he's decaying.

"I have an idea. One way to find out for sure." I grab onto him and give him a strong shake. "Connor Kenton!"

It does the trick. Connor starts writhing and hitting at me. On cue, the massive shadow rears its ugly head again, spreading out behind Connor and curling above him. I quickly eye the seeping shadow and find exactly what I expect—dark tendrils are spreading from it, skimming across the jungle floor and forming the veins undercutting the island.

The shadow turns its large head, hollow eyes locking on me, and hisses in a voice that spews from Connor, *"Get back!"*

For a moment, Neverland disintegrates. The rosy sheen

masking this place as the paradise it used to be fades, and I can see charred, twisted trees and broken ground. Just behind us, where the shadow is spreading out, is the star at the center of Neverland, which is now only a shriveled pool of oozing, dark liquid.

And just as quickly as it had gone, the film snaps back into place, the broken, fractured Neverland hidden by bright colors and a mask of normalcy.

"Was that his shadow?" Claire scoots closer to me, voice unsteady. Connor turns away from us as the shadow sinks back into him, and now he curls into a little ball. Claire's mouth quivers. "He doesn't even remember me," she adds brokenly.

I sit in the grass beside Claire and watch Connor. "Aye. It's his shadow-self. When Paige tethered his shadow to the star . . ." I'm uncertain even how to explain this. "Well, you saw what he was like before. When the shadow was inside of him, bleeding out. Imagine that, but ten times worse. His dark reflection now has more magic than he could have ever imagined, and it's taken control. It's feeding off him, off the island, and destroying them both from the inside out. Much longer, and Connor won't have much of his original self left."

A shiver sweeps over Claire. "So he's possessed by his own darkness? How can we even begin to stop that?"

I get to my feet. "I've found that the only way to truly defeat a shadow is to face it." I glance back at her. "We have to get him to wake up, Claire. Connor is the only one who can face his own shadow—and even cut it away."

She nods mutely, as if unsure how to proceed, so I take the first step. I sit beside Connor and grip his arm. He tries to wrench away, refusing to look at me, but I hold on stubbornly.

"Ho, lad. I know you don't want to—but you have to face it."

He shakes his head fiercely and twists, trying to escape. I tighten my hold. "Connor, look at us!"

He jerks his arm free and attempts to crawl away.

"Oh, no you don't!" I grab for him, but suddenly he swings around and slams a fist into my jaw. And he's not done. The darkness swells out of him again, towering over the boy, mouth open, but its words come out of little Connor's mouth.

"We want this! Leave us alone—or we'll make you leave!"

I lift my chin, cross my arms, and glare at Connor's blooming shadow-self throwing a tantrum.

"Just you try!" I spit back at it. Claire gasps behind me. But I'm not letting Connor just bury his head and let the rest of us burn. I latch onto the boy's shoulders and shake him hard. "Connor, you have to stop hiding! You have to face it! If you don't—*everyone* is dead." My voice rises in volume as I shake him harder, desperation and frustration roiling together. I sweep a hand toward my Pixie-Girl, shouting at him: "You are going to kill Claire if you don't wake up!"

At that, Connor freezes, eyes going wide, mouth going wider, and then he screams. "No!" He yanks away and races off through the jungle.

I am about to run after him, but Claire holds me back.

"You're scaring him, Peter."

I swing toward her. "I blooming hope so! This whole blasted mess is scary. *I'm* scared." I'm practically vibrating, and I can see from her bloodshot eyes that she can relate, but she's shaking her head.

"I don't think that's how we can get through to him, though." She takes my hand. "We have to remind him of the same things you and Lily first reminded me. There is still light."

I look at her a moment, then nod. "I guess you're right."

We move farther into the jungle, the color fading from the tropical vistas around us as we draw near where we saw Connor disappear. He's watching us from the taller branches of a tree.

"Let me try." Claire climbs through branches until she pauses on a branch just below Connor's. Her voice is soothing and low when she speaks to him.

"Con? We just want to talk." A few flakes of dust begin to lift from her skin, mingling in the air, and drift toward him.

But the minute Claire's gleaming, shimmering gold dust touches him, he recoils with a shriek, as if stung.

Claire gasps, pulling back as Connor frantically brushes the seeds of gold away. I can see darkness seeping and swelling around him as Connor jumps out of the tree and heads off into the jungle again.

I follow after him, not about to lose him again.

I catch a glimmer of a few stray pixie dust remains clinging to him. He's noticed, too, and instead of ridding himself of them, he slows to a stop. As we come up to him I study the way his face flushes and how he doesn't look at us and the way he's chewing on his lip.

I've seen that look before. On other Lost Boys, but mainly in the mirror.

It's the expression of a little boy who has been hurt and doesn't want to recall his pain. Just wants it to end.

I put a hand on his small shoulder. This time he doesn't move. He's staring at the few flecks of dust. Claire intakes a quick breath, and her eyes widen a bit. She looks at me, and I nod.

She lets her pixie dust drift from her hands and waft all over Connor. He starts to shudder and quiver, face drawn in pain.

Suddenly, I can feel it too. I stare down and watch thin, dark, spidering veins spread from him onto my hand and up my body. Carrying with them a deep, ripping ache.

I gasp for air, forcing myself to not let go, even though the pain makes me want to jerk away. And this is just a taste of the pain that's been tearing at his insides for months because of that shadow.

Connor's breathing grows heavy. Suddenly, he arches his back as more dark veins skitter across his body, his skin growing chalky white before our eyes—and, all at once, we can see it. Seeping out of him, spilling across the dull ground, much larger than a shadow should be. Even if it was a reflection of his more adult stature.

This is the part of him that is tethered to the island. The part of him Paige twisted in order to poison the star and create the fantasy world he wanted. This is all of Connor's fears and faults poured into a dark reflection on steroids.

And it's not happy.

But . . . it's no longer *inside* of him. Which may be our only chance of actually helping Connor face it. Overcome it.

Claire lets more golden dust pour out of her body, filling the air and washing over Connor. He grunts when the flakes of gold sink in. As they do, the dark veins seem to pulse, trying to push back the light.

Connor rotates to face the monstrous shadow that is seeping up the side of the darkened trees and still towering over him. He's not speaking to us.

Connor's shadow hisses, rearing at him, spindly fingers wrapping around his neck. *"Coward . . ."* it hisses.

Claire's pixie dust spirals around her like a bright light, a torch, and she shoves it toward the shadow. It screeches and lurches back from Connor just enough for him to be able to breathe and speak again.

The shadow is rearing and spewing curses, trying to reach for Connor, sink back into him, but with Claire standing between them, it can't. It can't move past her light.

"This doesn't have to be the end, Connor," Claire tells him. "You're not alone."

I grip his wrist. "She's right, lad. If I can change and try to fix all the blooming messes I created—anyone can."

He takes in a deep breath and then looks beyond Claire to his shadow that is leering at us. It continues to hiss words, threats. But Connor pulls his shoulders back, lifts his chin, and says four words that shake the entire island:

"I don't need you!"

And just like that Connor severs his connection to Neverland. To the star. It's like an invisible line snaps. Connor's whole body convulses, and he's thrown backward. The island starts to groan and vibrate again, the earthquakes rumbling to life.

Once his connection breaks, Connor's shadow begins to change. It shifts, grows smaller, and as it does, Claire and I let go of Connor.

We step back and watch as the thin haze coating him dissolves, and suddenly there he is. A young man with gaunt shoulders and sallow skin, in a ragged blue T-shirt and baggy cargo pants. He looks like he could be blown over but manages to stand on his own. When he lifts his head and I can see his eyes, I find a well of raw, aching pain and anger boiling under the surface. But the edge that had always followed Connor, even when he put on a brave face for Claire—the edge that wanted to damage anyone who threatened him—that edge is gone.

Instead, Connor just looks hollow. But there's a small spark of hope there. Especially when Claire rushes forward and wraps him in a hug, and he collapses in her arms.

Beside them, I watch Connor's shadow shrink until it's the size it should be. The thick darkness that had filled it begins to ooze out, streaking across the ground, bubbling and arching. Like a dark mire searching for a new hole to crawl into.

With an exhausted tremor, Connor's knees go out, and Claire helps him gently settle to the ground.

The world around us continues to dissolve, and as the vibrant jungle fades, I can see the broken, craggy Neverland coming back into view. And it's not in good shape. The massive schisms in the ground seem to have grown wider, and most of the trees here have fallen to become shriveled kindling. Without the connection to a child heart, the island may survive for a short time longer on its own, but eventually it will begin to just . . . fragment, without a heartbeat. It has already crumbled so much. The sky is dark, filled with storm clouds. There's a dim flicker of faint light at intervals, and I finally make out what they are.

Pixies. Dying pixies.

And standing in the middle of the field of magical, winged creatures whose lights are blinking out is a woman with stringy red hair and a wild, raging look in her eyes. "You can't do this!" she hisses, glaring at us. At Connor who's nearly passed out on the ground beside us.

She holds a knife, but it's not Paige that makes my stomach curl. It's a certain dark silhouette slithering across the jungle floor beside her. A silhouette whose boyish form mocks me, and who knows every move I will make.

Shadow. He's with Paige.

My malicious, boyhood self has teamed up with the sister I had forgotten.

And both of them look like they're here to tear me apart.

25

CLAIRE

Neverland

Paige is unhinged.

She's wild with fury that we've stolen her chance of escape. She shrieks at Peter, screaming at him, "You can't do this!"

She kicks the carcasses of dead, shriveled pixies out of her way. The pain that reverberates from Paige, the way Connor's shadow-self has leached this island of all its color—it's all too much for the pixies. Their lights blink out all around us.

I believe. I *do.*

It's no longer enough.

A shiver comes over me, and I realize that the spilling pool of darkness has started to encroach again. Shoving back the bile rising in my throat, the hopelessness, I focus on doing the one thing I can—use my light to keep the darkness away from my brother.

Connor is unconscious on the craggy ground. The darkness that bled out of his shadow is like a small lake of acid, burning and sparking and charring the ground, turning the air putrid as it tries to flow back to him.

I pour more pixie dust from my fingertips and palms, letting it flow from my skin in a steady stream that creates a barrier between its darkness and those I can still protect. At least for this moment.

I have no idea how we bring Neverland back from this.

My mind suddenly shifts. If the pixies' lights have gone out, what has happened to Lily and her people?

My vision starts to dim, a panic attack swelling, but I force back the fear. Right now I have to hold on to the last shred of a happy thought that I have like a lifeline, a weapon, and force this crawling bog of darkness back. *While there is life, we have hope.* I stare at the remnants of the dark magic still connected to the star but no longer inhabiting Connor's shadow. The longer we stand here, the more the darkness seems to grow. Seeping into the ground and spreading thick veins across the dusty jungle floor. Drawing from the oppression that fills this place thicker than air.

Don't let go, I tell myself, thin flakes speckling my skin and filling the air. I move just enough to gaze at Peter. *Don't stop.*

"You can't do this to me!" Paige is shrieking again as she draws near.

Peter's hands are up, and his tone is cautious, coaxing. "Whoa there! I'm not sure what you mean."

Paige stops in front of Peter, one hand gripping a knife. It's quivering far too much for comfort. Peter's treacherous little shadow has followed her, slithering across the ground. It tries to grab at Peter's ankles, but he kicks it away.

Paige waves the knife around at the decrepit landscape of Neverland. "Why couldn't you let Connor have his dream world? Why couldn't you just let it be?"

I speak up before Peter can. "Because that world isn't real, and it's dying." I maintain the barrier of pixie dust but keep an eye on how close she is to my unconscious, defenseless brother. "If Connor's world stayed, he and the whole island would have rotted from the inside out."

Paige only shoots me a fiery glance. "Don't tell *me* what's real and what's rotten." The hand with the knife twitches. "Let me go, Peter."

The color drains from his features. "What?"

"All I have ever wanted was to escape from here. To leave. But you could never let me, could you?"

Peter is watching her warily. "What do you mean?"

"Silly little brother." Her tone is dripping. "Little Peter. Always so selfish. Always wanting things his way."

He glances down at his childish shadow coiled at Paige's feet, like a snake waiting to strike. "You wanted your own life," Peter agrees. " And if it's still what you want"—he switches his gaze up to her—"can't you just leave?"

Paige's whole body goes rigid, and her eyes spark. "If I leave the island, I *die*, Peter. Connor rewriting Neverland was my only chance of severing that tie. But now you've ruined it all!" She slaps him hard across the face.

My whole body is humming with tension, and that familiar thrum of panic speeds up my pulse again. I fight holding onto this barrier, holding back the spreading darkness.

"You let me drown, brother." She spits that last word at Peter like a curse. "It's Neverland that brought me back, using the remnants of magic from my connection to the island." She's swaying a bit as she talks, and I'm acutely aware of the knife still in her hands. There's an edge of insanity in her tone. "The sirens didn't know, so they took me to their graveyards at the very edge of the Neversea."

"I almost *drowned*." Her voice grows more fractured. "And any time I try to leave, it happens again. Water, filling my throat . . ." She lifts a pale hand to her neck as if she's actually struggling for breath.

Watching her through my wall of pixie dust, I realize something that I hadn't seen before. Peter might have thought Paige had drowned and run away from that memory, but it was his Neverland that kept her from drowning. In his creation of Neverland, care and love for her was there—deep within.

Suddenly, she straightens and places a hand around the front of Peter's neck. I wait for Peter to react, but he holds very still. "I almost had it this time. When Connor was connected to the star. I was actually able to fly past the boundary of Neverland. But then, then you stopped it all." Her voice is high-pitched, frantic. "Do you have any idea what it's like?" Her grip on his throat tightens, and now Peter starts to pry at her fingers. "To not be able to *breathe*?"

"Paige . . ." he chokes out.

"Let go of him." I keep my voice low, controlled. "I'm sorry you weren't able to leave, but I won't let you hurt him."

Paige surprisingly lets go of Peter's throat and steps back, scrutinizing me. "Your new pixie companion looks like Mother, you know," she remarks. "You were always like her, Peter. She had magic too. She would have believed this place was a gift. But it's not." Her eyes narrow at Peter. "This island is a curse. And the only way for me to escape it was to remake its rules. But you keep taking that away from me." Paige spins toward me. "*You* have taken it from me, Claire Kenton."

Her blade flashes, but Peter is there in an instant, catching her wrist and pinning her hand back.

He tries to wrestle the knife out of her grasp. "Would you really sacrifice all of Neverland and every creature here just so you can escape? Will that really solve everything?"

At his words Paige's mouth parts a bit, and I can practically see the wheels turning behind her forehead. As her shoulders start to droop, my eyes widen. Is it possible he's actually getting through to her?

"I don't know anything else, Peter."

Her fingers go limp on the knife, and Peter takes it safely out of her grasp, and she stumbles forward a bit and crumbles into him.

We can't trust her . . .

My brows rise, uneasy. Peter has put his arms around her and is speaking earnestly. "I can help you. We can help you. You can start over right here. If we can save Neverland, we can change things. There can be a fresh start, and you can have the freedom you want so badly."

She leans forward, face against his shoulder. Every hair on my arms stands on end. Something is very off about how quickly she's gone from talking about our destruction to falling apart in her brother's arms.

But then I think about Connor.

Could there be a chance for Paige too?

Peter is still talking. "Or this island could be your home, if you let it."

"Really?" asks Paige.

Peter nods. "Yeah. I can make you a right ol' Lost Girl."

Paige leans in a little deeper, and I hold my breath, not sure what—

Suddenly she darts out a hand and reaches around Peter for her knife he has hidden behind his back. She grasps it and jumps up. Spewing curses, she glares down at her brother.

"I'll never be another of your little playthings."

It's clear that she isn't willing to surrender her own pain to make the most of a world she blames for it. She'd rather see that world burn with her.

This time, I'm ready when she streaks toward Connor, knife raised. I make a quick decision. I let my hands drop and run for my unconscious brother.

As I reach him, Paige halts. She steps over Connor's body, and her eyes meet mine.

"You're the only thing standing between rebirth and oblivion." There's something chillingly calm about the way she says it, the way she suddenly seems perfectly, impossibly sane. I can almost see the woman James Hook fell in love with in her dimmed green eyes. Can almost see the sister Peter grew up with in the freckles and planes of her face.

But Paige's expression turns stone-cold.

"It's too bad pixies have such short lifespans."

She sets the razor-sharp edge of her knife against my throat. Peter screams my name. I feel sudden pain.

The world moves in slow motion.

This can't be real.

This must be a nightmare.

But I'm not waking from this dream. This fairy tale.

Crimson spurts out, showering my dress, staining my dust red.

I fall to the ground, writhing, wracking, overwhelmed by searing pain. Suffocating. My vision spins, darkness seeping in at the edges, while spots of white-hot agony cut through every nerve.

Paige is standing over me, just watching. "Don't fight it. You'll die faster if you let it take you. Trust me, it's less painful that way."

My fingers are digging into the craggy ground, raw skin breaking across my fingertips. I somehow manage to turn my head, hair sticky and thick with blood. Across from me I can see Connor, still out cold.

I'll never get to say goodbye.

Peter is on his knees at my side trying to staunch the flow of blood with his hoodie.

Something slithers across the ground. A boyish shape, laughing at me.

Darkness is here too. Spilling toward Peter's shadow. Pooling around us and swallowing up the ground again without my dust to hold it back.

My body is so, so heavy. And it takes all my courage just to force my weighted eyelids back open, wanting only to see Peter.

To let his big, beautiful green eyes be the last thing I see.

But it's not Peter that fills my vision. It's a shadowed silhouette, dripping blood and streams of darkness, rising from the ground and towering over me.

I want to warn Peter, want to scream, but I can't even feel myself anymore.

They're all hazy figures now. Peter tries to duck around Shadow that is now dripping the dark magic that used to inhabit Connor. Peter's fingers touch me—but his shadow is too fast. The last thing I see is Shadow throwing himself at the redhead, clawing at his face and hissing, trying to squeeze the life out of Peter Pan. Peter's worst enemy: himself.

And then it's gone. All of it. Neverland, Peter, the struggle of light and darkness. In an instant, wiped away. My pulse slows, my chest no longer rises, oblivion taking me.

The shadows win.

26

PETER

Neverland

Claire's blood coats my skin and drips from my hands as I punch at Shadow and try to shove him away so I can get back to her. Tears blur my vision, and every time I manage to duck around him, he's there. Faster than me. More concrete because of the dark magic pulsing through him.

"Let me go!" The words rip from my throat in a guttural scream, and my knuckles are raw and bleeding from the amount of times I've dashed them against this blithering shadow. This awful reflection of myself, all my sins, holding me back from her.

From Claire, lying there, choking on her own blood. I watch her writhe as I scream and kick at my shadow, tearing at its dark hands as they claw at my face and neck. But then Claire stops moving. Her eyes go glassy.

Every single bone in my body feels like it shatters. The pain overwhelming, exploding from my chest.

"*No!*" I scream, too desperate now to care. I kick at Shadow's almost translucent knee and manage to sweep his legs out. I throw myself toward Claire, landing on my knees beside her. I fumble with her wrist for a pulse with one hand, the other grappling with my hoodie that presses tightly against her neck. But the green fabric is already soaked with red, and it's flowed down her chest, over the dress the pixies had made her.

No, no, no, no!

This can't be possible.

There's so much blood. Far, far too much.

Her light has completely dimmed.

I have never been so insanely terrified in my life.

"Claire!" I gather her in my arms, still trying to staunch the blood. Her dust has vanished, and her skin is becoming cold. "Claire, talk to me. Please, please . . ." My voice breaks, words breaking, heart breaking.

Shadow jumps on me, trying to drag me away from her. As I fight against him, my eyes catch on Paige standing a few feet away. Her face is expressionless, her voice flat.

"I thought the darkness would go back into Connor. I thought everything would be reset again so I could escape."

I shove an elbow into the dark visage behind me, and Shadow's grip lessens just enough for me to scream brokenly at her, "Why not me? Why couldn't you have killed *me*?" A sob wracks my shoulders, and the fight drains from me as I stare down at Claire. At her body, far too still.

Paige turns away from me. All my sympathy for her has drained into her pool of darkness.

Shadow has again climbed on my back, his arms strung around my neck, cutting off my air. I want to throw him off, but he's too wiry and strong. Just like I was.

But now I feel anything but strong. My very bones feel hollow and frail enough to snap from the weight of my grief.

Shadow's grip tightens. I'm not quite sure why he's doing this, until the thought comes. He does hate growing up, after all. I am everything I never wanted to be.

"*Peter!*"

At first, I think the voice must just be a hallucination. Something cannons into me, knocking Shadow off my back. I gasp for air. Vision clearing. I sit up to find Tiger Lily rolling to her feet. She raises her staff and points at Shadow.

He stands far more solidly than he used to, actually upright, not just sliding like a piece of paper across the ground. He hisses at her.

Tiger Lily's whole body is postured for fight. Her dress is in tatters, cuts and bruises are everywhere, and her braid is tangled and matted.

She glances at me, and I see eyes that carry the most wear. "Is Claire . . . ?" She can't even finish it, and I don't want her to.

I don't want any of this.

I limp back to Claire but am shocked to discover that Lily isn't the only person who has appeared. Captain Hook strides across the cracked ground, his crimson coat gone, and his white shirt shredded and stained with blood. There's a pistol holstered at his side, and he holds his sword in one hand. He looks like he's been through as much blasted hell as the rest of us.

As I sink to my knees at Claire's side, Hook stops in his tracks. The look of utter desolation that crosses his face is the most real expression I've ever seen him wear.

I gently take Claire into my lap.

A sob wracks my shoulders as I cradle her, brush back her blood-stained curls.

"Did you do this?" Hook is glaring at Paige, his voice edged with a dangerous growl. He stabs the end of his sword into the ground, leaving it sticking out of the rough earth. He steps forward, eyes fixed on her and asks again, "Did you do this?"

Paige wavers, like a mirage in the wind. Her eyes plead with him. "I thought I had to. For us to escape, James."

Hook's eyes travel to me with Claire cradled in my arms, then over to Connor, lying unconscious a few feet away.

My shadow tries to lurch at Lily but she bats it away with her staff. It's becoming more and more agitated. She won't be able to hold him back for long.

Hook turns those gray eyes on me again. He reaches for his side, and for a moment, I stiffen, thinking he's going for the pistol holstered at his hip, but instead he pulls something out of his pocket. Hook tosses a small drawstring pouch at me. I catch it, cradling the small pouch in my hands. I don't have to look inside to know what it is. It's almost lifting off my hand.

I raise my eyes to the pirate. "Claire's dust?"

He nods as he comes over to us. He tenderly trails the edge of his misshapen hook over her cheek.

"She really was magnificent." When I see his eyes fill, I lose it. I bury my face in Claire's silky hair.

Sobs wrack my whole body.

This is worse than death.

Hook's hand is on my shoulder. "I'll deal with Paige. You need to destroy that shadow somehow, Pan."

I numbly lift my head to him. This foe suddenly turned almost a friend. "How? What good is any of it anyway?"

Hook looks down at Claire. "We have to try, Peter. We have to try. She wouldn't want the island she gave everything for to die without a fight."

My skin bristles at the way he talks about her, like he actually knew her, like he actually cared. Maybe he did.

Because he's not wrong.

Claire wouldn't want me to let things end here.

I nod and glance over at Lily. Slamming her staff hard into Shadow. Over and over, beating him back, but he's learning, getting faster. He's starting to duck and dart around her swings.

I'm the only one who can stop him. I weigh the little bag of pixie dust in my palm and then gaze down at Claire.

"I'm sorry, Pixie-Girl," I tell her. "I have to help Lily with Shadow."

This reflection of myself. The me I used to be.

The me I would have become if it weren't for her.

I realize just how much I owe this girl. But, it's more than that—

Much, much more.

I take a ragged breath and gently brush her hair out of her eyes. The scent of metallic blood clings to the air, and far too much crimson stains the ground and her hair and our clothes. I lean forward and whisper only for her to hear.

"I love you, Claire Kenton. I should have said so a whole blooming lot earlier. I love you." Tears stream down my cheeks again. I press a "thimble" against her lips, the kiss hesitant and wet with my weeping. "I'd gladly grow old with you if we could."

And I mean it. More than I've ever meant anything before.

I cup her face with one hand, touching her one last time, and then I reluctantly ease away. I get back on my feet and start toward Tiger Lily.

I untie the string on the Hook's pouch and drizzle out the pixie dust into my hands. My chest feels like a gaping, raw wound, which is made more painful as I see the soft glimmer of Claire's dust filtering through my fingers, lifting me from the ground.

I glide over beside Lily. From the way her arms droop, she's exhausted. Shadow focuses on me, growling I nudge Lily's shoulder.

"I've got this."

She drops her staff on the ground. Her brown eyes glisten. "I'll stay with Claire."

I can only nod.

I brace myself opposite Shadow. "This is between us."

Before he can respond, though, I hear a weird guttural moan from behind us. Both Shadow and I turn to look, and I realize that Hook has stepped up close to Paige. And she's stumbled into his arms, shaking.

"You can't leave. It's impossible now, love," he's telling her, and I'm surprised at how gentle his voice is. He rubs her back with the curve of his hook. "Stay with me, love? Stay here? Try again?"

But Paige is shaking her head. A wail tears from her throat. "I can't. It's too much, James. I want to escape."

Her eyes are wild, and she's grasping at him, at his grimy and torn undershirt, reaching for something tucked in an inside pocket. Hook's mouth parts, but no words surface, and he instead grabs her shaking, desperate hands and pulls her in close. He holds her for a long moment, so quiet, then whispers something in her ear.

She nods.

And he pulls a slender vial out of his pocket. A curving silver snake makes up the tight cork of the bottle, and a deadly familiar green liquid sloshes about inside.

Before that can fully sink in, Shadow attacks again.

I leap into the air, letting Claire's dust lift me higher and higher. Shadow starts to follow and then stops. Without warning, he darts across the ground toward Hook. The pirate captain grabs his pistol and raises it. But Shadow isn't interested in Hook. Instead, the ghastly thing grabs onto the large, curved sword stabbed into the ground. Before the pirate can react, Shadow snatches the sword and heads back to me, dragging the clattering weapon behind him.

I draw him away from everyone else. It's chilling how fast he is, keeping up with me over ground as I travel above.

I don't know how to undo any of this. I'm not sure of anything anymore.

Even if I manage to destroy my shadow and the darkness along with it, it won't bring my Pixie-Girl back.

But still I fly. I soar back over the island, past the stretch of what was once rich jungle where the hanging villages were but is now only collapsed trees. I halt midair at their splintered remains. Jagged pieces of wood and collapsed roofing are all stained red. My gut turns when I see hundreds of bodies strewn among the fallen villages. The village has crushed everyone under the trees. Lily's brave warriors surrounding the star were only set in place for their own deaths.

I don't know how Lily even survived.

If that's what you can call any of this. It doesn't feel like survival.

It feels like a waking sort of death. I falter. I can't take anymore.

But I catch a gleam of Claire's pixie dust around me and continue on.

I aim right, veering away from the jungle, Shadow staying close, skimming over the charred ground. As I see the edge of the island, I realize that Neverland has split right down the middle. Water bubbles through the massive crack in the dry ground.

But it's not normal Neversea water.

This water is dark and murky with half-fish, half-human bodies afloat in it. Sirens. Dozens of them. The crocodile has washed up on one of the rocky shores.

Dead. Dead. Dead.

All of it.

The word hammers through my chest, and I drop out of the sky. I can't find a happy thought. I fall toward the splintered world below, toward the shadow that is skittering across the ground and dragging Hook's blade with him.

"Not like this!" I moan hoarsely. That fragment of a thought is enough to help me fly again. The sky is overcast, angry storm clouds blocking out the stars, and suddenly I hear the cannon of thunder. Lightning streaks across the clouds.

Just perfect.

I shoot out past Neverland just as the first big raindrops start to fall.

I swivel, hovering over the Neversea, watching Shadow pause at the border of the water. And then I sight what I was looking for. Skull Rock, just to the right of us, is mostly submerged and tipped on its side. But a large pirate ship has been thrown against it by the raging, crashing waves hammering at the island.

The *Jolly Roger* is a shattered wreck. Its sails are ripped and mostly gone. There's a massive hole in its hull that is quickly taking on water, and a few of the masts are splintered and lopsided.

But the main mast still stands with a few lengths of rigging.

It's enough.

I head toward the *Roger,* soaring quickly over the angry, rocking sea. A glance over my shoulder shows that Shadow has somehow managed to follow, cutting across the waves, albeit slower. I land on one of the *Roger's* crossbeams just shy of the very top of the mast. My feet fight for purchase on the wet, splintered wood. I grab onto a length of salt-crusted rope and hold on to the rigging to stay in place. Claire's dust still flecks my body, and a few specks still fill the air around me, but the rain is driving some of it away.

As the heavy downpour batters against me, I watch as Shadow climbs up the side of the hull, up over onto the deck, and then starts to streak up the mast toward me. He's shorter than I am, with an outline of thick unruly hair and a lanky, boyish frame.

A reflection of the Peter who swore he'd die before he'd grow up.

Shadow is here to make good on that promise.

I brace myself as I watch him climb. Hook's sword is clenched in Shadow's teeth. Dark magic drips from Shadow's wavering form, and charred veins spread out across the ship.

I have no idea how to stop this thing. He's me—he knows every move I make. And he's filled with dark magic. If Claire's light couldn't even destroy the dark magic, what am I supposed to do?

But as the rain beats down on me, and lightning flashes through the sky, brightening the skeletal *Jolly Roger*, there is one thing I do know.

If Peter Pan is going to die with this Neverland—

It's going to be by fighting until my last breath.

27

PETER

Neverland

The rain pounds down on me like a hail of bullets, the sky lanced by lightning and thunder that shakes the splintered mast I'm perched on.

My grip on the rough wood is slippery. As another vault of thunder rumbles through the shipwrecked vessel, I continue to watch the dark figure scaling up the wood.

Shadow has Hook's sword clenched between his teeth like some blooming pirate, and his lithe form is so quick he's only a foot below me. He takes a swing with the sword, and I jump out of the way, landing on one of the remaining crossbeams. Weathered strips of rigging snap and sway in the harsh wind, and the entire ship creaks loudly.

Shadow clambers up onto my section of wood and sweeps the sword again. I dance backward until my heels are hanging off the end of the beam. I'm armed with the remnants of Claire's pixie dust but no physical weapons. The little devil scampers across the beam at me, sweeping and slicing the sword like a child with an oversized plaything—and he's blinkin' fast.

I narrowly manage to jump and duck around him. Using the dust still clinging to my clothes and lightly flickering nearby, I vault through the air to land behind Shadow. I hurriedly climb back down the mast, searching for something to fight with.

There's some large chunks of wood and the fraying strips of rigging, but nothing that would hold out against Hook's sword.

Shadow is already on my heels, and I almost think I hear a wild little boy's laughter in the wind. It's chillingly eerie the way he moves in exact reflection of my movements. I step, he steps. I go to jump, he's poised to follow.

Shadow lurches toward me, ramming Hook's long cutlass right at my chest, but I expect it. It's the exact move I would have made. I leap into the air, use the last of Claire's dust to give me a few more inches, and grab onto a long stretch of rigging. I swing on the rope, crashing back to kick at Shadow's hand, trying to dislodge the sword. He doesn't quite lose his grip, but the move surprises him just enough that I can pull off what I try next. My feet skid across the thick crosspiece of the mast, the rope in one hand. I quickly swing it around Shadow's small fist. Once, twice, so fast he can't react—and then I pull it tight.

Shadow, drops the sword, hand caught in the rope and wrenched to the side by a gust of wind. I quickly grab Hook's sword before it tumbles over the edge. I place the end of the long blade against Shadow's thin chest.

"Give it up, mate! You've lost."

Shadow goes very still, and then he lifts his head. His dark eyes narrow at me, teeth bared, and then he lets out a guttural growl.

Shadow wrenches his arm out of the rigging and launches at me. I try to swing the sword at him but it doesn't seem to affect him.

Blast, blast, blast!

Another burst of thunder and lightning severs above. Shadow jumps at me, clawing at me with his fists. Using my hand to protect my face, I thrash at him with the sword, though it obviously can't do a blithering thing.

Shadow screeches again with a lunge, and suddenly the sword is out of my hand. The darkness from his feral little body seems to lash out at me, dripping down the mast and spreading like spindly veins across the ship. The *Roger* creaks as the whole ship begins to collapse inward. It's slowly breaking apart and bending in on itself and almost knocks me out of the rigging in the process.

The waves slamming against the hull are growing even wilder. Neverland is coming apart at the seams. Crumbling without the pulse of a heartbeat. Without being connected to anyone. Just as the *Jolly Roger* is splintering and sinking and close to collapse, this island won't last much longer.

I back up on the shuddering beam, trying to get out of the way as Shadow reclaims the sword. He lifts the weapon and I realize he's pushed me to the very edge. I'm practically on my back, hands pressed against rough wood to keep from slipping. A glance over my shoulder only reveals the splintered, jagged remains of the deck caving upward.

Not a fun fall.

My head turns back to see Shadow standing over me, the sky splitting with a bolt of lightning that reflects off the blade he's holding to my throat.

"Whoa, now—"

My boyish reflection parts its thin, stained lips and mouths three words:

No grown-ups here.

I meet the shadowy eyes of the boy who was once Peter Pan. "I've always thought to die would be quite the adventure." I force myself to stare at him, watching until the last minute. I'm many things, but a coward was never one of them. "And at least now I'll get to see Claire. She gave everything because she believed in this island." The words catch in my throat, but I have to get this out if it's the last thing I ever say. "Because she believed in me. And if that means I have to fight for our world until my last breath"—I lift my chin, wild determination filling each word—"do your worst."

Shadow snarls. I flinch but don't look away, preparing for the final blow.

Then suddenly something ripples through the whole island. It shakes the ship and skims across the frothy water, making even Shadow stumble back a step.

I hold my breath, listening. Every fiber of my being straining . . .

And I feel it. It's faint, but it's growing. The gentlest whisper of a pulse, beating through the island. Humming beneath my palms. Filling my own veins, moving in time to my heartbeat.

My eyes shoot wide. *Is it possible?*

Unease is on Shadow's vague features. There is a flicker of fear. Then panic as he tries to run at me again.

But he's too slow.

And the island is blooming to life.

By the stars, we're *alive*.

I duck under the sweep of Shadow's sword. It glances off the edge of my shoulder, but I don't even feel it. I race across the beam and brace myself with my back against the thick curve of the mast. The icy weight in my chest thaws out as I watch the island begin to thaw too.

The rain slows and settles, and the dark storm clouds are cut through with vibrant shafts of sunlight. The writhing, angry sea slows its vicious beating against the wrecked ship and soothes back into the soft whisper of waves against the rock.

I watch Neverland inhale.

I know what comes next.

From the terror on Shadow's face and the way the darkness is filling the air around him like a seeping mist, he does too.

But he's too late.

And I'm not alone. I can feel it in the pulse that hums through my bare feet and sings a quiet song across the wind and the whisper of hope in the air. It's not only my pulse filling this island, knitting it back together. Waking it back to life.

Lily said there was another way to form a bond with a Never Never Land.

Deeper than any other.

Born out of a deep sacrifice.

Stitching your soul to another's—and to a place.

Please, please, please . . .

The word chants through my head as I hold my breath, gaze locked on the shore of Neverland. I watch the island groan and rock and start to come back together and watch the sun begin to rise. Only it's not the sun.

The ball of light lifts above the tropical foliage that has begun to regain its color, and my mouth opens from just how stunningly bright it is. *She* is. A vibrant light, shimmering gold but with an almost pink hue, sweeps across the shore of Neverland and flies out over the sea. I see a small foot skim the top of a wave, watch streams of shining dust spill behind her, and then she's close enough that I can make her out.

There is a young woman shining at the center of the blast of light. Her skin is practically glowing, and the rosy color of dust spills from her, pixie dust brighter and more glorious than I've ever seen. It's like her magic has been fully let loose, rippling her body in a kind of shimmering dress that leaves a wave of shining magic in her wake.

Claire's hair is flowing free around her face, and her blue eyes are sparkling with life.

Shadow suddenly screams. He goes into motion and charges me, but he's afraid. I can feel it. When he swings, I just jump off the beam.

Claire's dust catches me. Even though she's still a few feet away, she's creating so much vibrant, rosy dust I'm swept up in the air. Facing Shadow, I wave a hand. "I guess this place can still do the impossible after all."

Shadow hisses, and the darkness oozes out even wider as more dark veins shoot across the wood and drip toward the deck below. Claire glides through the air to me.

I grin at her like a blithering idiot. "I love you."

She almost drops, but her eyes shine.

She places a foot on the beam, inches from Shadow, and the darkness suddenly recoils. The dust that cascades down her body like a waterfall spills over the side of the beam, and Shadow screeches, reeling back until he's the one standing at its very end. I plant both my fists on my hips and stare at my darker reflection. The little boy who had spent so long hiding in the light of the stars, only to find that the darkness was inside him all along.

But not anymore.

"Don't you see? The shadows will never win." I tip my head back and let out a long crow. "Not so long as there's faith, trust, and . . ."

"And pixie dust." Claire comes right up to Shadow.

She kicks the sword out of his hands. "Fear and darkness have already done far too much damage to this island. No longer."

Shadow hisses, the darkness clawing out from him and trying to snap at her, but the rosy dust pushes it back. Claire glances at me floating in the air beside her. "You know what I've learned in all this? My pixie dust doesn't just create light." She puts her hands together and creates a thick ball of shining dust. She fixes a fiery gaze on Shadow, and the swelling dark magic clinging to him like a cloud. "My dust is also a weapon."

She throws the large ball, and it explodes over Shadow, cascading across his body. He shrieks, clawing at himself and at the shining dust that clings to the planes of his form and soaks into the snapping and sizzling dark magic.

Claire leaps off the beam and grabs my hand. We hover together above the *Jolly Roger* and watch as the darkness seeps out of Shadow and grows so large that I can't even see a trace of my silhouette anymore, just a thick haze.

Claire creates another ball of dust and hurls it at the haze of darkness. Then another, and another, and another. Until her pixie dust completely covers and coats and sinks through the sizzling blackness. Claire lifts her hand as she observes the pixie dust mingling with the oozing darkness, its threads of light cutting through the black.

"This is *our* Neverland." She clamps the hand into a tight fist.

Her pixie dust immediately goes dark gray. Burning, acidic.

It burns right through the dark magic. Tightening and contorting and swallowing it up so quickly that I almost can't believe it. In a flash of sparks and the scent of burnt wood, all that is left is the sizzle filling the air, and Claire's dust littering the *Roger* in singe marks. The ashen dust is already filling with color again.

The black magic and my shadow are nowhere to be seen.

Claire suddenly looks at me, concerned. "I didn't realize your shadow would completely dissolve."

I give her a lopsided grin. "I couldn't care less about my blooming shadow when I have you back." I lean in and press my mouth against hers. I feel almost as weightless as her dust as Claire puts her arms around me. I melt into the sense of her, warm and wondrously alive.

I trail small kisses up her nose and across her face. "I'm so glad you're here." My voice is uneven and trembly, and I don't care.

She drifts back just a bit and sweeps hands across her dripping dress of pixie dust. "I don't quite remember what all happened."

"That may actually be for the better."

"How am I even here?"

My gaze goes beyond her to Neverland. I take her hand and pull her away from the skeletal remains of the *Jolly Roger*. "I think it may have to do with the same reason the island is coming back to life."

We fly side by side, her dust filling the air and curling around me.

I guide her higher, and we soar across the shore of Neverland, looking down at the island as it blooms before our very eyes. The craggy ground is now knit back together, and emerald grass is spreading across the jungle floor like a rolling carpet. The jungle itself is flourishing awake, trees springing up and growing taller than before, large, exotic plants filling the world with new color, and streams rushing with crystal clear water.

It's Neverland—but also not.

We soar ever higher, getting a bird's-eye now, and I realize the island is growing. Slowly getting bigger. New mountain crests are rising toward the clouds, and waterfalls and rivers are flowing over the land. The sirens' lagoon has expanded. A dozen more waterfalls tumble and turn down into the pocket of water. Whole stretches of tropical foliage flicker, alight with the glow of pixies.

Claire and I come to an abrupt halt, hovering. Her voice trembles. "Lily? The Lost Boys?" She asks the same question that is twisting my gut.

But as we drift lower, we suddenly see the tribal queen emerge through the trees. Relief floods through me. I soar higher and spot more villagers exploring the new expanding corners of the island.

Lily and her people are native to this place, born with its inception like many of the pixies. All a part of this world that is yawning and stretching awake again.

I catch sight of a small group of bedraggled Lost Boys that look like they're in an argument with a group of pirates trying to cast off in a rickety rowboat. I let out the other breath I didn't know I was holding. I can't make out how many of the boys there are, but at least some of them survived.

"What is happening?" Claire asks me in a hushed voice.

I tighten my hold on her as we continue to fly, the sun warming us both. "I think it's our bond. The Soul Bond. It's bringing the island back to life, just like it brought you back. But this is"—I brush a hand over my eyes, unable to even believe what I'm seeing—"this is so much bigger than it used to be."

Claire's eyes shine. "Maybe this is how it was always meant to be? Maybe Neverland was never meant to stay so . . . small. So childlike." She floats in closer, and I put an arm around her shoulders, pulling her against me. "Maybe, like us, Neverland was meant to grow. It was meant to bloom more beautifully and more colorful than before."

I know she's right. I kiss the top of her head. "I think because of our connection to it, the magic of the island brought you back. A Soul Bond must have formed when you sacrificed yourself for Connor and me and for the island. Plus I stopped being a fool. There's something about the magic of this world that is within us, Claire. It may have taken a bit of time to really sink in." I gesture to the world beneath us. "Neverland has become a part of you."

"Now it's a part of both of us." Claire laughs. She sparkles at me. "This place is truly my home."

I soak in those bright blue eyes. Forget thimbles. The kiss I give her is quite grown-up.

28

CLAIRE

Neverland
Quite Some Time Later

Connor sleeps a lot.

I knew something wasn't right that day all those years ago, when I flew and landed beside him on the shore of Neverland. I watched the island inhale and begin to heal—but not Connor. Not quite. When he gained consciousness, my brother was so physically and emotionally broken he was hardly coherent. I offered to help mend all his wounds with my pixie dust.

Tiger Lily said no.

Connor had healing to do, deep healing, and it wasn't the kind of thing one could do with magic. She took him deep into the jungle to be with some of her people and their healer.

When he's not sleeping, he's painting. He is using watercolors to bring memories and emotions to life.

I can't visit him yet, but I know all this because I can see Connor in my dreams.

When I close my eyes, it's as if we're sitting side by side, and Connor tells me how he's doing. His healing is not fast or magical or easy. But it's good. He is in the company of those who truly want his best, not their own selfish agenda. Lily's people are teaching him to read the stars and find the destiny the Ever One wrote for him there.

The bright light of the morning sun teases my eyelids.

I yawn and roll over in my bed, instinctively sliding a hand across the space beside me, only to find it empty. I blink sleepily down at my hand where a ring sparkles against the warm, yellow sheets. The place where Peter is usually snoring or murmuring is empty.

He's not here. Not yet.

Excitement starts to sing through me as I stretch and kick back the covers, the familiar pulse of Neverland and the sound of the island waking with me. I can hear the distant coo of birds and the howl of a Neverbeast. I smile at the lyrical chimes of pixies darting past my window.

I put on a dress made of woven leaves and a silky pink sash the pixies crafted for me and loop a small pouch of worn leather on a string about my waist. Flakes of dust begin to drift into the air around me, making the dress glisten and immediately brightening the room. My bare feet glide across the floor to the door set into our round little thatch house. I nudge it open and soon am dancing on air.

Our home is at the edge of Neverland, facing the second star to the right, so that I can always watch for Peter when he comes home to me. The little round villa hangs suspended in the trees, built by Lily's people, but unlike their hanging villages, our home is free-floating. No need for ladders or bridges. Nestled like a little acorn in the lush jungle.

I whisper good morning to Glimmer, who is sound asleep in one of the bows of thatch woven into our roof. The little pixie instantly arises and shoots after me as I soar away from the house.

The air is crisp and fresh and inviting, and a little thrill still comes over me as I fly over this vibrant island that I've come to know so well. The places where it slopes upward into mountain peaks, where rich tropical foliage is alight with colorful birds and the gleam of pixies, and spots where sirens sun themselves against purple-hued rocks.

There's a twinge in my chest, knowing that, while the Pan will get to see this beautiful homecoming every time he returns, Paige chose instead to leave it all behind. Hook's poison wasn't meant to kill, only incapacitate, and when she eventually awoke, even with the world reborn, she didn't want it.

So she took a bit of pixie dust and flew away. As far as she could—until she crossed past Neverland, into the stars, and the water began to drip from her clothes again.

Peter and I couldn't watch after that. She wouldn't let anyone help her. Flew as far as she could. And a part of me prays that somehow she was able to outrun her curses. But even if she couldn't, I think she wanted that. To live out the end of her life her own way.

Glimmer chatters in her singsong voice as she perches on my shoulder, burrowing between the leafy folds of the straps of my dress. I pick up speed quickly crossing the mottled green canopy below. Pixies pop their heads out or flit up to wave at me, their wings iridescent and glowing a little brighter as they catch sight of us.

I wave back as Glimmer continues to chatter in my ear, turning a bright pink from pride at being the one sitting on my shoulder and not merely one of the waving pixies.

"Are you excited to see him?" I ask her as we close in on the center of the island. Glints of wooden verandas and thatch roofs speckle the leafy foliage below. We've reached the hanging villages.

Glimmer does a happy little dance on my shoulder, tugging on one of my curls. "I wonder how many he's bringing us!"

"We'll see, but I have to get something first. I will only be a minute."

I scan the intricate spread of newly finished houses and crisscrossing bridges until I spot a familiar wraparound porch and the two figures sitting at its edge, their legs dangling down. I go through an opening in the branches around Lily's place and lightly land on the deck.

The two on the porch immediately glance up. Lily's eyes are the color of polished river stone, and they immediately twinkle at me. The silver threads of the elaborate stitching on her sleeveless teal dress shimmer as she leans forward. "Today's the day?"

"Yes! Did you get it?"

She nods, and glances at the young man sitting beside her. The Lost Boy nods and then shakes out his thick hair to look at me through those almond eyes. "It took a while, but our crew finally managed to track down one." Tootles is grinning, and once again I'm relieved at how well he is looking. It took a few months, but his full coloring is back, and he is no longer so gaunt. There's a new kind of light in his eyes.

It could also have something to do with the tribal queen sitting next to him, her fingers laced through his. Thank the stars, when Neverland bloomed back to life, the Dark Star reversed, and Tootles was able to come back as well.

Tootles reaches into the pocket of his trousers and pulls out something thin and red that rustles in the wind. I gently take the feather, feeling the silkiness of it against my fingertips.

"He's going to totally flip when he sees this." I don't fight the slow smirk that tugs at my mouth as I peer at its vibrant crimson color. I toss Tootles and Lily a grateful look. "Thank you for finding it for me."

Tootles shrugs, but his face beams. "Eh, no problem. The Lost Boys needed something to do, anyway. And we all saw Peter sulk for days when he lost his other one. Back when he was . . ."

"Younger." I finish.

He leans back on his hands, tipping his head up to the bright sky peeking through the leafy canopy. "Feels like a lifetime ago."

Tiger Lily gets to her feet, tossing her long braid over her shoulder. "But at the same time, it seems like yesterday."

I tuck the feather into the pouch slung at my side. "I'm just grateful we have a tomorrow to look forward to."

We look at each other, very quiet, thinking of the same thing. Of a Lost Boy with beautiful molasses skin and chocolate eyes who gave his life to try and rescue me. A life that couldn't be restored, even when Neverland was. We were only able to restore what was touched by the Dark Star, not the ache of those taken before it was created.

Some losses not even magic can change.

Some losses all we can do is grieve and promise to never forget.

I think Nibs would love this new Neverland.

Lily speaks quietly, breaking into my thoughts. "I've got to find Cres. We're meeting with the village elders about continuing the expansion, and also about Jeremy and Tansy's upcoming visit." She comes over to me and gently touches my arm. "I think this island is more than ready for some new blood. Go find that boy of yours."

I give her a smile. "Thanks. We'll see you soon."

She puts a fist to her chest. "You better."

I let dust drift from my skin and lift me into the air. Glimmer nestles closer to my neck as I fly back up through the trees and out into the vibrant blue sky. I turn toward the northern end of the island, the one facing the second star to the right, and squint at the horizon.

I pour on more speed, soaring over rippling brooks that race across mossy glades and past a little nook where a Neverbeast is playing with two small cubs. I reach the shore of Neverland and dip low over the water. My fingertips skim along the salty Neversea and soon skim over the rough scales of a large crocodile.

I pause just long enough to nuzzle the creature a bit, that ticking noise almost drowned out by the toss of the waves. Those reptilian eyes follow my every movement but slide closed in contentment when I scratch under his jaw. He stays like that for a while, then sinks back beneath the waves.

I notice a few dark forms gliding through the vibrant teal water. They poke up their heads and flash me toothy grins as they swish their tails.

I grin at the sirens, and Glimmer dives a little deeper into my bun as I drift closer to them. Strange that it's the sirens that unnerve her, not the massive crocodile I was just petting like some scaly feline.

I spot Nyssa at the head of a small pod that are leaping and playing in a surge of waves. She sees me at the same moment and raises a webbed hand in greeting. I wave back at the sirens and playfully kick water at them but bank away before they can sweep their tails and thoroughly drench me.

Glimmer mutters some choice words about the sirens, and I chuckle, flicking a few droplets of water at her. "You be nice. They're my family too."

Suddenly my gaze snags on a familiar pirate ship, bobbing in the water, suspiciously close to the outskirts of Neverland.

"Hold on!" I call out to Glimmer and dive swiftly to hover over the deck of the ship. Pirates bustle and rumble about the deck of the rebuilt *Jolly Roger*, and a certain scarlet-coated captain is standing at the prow, eyes lifted to the skies. He's holding a pouch filled to bursting with pixie dust.

"And just where are you going?" I ask, drifting just above Hook.

The captain quirks a half smile. "Just a quick jaunt to London. And don't worry—I traded with the pixies for some of their dust. I'll bring you and Pan back some pastries if you'll let it slide. You have my word we will be most discreet."

"Peter does love his chocolate cake," I concede.

Hook tosses me a salute, and with one last stern look at him, I'm off again. I do think he'll keep his promise about being discreet. So far, there's been a bridge of peacefulness maintained between the pirates and the rest of the island.

And Peter does love his chocolate cake.

More dust lifts from my skin and fills the air as I shoot upward, higher and higher, through the cloud layer and past the pull of gravity. I'm far enough to see the stars and swirl of galaxies beyond our floating island. The air up here feels thinner, different, and the stars that dance around us almost feel close enough to touch.

But I know better than to try and fly any farther.

I glance down at the world beneath me and am overwhelmed again at just how beautiful this place is. And how I spent so much of my life searching for somewhere to belong, somewhere to *be*.

Neverland chose me. And I got to choose her back.

Glimmer rustles from her place in my hair to sit on my

shoulder. She starts jumping up and down and pointing and shouting excitedly. The whole world becomes much brighter, the island a little greener, and the frosty caps of the mountains thaw as I watch a silhouette emerge through the stars.

He's surrounded by my gleaming dust, wearing a silky pair of pixie-woven trousers made of ivy and leaves with bits of the ivy climbing up his tanned torso and cascading over his strong shoulders. The closer he flies, I can see the way the ivy brings out the mischievous green of his eyes.

But Peter Pan is not alone.

He's brought a small procession of children with him. A little girl clings to one of his hands, while a small boy is sitting on his shoulders, a massive, toothy grin sprawled across his face. Three other children follow just behind Peter—a boy who looks a little older than the others, and a look-alike brother and sister.

My whole body thrums with excitement as Peter leads them closer to me. When he's within reach, I throw myself at him, embracing him into a tight hug, careful of the little boy on his shoulders.

"I've missed you!" I murmur to Peter and lean in to capture his mouth in a lingering kiss.

The little boy perched on his shoulders makes a gagging noise.

I let go of Peter and grin up at him. "Oh, you'll do just fine here."

He lifts a brow. "Who are you?"

The other children have spread out to float on either side of Peter, all peering wide-eyed at me and at Neverland sprawling below. Peter grins at them and gestures toward me. "Mates, I'd like you to meet my wife."

He sounds so happy to say it I want to cry.

I reach up and gently dislodge Glimmer from where she's

hiding in my hair, suddenly shy. She climbs into my palm, and I bring my hand forward to let the children have their first glimpse at her. She gives them a little curtsy, and the children all gasp.

My eyes shine as I smile at them. "This is Glimmer. She's a pixie. And my name is Claire. I'm part pixie."

The children gape at me, and I laugh, sweeping a hand to send swirls of golden dust through the air. Their eyes grow round as saucers.

My eyes catch Peter's as I reach into the pouch at my side. "I have something for you."

"For me?" His features shine with that boyish curiosity as he gently rocks the little lad back and forth on his shoulders.

I carefully remove the red feather from its hiding place and proudly present it to Peter. "I thought you might want to have one of these again."

His face bursts into a massive grin. "A Neverbird feather? Claire! How did you even get it? They only molt this color once every seventy years!"

I lay the feather in his hand. "Tootles and the Lost Boys helped."

The little fellow peering out at me from over Peter's wild curls exclaims, "Lost Boys? They're real too?"

Peter chortles, shoving the feather into his hair as if he were wearing a cap. It sticks out at a slightly ridiculous angle, but it's too cute for me to say anything. Peter spins the little boy around and says in a singsong voice, "Real as rain, chaps! And now you all are Lost Boys and Girls." He pauses, looking a little dizzy, and surveys the young faces watching him spellbound. "That is, if you want to be Lost Boys and Girls?"

Slow, hopeful, daring smiles appear, and the children nod quickly. "Yes!"

The boy on Peter's shoulder flicks at Pan's feather. "Well, we've come this far, haven't we?"

He's snarky, this one. I love him already.

Peter rubs at the side of his jaw, taking in the group of children again. "Well, you lot want to see the island? It'll be your home until it's safer to go back."

Cheers rise from a handful of little ones. However, the small girl clinging to Peter's hand doesn't make a sound. She's practically hiding behind him, peeking out from behind his leg to stare at me.

I drift closer and crouch down until I'm level with her. "Hello, sweetheart. What's your name?"

Her lips pucker, and her whole body quivers. She finally whispers, "Nora."

I notice the bruises that pepper her skin and the dark circles under her eyes. Peter must have plucked her out of a pretty difficult situation. I don't reach for her, just kneel there in the stars, golden flakes of dust filling the air around us. "You're safe here, Nora, sweetheart."

She nods slowly and then inches out from behind Peter, who is watching her closely. Her gaze slides past me and latches on Neverland far below.

"What *is* this place?" Her voice is hushed with a hint of wonder. My heart lifts in my chest just knowing how much good it will do her to step into this safe world filled with such magic and whimsy. To get a bit of her childhood back.

I reach out my hand for her to take if she wants. She hesitates, glancing up at Peter. He nods reassuringly. Her tiny hand is quivering, just like the rest of her body, but she slowly lays it in mine. I give it a light squeeze and cast a few shimmering flakes of dust over her skin. They soak into the bruises across her arms and sweep away the discoloration. Peter puts an arm around my shoulder as I bend in front of the little girl, and the rest of the children drift in closer too.

My dust fills the air, shining like drops of sunlight against the sprawling canvas of space and spinning stars.

"Welcome to Neverland, Nora," I tell the little girl whose small hand is nestled in mine. I smile as I watch glimmers of my gold dust reflect in her wide eyes. The start of a slow, small smile breaks out like a sunrise across the child's face. I can feel Peter's joy beside me.

My heart fills as I look into those dancing green eyes.

"This is a place where lost things are found."

ACKNOWLEDGMENTS

I fought some shadows this year.

In case you couldn't tell simply from the weight of the book in your hands.

And so did you, friend. We all did.

But you know what? *We're. Still. Here.*

And that is victory.

Each of us has had to decide what that spark of light is that we'll cling to. That bit of hope we'll cup in our hands like liquid gold, fan the flame—and trust that in time, it will grow. Because it does. No matter how cavernous the shadows, the light will always ignite and pour through the broken cracks.

And we will still be here.

So, as with *Dust*, I dedicate this book to you first, reader. I may know you by name. I may not. But the one thing I do know is that you fought hard, you wrestled your own shadows—and I'm so proud of you. Peter would be proud. And while I wish I could whisk you away to a beautiful island in the stars where you could have adventures with sirens and Lost Boys and leave the weight of this world behind—I can give you the novel in your hands.

A bit of my soul and a bit of whimsy impressed into the pages. A reminder that there is always a bit of light to chase back the shadows.

I would never have gotten here alone. There are far, far too many thank-yous to fit, but here are a few . . .

To my family: For supporting my journey and giving me the courage to fly. Love you!

To RJ and Orrie: I thank God every day for you. You are my heart. The shadows would have probably drowned me if God hadn't brought you along to crack the sky. Love you forever.

To Gram: For being the best roommate and cheering me on and sparking this love of writing in the first place.

To Alex: For being such a dear friend and always cheering me on. You are one of the bravest people I know.

To the Disney-boy (you know who you are): Our story is so precious to me. Thank you for seeing me, treating me like a queen (Lily would approve), and being so fond of Peter. You are a light.

To Sharilyn, Joanne, Hadassa, and Kezia: Thank you for all the retreats and long walks and heart talks and supporting me for so very long. I treasure each of you dearly.

To Aleigha: For being the most amazing support and always chasing the stars with me. You are a gift.

To Mary, Nadine, Sara, and Ashley: I'm so grateful to call you all my friends. I look up to each of you so much and am grateful for the chance to see such beautiful, strong women telling powerful stories and living even more powerful lives. I want to be you when I grow up. xoxo

To the many, many other incredible author friends: This community has absolutely blown me away. I get teary just thinking of all your dear faces. Thank you to everyone who has guided and cheered and supported me on this journey. You all have been like stars pointing the way.

To Brett, Jaquelle, Josiah, and Marita: Wow. It has been such a huge privilege to see The Young Writer grow and continue working with each of you. Thank you for being such an incredible team—and Brett, for being the best big brother and fellow author coach I could ask for. I am blessed beyond measure to get to guide young storytellers alongside y'all.

To Steve: My agent, my publisher, my friend. For believing in *Shadow* and trusting that I could pull off this crazy idea. Working with you has and will always be an honor. Thank you for taking such good care of this girl and her stories.

To the Enclave team: Lisa, my amazing editor, for deftly helping Peter and Claire truly shine. To Trissina and Jordan—you both are marketing superheroes. To my Enclave author-family and everyone else involved—I'm so honored to get to tell soul-stories with you all.

To J. M. Barrie: I hope you don't mind that I gave Peter a sister. You did have him live with birds as a child, so I think we're even when it comes to unusual plot choices? I'll always be grateful for the boy who never grew up that came knocking on the window of your imagination.

To my Jesus: the Ever One, the holder of my heart and my strength when I am weak. Thank you for finding me, for loving me more than I can possibly fathom, and for allowing me to shine your light in a broken world. May I never forget just how much you are bringing all things to glory in your timing. And chasing away every shadow.